BRAIN**STORM**
A MEDICAL MURDER MYSTERY

SHELDON COHEN

authorHOUSE®

AuthorHouse™
1663 Liberty Drive
Bloomington, IN 47403
www.authorhouse.com
Phone: 1 (800) 839-8640

Published by AuthorHouse 05/19/2015

ISBN: 978-1-5049-1298-3 (sc)
ISBN: 978-1-5049-1297-6 (e)

Print information available on the last page.

Any people depicted in stock imagery provided by Thinkstock are models, and such images are being used for illustrative purposes only. Certain stock imagery © Thinkstock.

This book is printed on acid-free paper.

Dedication

I dedicate this book to
Betty
Gail, Paul, Marci
Amanda, Shane, Megan, Travis
Carly, Alexa, Ethan, Emily,
Derek, Rylie, Benjamin

CHAPTER 1

George Gilmer bolted upright gasping for breath as his heart pounded and sweat trickled down his forehead. Awakened from a horrible dream, he glanced at the clock on the dresser—7:10. He took a deep breath trying to clear his mind full of jumbled disconnected thoughts.

Why would I have a dream like that, he thought? About fire? Could it be because of the recent fire at work? But that was a tiny one controlled by a few squirts of a fire extinguisher. It's funny how little events become bigger with dreams. The worst part was where the flames trapped Gail and the girls.

The fear he felt in his dream was as real as if he was there in the flesh; the look of terror on his two daughters' faces, his wife's panic. He hoped it would all fade from memory soon. He could still feel the smoke of the dream that seared his lungs and irritated his eyes. The power of the brain is amazing he thought, but he was awake now and the sensations were still there. Why? Could this all be part of the way I've been feeling? Why have I been so tense and anxious lately? He felt as if he was detached from his body. Simultaneously he looked at himself in the dresser mirror. That's my face he whispered; blue eyes, my mother's pointed nose, same wavy black hair. Yes, that crazy dream was mine! He thought back to before he was married and his future wife's girlfriends used to refer to him as Mr. Tranquilizer. I sure as hell don't feel calm like that now. Why the change? What the hell's going on?

"George, what is it?" said Gail.

The sound of his wife's voice stunned him. He turned and looked at her sitting next to him in bed, his mouth wide open as his eyes searched her beautiful face. It's Gail, he thought. No words came from his parted lips as he felt his anxiety dissipate. He breathed a sigh of relief.

"George?"

"Uhh, nothing…I…" My God, he thought, that was the worst dream of my life. What's happening?

"You look so weird. Is anything wrong?" said his worried wife.

"I…uh, I had a bad dream…that's all, just a bad dream. It's nothing."

His facial expression concerned her. "What was it about?" she asked

"Just stupid…that's all. It's, it's…I'm late. I better get moving." He shook his head, turned, got out of bed and stumbled toward the bathroom.

Gail noted the abnormal gait, but before she could say anything, he had closed the bathroom door. Although unsteady on his feet, he took a shower. As he shaved, he observed himself in the mirror. I look okay, he thought. I hope I never have a dream like that again. He shuddered as he dressed in his work clothes and went down to the kitchen where his wife was making breakfast.

"I'll just take a piece of toast. I'm late," George said as he rushed out, leaving his wife to ponder his unusual behavior. "Take some milk," she said as he faded out of sight

He could not forget the unusual dream at work, and it effected his concentration to the extent that he cut a two by four too short to fit. Damn, he thought, when the hell have I ever screwed up like that before? No one saw, he said to himself. He redid the cut with another two by four and resolved the problem. He completed the rest of the day's work without mishap and left for home, still feeling a bit nervous.

He picked at his food that evening at dinner and noted his wife staring at him with her wide blue eyes. "What's wrong?" Gail asked, obviously still concerned.

He shrugged his shoulders. "Funny. My stomach's kind of queasy tonight."

"Anything else? You looked a little unsteady on your feet this morning."

"No, that's all. I just got sort of a dull pain right here in the pit of my stomach. I'm walking okay. Work was no problem."

"You're not eating. Doesn't it taste good?" Gail asked.

"No, it's good. I'm not too hungry, that's all."

"First time I ever heard that from you," Gail smiled.

"Anyhow, I better go downstairs. I got work to do."

George went to the basement where he started working on a fireplace mantelpiece. Gail, startled again at his abrupt departure, could only wonder as to this sudden change in her husband's routine the last few days.

His reputation was spreading by word of mouth from satisfied customers. No sooner did he finish one mantel then he started on another. He worked on these whenever he had the time from his regular work for a large Chicago construction firm. He loved all aspects of carpentry, but the fine, detailed work required to make items such as mantle pieces and tables or chairs was his favorite.

He was an average student through grade and high school, but he excelled in art. Every chance he got he would work in his finished workshop basement stocked with power tools, easels, paintbrushes, oils, watercolors and whatever necessary to feed his artistic cravings. When finished with his current task he went upstairs to bed. Gail was already asleep.

He awakened the next morning feeling as if he needed more sleep. Damn, is it morning already? I feel like I just went to bed, he thought. He went to the bathroom, stared at himself in the mirror, noticed dark rings under his eyes and messed up hair. Must have had a restless sleep, he thought. He cut himself shaving and placed a piece of tissue on the blood. At breakfast, he noted that his appetite still was not what he thought it should be. He picked at his food.

Gail said to him, "Am I going to have to start shaving you?"

"Ha, ha, funny," he answered while tousling her long blonde hair.

"Thanks a lot," she said. "I still can't believe you weren't hungry last night. Are you sure dinner was okay?"

"It was great. I just didn't have any appetite," he said, managing a weak smile as he glanced up from his plate.

"You mentioned a queasy stomach."

"It's nothing. My stomach was upset, but I'm good now."

"All I know is, you usually wolf everything down, but now you're just picking. I don't know; seems to me, you're losing your appetite," said Gail.

"Nah, I'm good." He gulped down the remaining food. "Look how I finished off my breakfast," he said, holding up his empty plate. He pushed himself away from the table and stood up. "Time to get to work. I'll be late tonight, so don't worry. I have to see Mr. Worthey with the final mantelpiece drawings. He's got some good ideas, and I think I know what he wants."

"Okay," she said, "but…"

He interrupted her by planting a kiss on her lips.

"You sure know how to quiet a gal down. That hasn't changed, I see."

"The only time that will change my dear wife is when they put me in the ground." He grinned and headed for the door. "See you later," he said, glancing over his shoulder before rushing out.

Work was uneventful that day and the nausea did not return although he did notice a lack of appetite again at lunch. The dream surfaced again in his thoughts. Most of the time he could not remember the details of a dream when he awakened, but this one was vivid—in living color yet.

When he arrived home after work, Gail looked at him concerned and said, "How do you feel?"

"Good, why?"

"Your queasy stomach. Remember?"

"It's gone."

"You sure?"

"Yeah."

"Good, your dinner's ready."

"Thanks, in a minute." He hurried downstairs with the plans for Worthey's mantel under his arm.

He continued working downstairs through dinner. Gail sighed, ate with the children, let the girls go to their rooms to play and then walked down stairs. She found George at his workbench staring into space.

"George?"

He continued looking straight ahead.

"George?" repeated Gail.

He finally turned to look in her direction. "What?" he said with a blank expression. I got tied up with these plans. I'm trying to figure something out for Mr. Worthey."

"You didn't eat anything."

"I'm not hungry."

"Hungry, not hungry, hungry, not hungry," she said. "What's going on?"

"Nothing," he said with a twinge of anger in his voice that she detected.

That silenced her, but he was already working and deep in thought. It would just be one of those evenings, she thought; the frustrated artist would spend all night cooped up in the basement detailing another masterpiece. I wish he would do more artwork for his own enjoyment, but he was always "too busy." Maybe he's working too hard. Could there be some problem at work? I hope not. He needs more recreation time doing what he loves to do in his private workshop where he has always been calm and relaxed. Gail went back upstairs to prepare for bed.

As she was getting into bed, George came up and joined her. He fell asleep in minutes, but during the middle of the night, a sudden severe nausea woke him up. The urge to vomit overwhelmed him, and he leaped out of bed and ran to the bathroom. When he did so he awakened Gail, and she found him on his knees with both hands on the toilet seat and his head hanging over the bowl.

"George! What's wrong?" She knelt down beside him. He was unable to answer as he continued to vomit. The retching was loud and vigorous; his face was ashen and perspiration covered his forehead.

"Oh, man." Bracing one hand on the sink, he pulled himself up to a standing position, but his knees buckled and Gail grasped his elbows.

She steadied him with both of her hands. "I knew something was wrong," she said.

He shook his head and wiped his mouth with a towel. "Damn bug!"

"I've never seen you so sick." She felt his forehead. "You don't feel warm. Does anything hurt?"

"Yeah, a little pain here," he said, pointing to the center of his upper abdomen.

"That does it. You are going to a doctor. I'll call Eve and see who she recommends."

"No. I'll be okay; in fact, I'm better already. That vomiting did the trick. I think it's just the stomach flu. I've got lots of extra work to do. I told Mr. Worthey that his mantle would be ready in about ten days."

"Yeah, but…" she said to his back as he walked away.

They returned to bed. He tossed and turned all night. She lay awake wondering what was happening to her husband. He had never been sick a day in his life, or at least not the years of their marriage. She never heard a complaint from him in all that time. Something was happening. This was not like him. She joined him in tossing and turning much of the night.

She was the first to rise and she dressed and went down stairs to prepare breakfast. George followed in twenty minutes. The children were already on the way to school.

"Feeling better?" she asked, attempting to sound cheerful.

"Sure," he shrugged.

"Hungry?"

"Not much. A glass of milk is all I want."

As George sipped, he became aware that the abdominal discomfort that he chose not to tell Gail about was easing. He kissed her goodbye and drove off to work. He looked back to see his wife standing at the window watching until his car was out of sight.

While at work, his abdominal pain worsened. A fellow carpenter saw him rubbing his abdomen. "Looks like you got pain," the carpenter said.

"Yeah, it hurts right here in the pit of my stomach."

"Why don't you try some of these," said the carpenter reaching down into his toolbox. He handed George some antacid tablets. "Take a couple of 'em. It helps me when I get some acid."

He took two and within ten minutes, his symptoms were gone.

That night, at dinner with his family, he felt better, but only because of continued use of the antacid tablets purchased at a drug store during the lunch break. He could see his wife looking at him with a contented look on her face. She knew nothing of the antacids in his tool kit.

"I spoke to Mr. Worthey about some new ideas for his mantelpiece. He liked it even though it hiked up the price," said George.

"That's good," she nodded.

"I got a few more things to buy, and I'll work Saturday so maybe I can finish earlier than I promised."

Gail was relieved. He was talking and acting like his old self.

CHAPTER 2

Burt Crowell, a young board certified internist, is on a first date with Eve Worthey at an up-scale restaurant in Chicago. Colorful modern art lines the walls. He feels comfortable in her presence, immerses himself in the relaxing ambience, and opens his life to her full scrutiny. What he does not know is that his date, a nurse who works at the hospital where he is a medical staff member, will soon refer a fascinating medical case to him setting up a chain reaction that will educate the young doctor, the nurse and the new patient in ways none of them ever dreamt possible.

When he first saw her in the Covenant hospital cafeteria, she was sitting alone holding some papers in her left hand and eating a salad with her right hand. She immersed herself in whatever it was she was reading. He was able to see her in profile and thought that she looked familiar. As he progressed down the line, he glanced again in her direction and was able to see her face from a frontal projection, and then knew who she was. He recognized her from his past residency days at Illinois General Hospital. She was a medical nurse there and although he had had very little contact with her he did not fail to remember that she was very attractive with the purest blemish free skin, faintly painted high cheek bones, perfectly coifed medium length dark brown hair, and brown eyes framed by long eyelashes He was married at that time, so the thought remained buried in his mind never to see the light of consciousness again. However, things were different now, so he paid his bill and walked to her table and asked if he could join her. She looked up at him and her expression told him that she too recognized him. "Sure," she said with a smile, "What a surprise, but I have to be back on the floor for a meeting in two minutes."

"Well okay," he said. "Eve, isn't it?"

"Eve Worthey. Good memory, Dr. Crowell."

He laughed. "It's Burt, please. Okay, take care of your meeting, but let's talk about old times at dinner tonight. How about seven at Silvestri's?"

"I'll meet you there," she said with a nod.

His eyebrows lifted as her warm smile made him feel an emotion he had not felt for almost a year. There was something to look forward to this evening. After he and his wife divorced, he had wanted to socialize, but there was so much to do: work, study for boards, get established in his new practice, join a new medical staff. Women would have to wait. However, those days were over now, and Eve sure looked pretty sitting there immersed in whatever it was she was studying.

They met in the waiting area of the restaurant. She was already there when he arrived. More than prompt, he thought. I like that. He was anxious to continue the introductory phase of their new relationship.

After they sat, he said, "I want to hear all about you. What are you doing here at Covenant?"

She smiled and said, "I got a supervisory nursing role on the third floor. I couldn't pass it up. But you tell me about yourself first," she said.

He nodded and sipped his Martini. "Okay, I'll get right into the nitty-gritty, what there is of it. What do you want to hear first: professional or personal?"

"Let's save personal for the last," she responded with a smile that took away Burt's concentration.

"Well?" she offered.

"Uhh, yes, forgive me. That smile dazzled me for a minute. You are a very attractive woman, you know."

"Thank you for the nice compliment," she said careful not to smile again.

"Anyhow, after I completed my internal medicine residency, I went into practice here at Covenant. It's the only hospital I use. That makes things a lot easier as opposed to many of the doctors who run to three or four hospitals."

"Yes, circuit workers we used to call them," said Eve.

Burt nodded. "That's a quick rundown of the professional side of it. On the personal side, I'm thirty-years-old and divorced one year from a wife of three years. If you spoke to my ex, she would tell you I ignored her. Never home she would say. It was tough for her not to be the center of attention at all times. We talked about how busy I was before we got married, but I think she never believed it. Anyhow, she wanted out and she got her wish."

"I've heard it before," she reassured him with a smile. "Are you over that trauma now? You look kind of sad."

"Yeah, I'm over it. When someone wants out as bad as she did, there's no use fighting it. I must have been the only medical resident who lived in an 800,000-dollar house, a gift from her father for her to live in while she worked in Chicago before she met me. A starter home, he called it. Eight hundred grand to him was like loose change. His net worth was over three billion. He made it as one of the early hedge fund pioneers. Anyhow, everything that guy touches turns to gold. When his daughter moved back to New York he sold the house for a million dollars and I moved to a nice little condominium overlooking a crystal-clear man-made lake."

"Was it a nasty divorce?" Eve asked, her face reflecting a combination of sympathy and interest.

"Not at all, it was easy. We had nothing to fight about. I didn't even hire a lawyer. My wife said, let's each take what we brought to the marriage, split our joint assets fifty-fifty and go our own ways. I thought it was her old man talking, but her financial savvy was good enough for it to be just her. I can't argue with fairness, I said, and I moved out. By that time, the residency was history and I went into a partnership with a very busy, older internist who promised to retire after one year of orienting me to the ways of private practice. The guy's got more money than he knows what to do with."

"What's his name?"

"John Wagner. Do you know him?"

"Do I ever. I worked with him many times at Illinois General. We used to call him Porschy, because that's all he ever drove were Porsches; I think a new one every year. We figured he had family wealth. No internist can make that kind of money."

Burt laughed and said, "Ain't that the truth, and while he was on the Illinois General staff he was also on the staff of Covenant, but when he made the decision to retire, he left Illinois General to concentrate on Covenant. That's when he took me in practice with him. Would you like another drink?"

"No thanks. One's my absolute limit. Anyhow there's the waiter coming with our food."

Well that is refreshing, he thought. Most of the women he dated years back were clueless compared to this gal and would never turn down a drink even after they got to the babbling idiot stage. Nothing turned him off more than that. His turn-on came from women with impressive intellects. He had met Eve when he would attend grand round medical conferences at Illinois General. Their relationship had been only a professional one when she took care of some of his patients. She was a medical nurse and was married then, but there was no ring on her finger now and that suggested she was unmarried, or perhaps was practicing good hospital infection control and no longer wears a wedding ring.

"Tell me about you now," he said.

She nodded her head and smiled a smile again that brought back the emotion he felt when he first saw her in the cafeteria.

"Our lives are sort of running on a parallel course. I'm divorced too. My ex was involved in extracurricular activities, if you know what I mean."

"I think I know what you mean."

"You're right, so I moved out and had a lawyer give him the news that I'm history. I had an easy divorce too. I promised I wouldn't make any waves if we just called it quits. He saw the wisdom of that."

That was concise and to the point, he thought. "Have you dated again?"

"You're the first."

Burt smiled, sat upright, puffed out his chest, and said, "It's not often that a man is recorded a singular honor such as that."

His eyebrows lifted again as she laughed and threw her head back. He liked her relaxed manner and the way she concentrated on his every word. Her facial expression was a model of attentiveness and a mirror of the emotion she may have been feeling at the moment. And those sparkling brown eyes staring into mine, he thought. She had dark brown hair coiffed to hang shoulder length in a graceful curve covering her shoulders. She stared at you as if nothing else mattered except hearing what you had to say. There was no makeup, nor was any necessary on her smooth, blemish free face. She was five foot seven inches in her high heels, probably five three or four in stocking feet and was trim and fit. He judged her height when she stood next to him. First date, first impression—this gal was class. Let's see what happens. The good news was that after her divorce she left Illinois General to take the supervisory nursing role at Covenant.

"Where are you from," he asked.

"I was born in Covenant, believe it or not. My parents live in Barrington Hills now."

Recognizing one of the most affluent suburbs in the nation, Burt said, "Whoa, have I met another gal with big bucks?"

"My parents have the big bucks, not me. They helped me with college for my nursing BS, but I paid for my master's degree. I'm self-supporting, my good man. A woman's in trouble these days without being able to support herself."

"You got that right; any serious man in your life?"

"But I already told you, you're the first date since my divorce. Anyhow why would you wish to know?" she asked with chin down and eyebrows lifted.

"Just trying to be sure I got a chance to get to know you. I'm not one who likes to beat his head against the wall. I kinda like what I see, but when I get turned down, it wreaks havoc with my fragile ego." He shook his head and put his hands over his eyes.

She said, "Aw...poor baby."

He stared at her mock, pitying face and tried to mask a smile. Eve Worthey, he thought, this could be the start of a beautiful relationship.

CHAPTER 3

George finished Worthey's mantelpiece earlier than promised. Feeling better, he didn't think to take the antacids, so the pain returned. He began to suspect some medical problem, but chose to dismiss it. Too damned busy to be sick, he thought.

In a few days, his symptoms quieted down. He delivered the signed masterpiece to Worthey who was very pleased. "George," he said. If your work is always this good, how would you like to build a patio deck for me?"

George was stunned, but delighted and said, "I could, Mr. Worthey, I've done decks before, but I don't have a lot of time. That's a full time job."

"It's Fred, George, call me Fred. Time is not critical for me, George. Take your time. Do it on weekends, day off. I don't care. There's no hurry. I've been thinking about doing it for over a year and my wife wants one too."

"Okay, Mr. Wor...er Fred, I can do it, but I'll have to hire another carpenter and a cement man to work with me."

"As long as you're doing the supervising, that's ok with me."

Worthey took off his thick spectacles and rubbed them on his T-shirt. "Look, George. You're a true craftsman. Do the job part time, whenever you can. I know I'll get a great product, so it'll be worth the wait."

"Thanks, Fred.

Fred Worthey was a multimillionaire and founder of an electronics firm. At sixty-six years of age, he was no longer active in company management, but continued to serve on the Board of Directors. He had a frontal baldness with penetrating dark eyes and a trim figure on a five foot eight inch frame. His background was as a Ph.D. in electrical engineering. Although trained in the early days of computers and electronics, he managed to stay abreast of the many advances that had so changed his industry and the world.

It was Eve, a friend of Gail and daughter of Fred Worthey, who asked Gail if George would be interested in doing some carpentry work for her father. She had seen some of George's work at his home when she was visiting Gail, and she raved about him to her father. On the strength of his daughter's word, Mr. Worthey hired George to construct the mantelpiece and their relationship flowered.

"Where do you want the patio, Fred?" asked George.

"In the back, George. Follow me."

George surveyed the patio deck site and drew a rough sketch. "If you like this plan, I'll take the sketches home and draw up a final set. I'll hire the cement man and a second carpenter to help me out. I'll get you good guys."

Worthey took the sketch, and studied it. George hoped he interpreted a look of admiration on Worthey's face.

"I'm sure your men will be good if you choose them, George. It's a deal. Bring me the final plans as soon as they're done." Then he held up the sketch. As he scrutinized it, he shook his head and said, "Damn, I'm looking at this sketch that you knocked off in a minute. You're one hell of an artist."

"Thanks, Fred. It's just a hobby. I'll bring you those final plans," he said beaming with pleasure. He felt on top of the world. It was exciting to think that a man of Worthey's reputation could think so well of him. But, why was this damn pain coming back?

That evening, George told his wife, "Gail, I got good news. Fred Worthy was so happy about the mantelpiece that he hired me to build a patio deck."

"That's great," she exclaimed. "But, when will you have time?"

He didn't reply.

"George?"

"What?" he asked.

"When will you have time?" she repeated.

"Time for what?" he said with a quizzical look.

She was shocked. "For what? For the deck. We're talking about the deck."

He glanced at her with a scowl. "Saturdays and my day off," he snarled, "and I'll need health."

This took Gail aback. She was startled. "Health? What do you mean, health?"

He took a deep breath. "What health? What are you talking about?"

Now she was frightened, but tried not to show her concern.

"You told me you'd work Saturdays and on your day off, but that you need 'health.'"

George gazed back at her for a good ten seconds. "I did? Help, I meant help, sorry."

"Maybe it was just a slip of the tongue," Gail said.

Then he suddenly bent over, his eyes closed, his nose wrinkled, his lips apart, and his teeth clenched. He began writhing in pain.

Gail leaped up. "George, what's wrong?"

His breathing was noisy and labored. His face turned white. He doubled over with both arms crossed above his upper abdomen. "The pain, it just started again." Gasping, he reached inside his tool kit for the antacids. He downed two of them. "Let me sit down for a minute. I could use a milk," he pleaded.

She rushed to the kitchen and filled a large glass. He gulped it down. After a few minutes, his facial muscles relaxed. He sighed and said, "Okay, I'm better now."

"You told me you were better a few days ago," she said with an anguished expression on her face.

"I am better."

She stomped her right foot. "That's a hell of a way to show it. No, you're not better. It sounds to me like you have an ulcer or something. I'm going to call Eve and see if she can recommend a doctor. God knows you never went to one in your whole life."

He looked at her and knew she was serious. "Don't. Not for the next few days. I swear I'll take these antacids and then we'll go. I can't take time off because I need to get this deck thing going. It's a big job, and we need the cash."

"Listen to yourself." What will we do if something happens to you?"

"The pain's going away," he said. "Like I said, I'll take the antacids every day, and as soon as I finish the job I'll let you call Eve. I promise."

Gail could see a less anxious expression on his face and recognized further insistence would be futile. "Okay, that's a promise," she said.

George shrugged, and went back to the basement. Moments later, he let out a scream and ran back upstairs holding his left hand with his right.

Startled, Gail said, "What happened?"

"C-can't believe it," George stammered, as he waved his thumb in the air. The nail was dark blue. "Hit my thumb with that damn hammer."

She reached for his hand. "Ouch. You've got blood under the nail. It's got to hurt like hell."

"Yeah," he grimaced.

"We're going to the emergency room. You've got to get that blood out of there or you'll lose the nail. Let's go. Maybe your finger's broken."

He offered no opposition as the pain was intense.

The Emergency room doctor drilled a small hole in the nail. George watched with surprise as a six inch high geyser of blood shot forth, and with it instant pain relief. An x-ray revealed no evidence of fracture. The doctor bandaged his wound and gave him instructions.

The following week proved uneventful, though he experienced intermittent abdominal discomfort. He said nothing to Gail and kept taking the antacids. After the discomfort turned into such severe burning that it woke him up two nights in a row, he agreed to have Gail call Eve for a physician recommendation.

CHAPTER 4

Gail was active in her church and greeted all new members. When Eve moved to her neighborhood, she joined the church and they became fast friends.

When Gail called Eve, she expressed the urgency of George's recurrent symptoms to Eve. "It's not like him," Gail said, "He's changed. He's complaining of pain in the abdomen that he prefers to ignore. One night he vomited and I saw him stumble and he was unsteady on his feet."

Eve said, "He should be seen by an internist. Since I've been at Covenant, I met a very fine one. He has an excellent reputation not only as a good doctor, but he has a great bedside manner. I see how he makes rounds on his patients. He's young and board certified and up on the latest medical advances."

"That sounds good," said Eve. What's his name and number?"

"Doctor Burt Crowell. Let me call him for you. When do you want your husband seen?"

"You can do this?"

"Try me."

"Oh, my goodness, you have such clout already. You can never talk to a doctor these days when you call. You get a computer. I know from my kids. And you can make the appointment? Sounds kinda suspicious to me, Eve."

"Now now, Gail, let's not jump to conclusions. You let me handle it. When do want the appointment?"

"George has a day off on Thursday."

"I'll call you later and give you your time."

"What if he's busy? This is such short notice?"

"I'm sure he'll do me the favor. Trust me, Gail."

"What's the doctor's name?" asked Gail.

"Crowell, Dr. Burt Crowell."

Eve was as good as her word, and when George arrived at the office in the doctor's building of Covenant hospital, the receptionist handed him a four-page medical history form to fill out. He minimized his problem, jotting down stomach pain on a question labeled chief complaint.

After about twenty minutes, George met Dr. Crowell. He shook his hand. At about five feet and ten inches, the doctor was impressive. A former baseball player in college, it was clear that he was making every effort to maintain the same musculature he had in his playing days. His white coat could not mask the circumference of his upper arms. His hair was brown as were his eyes. He had a cleft in the center of his chin. There was a warm smile on his face.

George had avoided doctors all his adult life, but he was impressed with the demeanor of this man.

"It's nice to meet you, Mr. Gilmer. How can I help?"

George put his right palm over his upper abdomen and said, "I've got stomach pains, and my wife nagged me until I would see you."

A typical story, Burt thought. Women come in on their own. A man's wife usually drags him in. Burt checked the medical history form while keeping a watchful eye on his new patient who was sitting at the edge of the examining table abutting the windowed back wall. He noted his patient fidgeting with his hands, his eyes darting all around the room. Burt sat down on a stool in front of a desk and side chair adjacent to a built in sink. He had seen similar behavior from other male patients.

Starting the medical history, Dr. Crowell touched George's upper abdomen, and asked, "Is this where the pain is?" He would zero in on the chief complaint and present illness, which he viewed as the most important part of the medical evaluation.

"Yes, that's right," answered George.

"Is the pain persistent, or does it come and go?"

"It comes and goes."

"Does it stay in the upper, middle of your stomach, or can you feel it other places in your abdomen or in your back?"

"Stays right there," George said, pointing to the same location.

"Can you describe the pain? Does it feel sharp like a knife, or a burning, dull, gnawing, or achy kind of pain?"

George thought for a moment before he said, "Mostly dull and gnawing, but sometimes burning."

"Is there anything that makes the pain go away?"

"Yeah, I take these antacids," he said as he took them out of his pocket to show the doctor.

Burt looked at them and nodded his head. "On a scale of one to ten with one the least and ten the most you could possibly stand what number would you assign to the pain?"

"Mostly four or five, but one time it felt like an eight."

"Does it ever wake you up in the middle of the night?"

"A couple of times," answered George abruptly.

"Have you had any nausea or vomiting?"

"Um…what did you say?"

Burt took note of his patient's sudden inattentiveness and repeated the question.

"I vomited a couple of times," nodded George while squirming. His answers were getting short, so Burt chose to scrutinize the history form again for any other pertinent information and said, "That's about all the questions I have now, Mr. Gilmer. Strip down to your shorts and I'll be back in a minute."

George did as the doctor told him. Surveying the room again, he noted three diplomas on the wall and a picture of a man seated at the bedside of a sick child. The picture, titled The House Call prompted a "Hmm," from George. He smirked. A framed collection of antique fishing lures hung next to the picture. He was still scanning the room when he realized that the doctor's minute was stretching into two, then four, then six. He struck his left palm with his right fist. He was struggling to suppress the desire to leave when Dr. Crowell returned and observed his patient's agitation. "Sorry, but I got a call from the emergency room. I had to be sure everything was okay."

George stared with unchanged expression.

Burt asked more questions while performing a complete physical examination and then told George to get dressed. "When you're ready, just open the door and I'll come right back." George got back in his clothes and this time Burt kept his word.

"What do you think?" asked George.

"Your physical examination didn't give me any real clues, and that's the good news."

"How about my stomach. What do you think is wrong?"

"My first guess would be an ulcer."

The wife was right as usual, thought George.

Burt continued. "There are other possibilities such as an inflamed stomach, a hiatus hernia, an inflamed esophagus, inflamed gall bladder and other upper abdominal problems. But, my money lies with the ulcer. We need blood tests and a stool specimen to rule-out the presence of a bacteria that causes ulcers, we're also looking for some other rare possibilities that can cause you to have these kind of symptoms. Get these tests as quickly as you can and we may also need to take a peek inside your stomach"

"What about my stomach pain? What can I take for that?"

"Here's a prescription. It will cut down the acid that your stomach makes and help with the pain. Take it morning and evening, twelve hours apart. You could also take the antacids if you need them. This paper I'll give you tells you what you shouldn't eat until we find out what's causing your problem. Take this order slip to the outpatient department and schedule the blood and urine tests and the stool test. You'll get instructions. In the meantime, don't drink any alcohol, don't miss any meals, don't take any aspirin and don't miss any doses of the medicine." Burt wrote the instructions out on his letterhead.

George felt calmer. If medicine could fix the ulcer, he thought, who needs all these tests? He extended his hand to Burt. "Thanks, doctor."

"Make an appointment to see me after the tests are complete. Call me if your symptoms get any worse. It was good meeting you, Mr. Gilmer."

George took the prescription to the pharmacy but didn't schedule the tests, electing to see how things went. After a twenty-minute delay at the pharmacy where he paced back and forth while waiting, he realized that since he developed this problem he'd been losing his cool a lot. Maybe that's why I'm getting an ulcer, he thought. He received his prescription and returned home.

"Well, how'd it go?" asked Gail.

"Good, he's a nice guy. He gave me some medicine."

"What did he tell you?"

"He said I'm as healthy as a race horse."

"So you need medicine to make you even healthier, right?"

"Correct. Man, I'm sure lucky to have a smart wife like you."

"And you know how to change the subject. Cut the bull, and tell me what the doctor said."

"He said I wasn't getting enough."

"Enough what?"

"I'll show you," he said as he grabbed Gail and wrestled her down on the couch.

"You've got a one track mind, Mr. Gilmer. I should have known. No deal."

George feigned disappointment. "Okay," he sighed. "If you insist, I'll tell you. He thinks I probably have an ulcer. So, who needs a doctor when I've got such a smart wife that could tell someone what's wrong without ever going to medical school?"

She smirked. "Is he going to take any tests?"

"He gave me an order for them."

"And?"

"I'll get them as soon as I can."

"You better, George."

CHAPTER 5

He awakened the next morning refreshed after spending an uneventful symptom free night.

Gail was already awake looking up at the ceiling trying not to disturb her husband. When he stirred and stretched. She asked, "No pain?"

"None, I feel great this morning. I don't know if it was you last night or the medicine that did it."

"It was me. I have that effect on all my men."

"I could understand why."

"So do they," she said with smile as she yawned and stretched out both arms.

His mind had already drifted off. "When I get home tonight," he said, "I'll draw up the plans for Mr. Worthey's deck."

"Don't forget to take your medicine this morning," she said.

"Oops. Thanks for the reminder," he said as he downed the pill, got up, dressed, had a small breakfast and rushed off to work.

That evening, after dinner, he sat down in front of the television set. Gail joined him on the couch.

"How'd you do today?" she asked.

"Good."

"No pain?"

"Gone."

"Good. What's happening with Mr. Worthey?"

"What about him?"

"His drawings."

"What about the drawings?" He looked puzzled.

Gail frowned. "Don't you remember saying you'd work on the plans for his deck when you came home tonight?"

"When did I say that?'

"This morning."

"I did?"

She looked away. How could he forget something so important to him, she wondered. Her worry returned.

"Yeah, right, I'll get to the plans right away," George mumbled.

Her anxiety made her feel tired. She got up and left the room. He resumed watching television. With TV, he could distract himself from problems of any nature. By the time he was ready for bed, she was fast asleep.

George stayed up late and managed to complete the plans for the deck.

The next evening they were engrossed in television when Amanda ran in front of the screen with Megan in pursuit. Megan was screaming, "It's mine." Amanda was answering in kind. George leaped out of his chair, grabbed Amanda by the upper arm and said, "Shut up. Give it to her now."

The sudden outburst so startled the girl that she burst into tears. Never before had she experienced this tone of voice, or such rough handling from her father. She dropped the toy and ran to her mother who comforted her. George stared for a minute and then his face reflected a realization of what he had done. It was as if he had just awakened from a bad dream. He frowned. He stared at Gail. Then he looked at Amanda and said, "I'm sorry, honey. Daddy's sorry. I didn't mean it." He walked over to hug his daughter. She let him, but she was tense.

Gail confronted him late that evening. "What about Dr. Crowell and the tests?" she asked.

At the mention of Dr. Crowell's name, he exploded, "No!" he shouted. "I feel fine and those tests are a bunch of crap."

Gail cupped her hands over her mouth. She thought, what was happening? His personality was changing. Why? He was abrupt, impatient, and restless. There was something serious going on.

CHAPTER 6

Monday morning George arrived early for work. On his way downstairs to the basement he rushed by his boss, Andy Simpson, Not until he was halfway down did he hear Andy shouting, "Where are you going?"

"Downstairs," he answered without looking back.

"For what?" asked Andy.

"I gotta finish my work."

"We finished down there, don't you remember?" Final inspection was last week."

George stopped, looked back at Andy and said, "Gotta frame in the doors," he answered.

"What? You already did that," said an exasperated Andy.

"No I didn't," answered George with one hand on the banister.

Andy motioned for him to come up, but George continued down.

"We worked on it together," Andy shouted.

"You're full of crap," loudly answered George in a voice Andy could not recognize.

"All right," said Andy. "Go take a look."

George spun on his heels and took the steps two at a time until he reached the bottom stair. There he froze. All the doorframes were finished. In fact, everything on the lower level was finished. Why could he not recall working on it? He forced himself to remember, but his mind was blank. He paced the floor, feeling more confused than ever. He went back upstairs, where Andy was waiting for him at the top of the landing.

"Well?"

No answer.

"Never mind," said Andy. "We've got work upstairs."

George bit his tongue, fighting to hold his temper. The whole thing had been a set up, he thought, a plot to get rid of me. He felt confused and uncertain. So much was at stake. He knew he was in trouble, but somehow he would have to fake it. Andy was ordering him back to work, but why? So he could mess up and give him the excuse to fire him? His only recourse was to continue work, but he could not afford to make any mistakes. His work had to be free from defects. It had to be perfect.

CHAPTER 7

George returned home that night moody and short tempered. He paid no attention to his daughters. Gail decided to confront him after the children were asleep. She braced herself and with a tremulous voice, she asked, "What happened today?"

He pursed his lips and glared.

"Do you hear me? Tell me what's wrong?" she entreated

George refused to make eye contact. "Nothing," he loudly erupted.

"You can't kid me," she roared back.

"Get off it," he snapped.

Gail now knew it for certain. Things were getting worse. Never before had he spoken to her like this. Could an ulcer cause a personality change? His explosive temper and sudden forgetfulness frightened her. He bore no resemblance to the man she had married.

The next few days, Gail studied her husband's mood swings in as thoughtful and calm a manner as she could, understanding the importance of what was happening. He was up one minute and down the next. He went from happiness to grief, from the dumps to agitation, and he was forgetful. When viewed together they suggested some underlying psychological or medical problem. Several weeks had passed since his appointment with Dr. Crowell who had called a week ago and asked Gail where George's tests were. He had not yet received them and he stressed their importance. "I'll do what I can, doctor, he tells me he's better, but I'm not so sure. I believe he still has symptoms. He's been so busy."

Meanwhile, George continued to work, but Andy needed to remind him to finish some projects. Whereas he had been outgoing and collaborative, he now was secretive and quiet.

Fred Worthey's deck job was also a work in progress. George hired a second carpenter and a cement contractor to help him. He took measurements, drew up the specifications and drawings, and calculated how much material would be necessary to complete the project. They went right to work as soon as they received the necessary supplies. This would be his first experience directing a construction project, and he enjoyed his new status as boss. If the three of them worked a full day on Saturdays and their days off, they expected to complete it within two weeks. Fred would act as the team's unofficial supervisor.

When the project was nearly half-finished, Fred again praised George for his talent and workmanship.

"I appreciate that. Thanks, Fred." Then as he reached down to shake Fred's hand he experienced a sudden and excruciating back pain that caused him to jump off the ladder.

"Oh, God," he agonized with eyes closed and teeth clenched.

Fred was startled. "What's wrong?" he said.

George stood stiff as a board, his left hand covering his flank as he spoke through his clenched teeth. "I'm not sure. I must have sprained my back. It just hit me when I reached down to shake your hand." As he spoke, he could feel the pain growing worse, extending into his abdomen, and threatening to render him helpless. With great care, he eased himself down into a sitting position on the ladder steps. Fred noted his distress and tried to be comforting, but George's pain turned his face white.

"I'm always spraining my back," offered Fred. "Sometimes it just takes a little movement the wrong way. Come in the house and sit for a while. You'll see how it goes. I've got some Tylenol or Motrin if you want it."

"Thanks," he murmured. "That's not a bad idea. Man, but this hurts. I never had a back sprain like this," he groaned. Even his hammered thumb had not been so painful.

In a semi-crouched position he followed Fred into the house, and they sat at the kitchen table. Soon his two associates joined them, and then all three began to hover over him. The pain was intense. It reminded him of Dr. Crowell's questioning when he asked him to describe the intensity of his stomach pain. If Crowell questioned him about this one, he would say it felt like someone had reached inside his back, grabbed hold, and squeezed with all his might. The pain traveled down from the left side of his back to the lower left side of his abdomen. Not only was he hurting, but also he felt frustrated because he could not afford to let anything interfere with work. He became impatient with all the hovering.

"Stop worrying about me and get to work," he lashed at his men. "I'll be fine." Although surprised by his response, the two men were quick to follow orders.

He squirmed in his chair, trying to find a comfortable position. He stood up and walked around the room, and after several minutes began to feel better. "I guess the Tylenol's kicking in," he said to Fred.

"Good. Now go home and use a heating pad. It will help you get over this thing. You know I'm in no hurry to finish."

He got up to leave, but not before reassuring his appreciative client that he'd be back on the job very soon. Meanwhile, his two associates continued working. By the time he arrived home, the pain was almost gone. All that remained was a dull reminder on the left side of his back. He kept silent about it, not mentioning a word to his wife. She had enough on her mind, he thought.

CHAPTER 8

George continued with his prescribed medication until he was symptom free, then stopped cold turkey. He finished Worthey's deck, and was delighted with the extra income, most of which he and Gail lavished on their children. Nevertheless, the abdominal pain returned and he refilled his prescription without telling Gail.

The following Saturday, he was free, so he took his family to a movie. Amanda was well behaved and attentive, but when Megan persisted in walking up and down the aisles, he became enraged. He tried first to scold Megan and then held her on his lap to placate her. Nothing worked, so Gail grabbed the child by the hand and led her out to the lobby, hoping to keep her occupied and away from her agitated father. She did everything she could to keep his environment serene but his strange behavior made her tense. She was wrong; things were not getting better.

On their way home from the movie, Gail noticed George driving in the wrong direction.

"Where are you going?" she asked loudly trying to get his attention, a task that was becoming progressively more difficult of late.

His mouth fell open as he stared straight ahead. "Home," he said calmly.

"But you're going the wrong way," Gail screeched.

George made no comment, just continued staring out the window.

"Stop," she shouted. "We're getting farther away from the house."

The car stopped abruptly as he slammed on the brakes and pulled over to the curb.

"I'll be dammed," he mumbled under his breath. He saw a look of fear on his wife's face. Moments later, he restarted the engine and stepped on the accelerator. "That's what I get for thinking too many thoughts at the same time," he muttered. Gail kept still. She looked away so as not to let him see her worried expression. He was driving in the right direction now, and she did not want to create a scene in front of the children. Not until after they were home and the kids were out of hearing range did she attempt to speak with him.

"What's going on? Gail asked. "You're forgetting things, you lose control, you get angry for no reason, and I don't even recognize you anymore. You're scaring me. I don't know what to expect." She was trembling. She stopped to regain control. Closing her eyes, she inhaled deeply before continuing. "What on earth is happening? I'm making another doctor's appointment for you. You never went back to Dr. Crowell, and you never got those tests like you promised."

"I don't need any tests. I got better, and the pain never came back," he lied.

"Yeah? Then something else's going on. You're different now. I'm scared to say anything or I'll set you off. What you're doing is nuts. Don't you care about your health?"

"Drop it." he yelled. "You made a federal case out of a wrong turn. I know my way home."

His anger was unsettling, and Gail felt she was losing him. This metamorphosis had been so insidious she didn't know how to react. Her mind was hoping it would be a temporary aberration that would soon disappear. Her one remaining tool was her vigilance. She would need to remain on guard. Why was he so irrational? Was his illness making him this way? They spent a very quiet few days.

The following Saturday they went marketing as a family. They each took one daughter as a passenger in their grocery cart, something both girls relished. Then, they went their respective ways with a separate list of items.

While Gail was at the dairy counter, she thought she heard loud voices. Seconds later, she heard the sounds of cans crashing down onto the supermarket floor. That would have been bad enough, but what really alarmed her was the piercing sound of a crying child: Megan! She rushed in the direction of her daughter's voice.

Several male employees were also hurrying to investigate. By the time she arrived at the scene, she saw George rolling on the floor with another man, their hands and feet flying in all directions, his face contorted with rage. A nearby employee rushed to telephone the police, and three others tried to separate the two combatants. She screamed at her husband and rushed to his side, but he never saw her. At that moment, he was too busy fighting off the three employees who were attempting to hold him back. The other man needed no restraining. Finally, George calmed down, but only with Gail's prodding. When a uniformed officer appeared on the scene, George appeared dazed.

"Is everything okay now?" asked Officer Doherty, shaking his head with disbelief as he regarded the spectacle.

"Things have calmed down here now," replied the store manager.

"What happened?" asked Doherty.

"These two guys got into a fight in the aisle," replied the manager.

George was sullen and remained mute, but his opponent spoke up. "This crazy guy he attack me," he said, pointing a finger at George.

"He hit me first," snapped George.

"Alright, alright. Hold on. One at a time. You. What happened?" demanded Doherty of George's opponent.

"My cart hit back of his foot. It was accident. Then this crazy guy he turn and swing at me. He throw me on floor."

"What's your name?" asked Doherty.

"Alberto Arroyo."

Doherty turned to face George. "What do you have to say about all this?"

George looked away.

"I'm talking to you," barked Doherty.

"Answer him, George," cried Gail. The tone of her voice seemed to shock him back to reality.

"Yeah, his cart hit me. It hurt like hell."

"What's your name?" demanded Doherty.

"George Gilmer."

Doherty confronted him. "Did you hit him first?"

When George failed to answer, Arroyo spoke for him. "Yeah, he hit me first."

"Any witnesses to the start of this fight?" asked the officer. By now, a crowd of curious spectators had gathered, but not one had witnessed the start of the incident.

"We just heard screams, and a crying child, and some cans crashing to the floor," replied the store manager.

Doherty took detailed notes. "Is there going to be more trouble here?" he asked.

"No." answered Arroyo. George remained silent. Gail forced herself to remain calm as she interjected on his behalf. "I'm Mrs. Gilmer, sir, and that's my husband," she said, pointing to George. "He's never been in trouble with the police before."

"Well, ma'am, he's in trouble now if he refuses to answer my questions." Returning his attention to George, he asked again, "Did you strike the first blow?"

He swallowed hard. "Uhh, yes, sir. I guess I did. Just lost it."

"Do you lose it very often?"

"No, no sir," he stammered.

Gail stared wide-eyed at her husband. She didn't know whether to be embarrassed or scared to death, or both.

George's expression softened and, for the first time, he seemed alert. "Sorry," he said.

Officer Doherty was now eager to wind things up. "Both of you finish your shopping, pay the tab, and get out of here. There better not be any more trouble. I'm gonna stay put for a while, just to make sure." Turning to Arroyo, Doherty continued, "If you want to press charges, sir, you'll need to come down to the station."

"Let's go," said Gail, still shaken. She paid the bill and insisted that George sit alongside her while she drove home. She could not trust him behind the wheel. For the moment, at least, she was unconcerned about the girls' welfare. They were playing in the rear seat.

Back home, with the children in the back yard, she wept. "Now, do you believe me that you've changed? Who are you, anyhow? Tell me!" she insisted. "What's happened? I don't recognize you anymore." Tears rolled down her cheeks.

George went pale. Perhaps for the first time he recognized her desolation, but felt powerless to help. "I just lost it," he said, his voice above a whisper. "It's okay."

"No. Nothing's okay anymore. Something's wrong, and you better admit it."

"Don't worry."

"Don't worry? That guy might press charges."

"But he didn't get hurt," he said.

"Oh? You assaulted him. Don't you understand what you did? You have never done anything like that in your whole life. You've got to see Dr. Crowell. Enough." Gail could no longer contain herself. She started weeping. From time to time, she reached out to touch George's hand.

Never before had he witnessed his wife in such a state, yet he realized he needed to act.

"Okay, okay," he said. "Set up the appointment, but you're wasting your time."

She knew that he was in denial, and insisted on accompanying him to the doctor's office. She also arranged for her mother to baby-sit the girls, recognizing she must not miss this appointment with Dr. Crowell.

CHAPTER 9

When they arrived for their scheduled appointment, they waited more than an hour before Dr. Crowell could see them. Gail had difficulty keeping George in his seat. Several times, he threatened to get up and leave. When it was their turn, a sullen George walked into the doctor's examining room.

Burt greeted them both before scanning George's chart and questioning his patient. He asked, "This visit is for you, Mr. Gilmer, is that right?"

"Yes," said Gail, before her husband could speak, "and I had to beg him to come."

The doctor glanced back at the chart, reviewing for detail. Burt recalled the abdominal pain syndrome most likely attributed to an ulcer. He noted that George had failed to follow through with the previous post-exam tests he had ordered during his initial visit, but elected not to mention it for the time being.

Burt stepped within inches of his sulking patient who was sitting on the examining table with hands folded in his lap. "Tell me what happened," said the doctor in a calm voice

"The wife dragged me here." he said. "She thinks something's happening to me, but I feel great. In fact, if you'd like the truth, I'm just trying to satisfy her. This is all a big waste of time." Dr. Crowell nodded and turned his gaze to Gail who was shaking her head no.

"Doctor, it was like pulling teeth to get him here," Gail said. "He's like a stranger. It's all so sudden, and I'm sick with worry. He loses his temper, he forgets things, and he even got lost driving home the other day."

George shook his head in defiance, but failed to get a word in while Gail continued. "He's nervous and irritable and barks at the children. We're all scared to death. Worst of all, the other day at the supermarket some guy bumped into him with a cart, and he started swinging and punching. The store manager called the police, and we're praying that the man won't press charges."

"That's quite a lot of complaints, George," said Dr. Crowell. "How do you feel about all this?"

"Nothing's wrong with me," he countered. "I've been busy at work, and took on some extra jobs. Just lost my temper in the supermarket, but I didn't hurt the guy."

"Hmm," replied the doctor," sounds like two different stories."

"Sure does," said George, with a wry smile.

"Gail, if you don't mind, I'd like to question your husband alone. Soon as I finish, I'll call you back in. Is that okay with you, George?"

"Yeah, sure."

Gail nodded and left the room.

"Okay, George, let's concentrate on what brought you here. I'll ask you questions and check you over again. Have you ever been in a fight like this before?"

"No. Well, maybe when I was a kid."

"Do you think you've been getting more nervous as time goes on? Is your wife right that there's been some change in you?"

"No, I don't think so."

"Has anything changed at work; any recent pressure?"

"Sure. Lots of deadlines, and my own work like the side jobs I take care of on Saturdays and my day off."

"Your wife thinks you're forgetting things. Is that true?" A distracted George did not respond. Dr. Crowell waited, permitting him extra time before repeating the question.

"Well, one day at work I was going to frame in some doors until the foreman told me I already did it. I was sure I didn't, but I checked to see and he was right. I just think he was putting me on because I know I never worked on those doors."

"Is the extra work adding to your stress?"

"No, like I said, I like it. The money's good, and I get the chance to do my own thing."

Burt paused, making sure he had eye contact before going on. "Are you happy in your marriage, George?"

"Sure, why not? I got a great wife and kids."

"Any problems sleeping?"

"None at all."

"Any problem concentrating?"

He paused. "I don't think so."

"What about appetite?"

"Good."

"Any headaches?"

"No."

"What about the stomach pain?" asked Dr. Crowell.

"It's good," Burt lie without eye contact. Suddenly George got up, walked over to the window, and stared outside. When he returned to his seat, his expression had changed. Burt had seen this failure to concentrate before. He knew it was time to stop. This was a different patient from the man he met on their first visit.

"It's a big waste of time—right?" asked George.

"Your wife's worried, so I'm glad you came. I'll step out of the room, and while I'm outside I want you to strip down to your shorts so I can examine you. As soon as you're ready, open the door a bit and I'll come right in."

The doctor did a brief examination, a repeat of the last time, before concentrating on George's neurological exam. He evaluated his motor abilities and did a full sensory exam. He checked cranial nerves and reflexes. He checked the strength of George's arms and legs. He looked into George's eyes with an ophthalmoscope. There were no localized neurological deficits. In short, his examination failed to reveal any evidence whatsoever of neurological change.

"All right, George. Everything looks good. May I call your wife in?"

"Sure."

When Gail returned, Dr. Crowell informed her of the results. "Your husband's examination was normal. I don't find any evidence of a brain tumor, or any other brain disease for that matter. In fact, I find nothing wrong. But normal findings can sometimes register even when there's a severe illness. What I'm saying is that everything is fine so far, but for a complete evaluation I'm recommending an MRI brain scan."

"What would that show?" asked Gail.

"It would eliminate any possibility of a tumor or other brain disease. I don't find such evidence on his physical exam, but we must look into every possibility."

"Brain tumor?" repeated Gail. George flashed a look of disbelief.

"I don't think there's a tumor, but I want to be thorough," said Burt.

George was staring out the window again, no longer paying attention.

"Anyhow, that's number one," said Burt. "Number two could be some psychological dysfunction: anxiety or depression to be exact. Not that George fits the exact mold of these diagnoses, but if there is any significant changes as you suggest we'd better check out that possibility. In fact," he paused to look at George. "I would like to recommend you see a psychiatrist for a second opinion."

George bolted straight up. "A shrink? No way. Never."

"Well, then my final suggestion is that you watch and wait." Turning to Gail, he directed the next comments to her. "Because of your husband's occupation, I'd rather not prescribe medication considering he works with nail guns, hammers, power tools, and climbs ladders. We need to get this all sorted out first."

From the corner of his eye, Burt saw George jump up to leave. "Thanks for your time, doctor."

"Hold it, George." The tone of the doctor's voice took both Gail and George aback. His facial expression was stern. "This brings me to number three. It looks like you never took the tests that I ordered the last time." Burt placed himself in front of the closed door. George got the message and stepped back.

"Right. You said I had an ulcer, and the medicine took care of it," lied George.

"I said I thought you might have an ulcer, but for a final diagnosis I needed those tests I ordered."

"I'll see to it that he takes them," said Gail.

"It could be too late, Gail. If the ulcer healed, and that's a possibility because your husband claims the pain is already gone, then the ulcer may no longer be there. Ulcers are caused by a certain bacteria, and I ordered tests for that, but apparently George never got them" he said to Gail while turning to George. "I mention this only because the time to take tests is when symptoms are present. I hope you'll learn from this experience and go from here."

George was noncommittal, but Gail soaked up every word.

"Here's a slip for the MRI of the brain, a full set of blood chemistries, a stool and blood test to search for the ulcer bacteria, and a blood count. Get them right away and I'll have the results in a few days. There's a lot of unusual things going on here and I need the help of these tests before I can pinpoint a diagnosis. You listened to my advice and ignored it after your first visit. I have no idea why you did that, but it made no sense. I'll never order a test unless it's necessary, George, and in your case there are some unusual things that could cause all your symptoms and they can't be ignored and I must, I repeat, must have these tests."

The doctor's stern comment was resolved and firm. Gail promised and George remained silent. They did not speak in the car on the way home. Gail prayed for a quick and simple diagnosis and cure.

When Gail raised the subject of medical tests George said, "I have no brain tumor, and I'm sure as hell not going to some shrink." When she offered opposition, George left the room. Distraught, but not surprised, Gail's only hope was that he might change his mind. But why was he being so resistant? His whole mindset was not rational. Why was he refusing to do what the doctor ordered? It's as if he never heard what the doctor was saying. What was happening? Things have gone on too long.

CHAPTER 10

George's emotional lability, fueled by his changing internal biochemistry caused by an unusual condition that altered his thinking in the direction of irrationality, could not alter the inevitable. His work showed signs of deterioration, not because of any difference in physical prowess, but because of the storm that raged inside his brain. Like a hurricane born off the coast of Africa, the storm was heading westward toward Florida and gaining turbulence, speed, and momentum. This was the cause of his confusion and forgetfulness, both of which affected his performance at work and his relationship with his family. Jobs were left unfinished, shoddy work had to be redone and he failed to remember assignments. His mental state changed so fast that his coworkers, and even the foreman, could not miss the signs. Andy Simpson summoned him into his office.

"Sit, George. We gotta talk. Sorry, but you have to know, if there ain't any improvement pretty fast, you're outta here. You always did great work, but it's different now and the boss knows everything. He told me to fix this problem either way. I got no choice. I'm under the gun, and I'm gonna watch you like a hawk. Understand?"

George was confused, but he knew enough to recognize that his job was at stake. He had all he could do to hold back and not vent. "I'll do okay," he said, trying with all his strength to muster the necessary control to keep his voice steady. "You'll see."

Andy, hoping for the best, dismissed him with a stern and unchanged expression.

The small talk between George and Gail had turned into silence. In fact, any meaningful conversation between them became more difficult.

He mixed up the children's names, and even they began to notice something wrong with their father.

Megan cried whenever he raised his voice. He spent most days staring into space, and even stopped working in the basement. Gail, reaching the breaking point, had had enough. She feared he was having a nervous breakdown, or worse. Could it be a brain tumor, she wondered? The unmistakable truth was that his condition was deteriorating. At times, he would respond to questions with answers that made no sense. She decided the time had come to give him an ultimatum: that he return to Dr. Crowell and level with him, or she would leave and take the children to her parents.

By evening, Gail heard a loud groan. She left the kitchen and went to the living room where she saw George sitting on the edge of the couch, doubled over and shaking. He had his arms crossed over his abdomen.

"Good God, what's wrong?" cried Gail.

"Can't talk…got a pain…can't believe it," George moaned.

"Your stomach?"

"No," he screamed. "It's here…and…and here," he said, placing one hand on the left side of his upper back and the other on his lower left abdomen. This was the same problem he had developed on the ladder at Fred Worthy's house. Only this was worse. "Call work and tell them I had to go to the hospital."

"Let me call Dr. Crowell," pleaded Gail.

"No, no, stay home with the kids. I'll leave now," he said, trying as hard as he could to stand up. "Gail, help me," he pleaded. "I can't wait. I need to get to the hospital…now." He walked out the door bent on driving himself.

Gail was distraught. Was realization starting to soak in?

CHAPTER 11

The Emergency Department (ED) at Covenant did not appear busy. Dr. Jason Pollard, head of the ED, had the rare luxury of an uninterrupted hour to concentrate on each patient. A more typical day in the ED boasted a high volume of patients, assuring Pollard and his staff an extensive and varied experience with every type of emergency condition. The Emergency Department, by volume, was one of the largest in the state. It saw over eighty thousand patients per year. It was a large rectangular shape with ten rooms on each long side of the rectangle, four rooms on one narrow side and the ambulance and patient entrance and waiting area on the other narrow side. Down the middle of the rectangle stood supply storage, counter, and desk space where the staff worked on record keeping, chart storage, patient dictation and consultation with each other on problem patients.

Both students and colleagues respected Dr. Pollard. He prided himself on a lean muscular frame six feet three inches tall honed by years of active tennis competition. He had a full head of black hair and dark brown eyes. His sense of humor and occasional mind-clearing breaks along with his time on the tennis courts helped prevent early burnout, so common in emergency medicine physicians.

He breezed in and out of rooms like a private practitioner, spared the disruptive emergencies that required immediate decision-making. Behind him trailed the usual group of residents and medical students.

"This is the time to shift into second gear," he informed his residents. "Slow your pace, give yourself time to think, and remember you're dealing with a sick, frightened, and conscious human being who needs your full attention. They will also be filling out patient satisfaction forms, and those forms are crucial. It's how we're judged by the Board of Trustees. Do I make myself clear?" Everyone nodded.

Since every resident on his or her first day at Illinois General received the same talk as part of Pollard's one-hour orientation lecture, former residents had already briefed most of the new ones. They knew you either measured up or risked removal from the program. It was due to such methods that Dr. Pollard's program received the best rating in Illinois and commendation from the Joint Commission on Accreditation of Healthcare Organizations..

George was in severe pain when he arrived at Covenant. The ED triage nurse greeted him and recognized his distress. Without wasting time, she ushered him into an examining room, had him lay on a cart, checked his vital signs, and took a brief medical history. He remained in pain the entire time. His answers were short and delivered behind clenched teeth.

When Dr. Pollard entered the room, George was unaware of his presence because he was lying on his side with his face turned away from the doorway. Pollard scanned George's chart before addressing his patient.

"I'm Doctor Jason Pollard. What brings you to the emergency room, Mr. Gilmer?"

George was beginning to notice some alleviation of the pain, and he turned to look at the doctor. "All of a sudden, I got a bad pain, doc," he said, pointing to his left flank. "And here too," pointing to his left lower abdomen.

Pollard made the diagnosis with a high degree of certainty. A good medical history could provide a diagnosis up to eighty percent of the time, and that is what George provided. More than one hundred years ago, the famous Dr. William Osler said, 'Listen to the patient, doctor; she's trying to tell you the diagnosis." George's verbal and hand-pointing description could place any responsible physician on a proper diagnostic path. Pollard suspected a kidney stone and mentioned the possibility to a surprised George.

"Mr. Gilmer, on a scale of one to ten, with one being the least pain and ten the worst, how would you now score yourself?"

George remembered the question from Dr. Crowell's office. Staring first at the ceiling, then at the floor, he said, "A ten when it first hit me, "but it turned the corner pretty quick and now it's a five."

Dr. Pollard noted that the patient now seemed calm, no longer suffering from severe distress. "Have you had this before?" he asked.

George did not answer, nor was it clear that he had even heard the question. Pollard moved into position to get better eye contact. He placed his hand on his patient's wrist. "Tell me, Mr. Gilmer," he repeated, "have you ever experienced this pain before?"

"Yeah, once when I was working I had the same pain. I was on a ladder and it hit me all of a sudden. It lasted about half an hour."

"Was it anything like today's pain?"

"It was the same kind of pain, but the one today started harder."

"Did you see a doctor the last time?"

"No."

"Are you having problems urinating?"

"No."

"Any nausea or vomiting?"

"No."

"Any chills or fever?"

"No."

"Are you normally in good health?"

"Yeah."

Pollard observed his patient's blank expression and abrupt answers and assumed that his pain must have abated.

"Are you allergic to any medicine?"

"Never."

"Never what? Never allergic or you've never taken any medicine?"

"I'm not allergic to any medicine I ever took, but that's not much."

"Could you pass me a urine specimen now?"

"What."

"A urine specimen. I need one now." He handed George a urinal.

"Yeah, sure."

"I'll examine you after you finish. I'll leave and close the curtains and you can pass the specimen right here. Urinate through this gauze, so in case you pass the stone we'll catch it."

Pollard returned, passed the urinalysis to the nurse for testing and proceeded to examine his patient. George's pulse rate was eighty-four, and his blood pressure of 136 over 80 was not bad for a man who had been in pain and was visiting the threatening environment of an Emergency Department. Eyes, ears, nose, throat and thyroid were normal. Carotid artery pulsations were equal. There were no abnormal lymph nodes palpable. Lungs and heart were normal. Integument normal. Genitalia and rectal exam normal, prostate felt ok. Neurological examination was normal. The only positive finding was some left lower quadrant abdominal tenderness, and a positive Murphy punch on the left. The Murphy punch is a gentle, closed-fist punch overlying the kidney region in the back. If the kidneys are involved, it may cause a sudden deep pain in a startled patient. Everything was consistent with his initial diagnosis of a kidney stone. The clincher was the urinalysis report of blood in the urine.

Pollard made the provisional diagnosis of a kidney stone. Based on the test results, he also recommended hospitalization. For the first time, George fixed his expression on the doctor and bolted straight up on the cart.

"Hospital? No way. I don't need a hospital. My pain is almost gone."

"Are you certain?"

"Yes."

Dr. Pollard continued. "These stones can pass by themselves. If you're sure you're better, I could chance it and send you home."

"That sounds good, doc," said George.

Dr. Pollard said, "I'll tell you what. Rest awhile. Maybe this stone is passing, or it might have already passed into your bladder. I'll come back soon to check on you, and if everything's okay you can go home."

"Okay, I'll wait," he said, "but I've got too much work to stay in a hospital."

Pollard conceded that it was better to let this patient have his way, since he was agitated and his symptoms might be letting up.

Patient volume was already picking up. In the next room was a frightened ten-year-old boy with a lacerated hand. Pollard placed four sutures, administered a tetanus injection, dressed the wound and gave the mother verbal and written instructions before sending them home.

When he returned to check on George, he knew his patient's pain had probably passed. He was pacing back and forth. "Feeling better?" the doctor asked

"Yeah."

"What about the pain?"

"It's gone. I can go home now."

"Your pain was five. What about now?"

"It's ZERO."

Dr. Pollard sighed knowing that George's emphasis on the score was his way of insisting on going home. He told his anxious patient, "Look I'm ninety five percent sure it's a kidney stone. Everything points to it. An x-ray could clinch the diagnosis. Sometimes the pain leaves and that could be temporary or permanent, but we can never be certain what will happen."

"Can I take some medicine and take my chances at home?"

Pollard sensed his question inferred an ultimatum.

"Do you have a family doctor?"

"No, said George, forgetting or failing to mention Dr. Crowell."

"All right, Mr. Gilmer. We can let you go since you are feeling better. Understand this means you might have passed the stone into your bladder or are just having some temporary relief. If the pain returns, come right back. In the meantime I'll give you the names of the doctor on call to follow up with."

"Sure thing, doc," said George knowing that he would ignore the information about the referred physician.

"Take these pieces of gauze," offered Pollard. "Urinate through it like before so if you pass the stone out of your body you will catch it on the gauze. If that happens, take it to the doctor so that he or she can have it analyzed. Now, before you leave I would like to get an x-ray and some blood tests. The x-ray may help us pinpoint the stone's location, and the blood tests may help us determine why you developed the stones in the first place. People develop stones for many reasons, including rare ones, and if you do have a stone, you have to find out why, and that takes tests."

"Thanks, but I'll see the doctor you give me and get them then," said George turning toward the door.

George's response and action came as no surprise to Dr. Crowell since his patient never stopped pacing the examination room, nor did he stop staring at the wall long enough to make eye contact with Pollard. He left as soon as he received written instructions, test requisition slips, and the name and phone number of the on-call doctor

Pollard watched as the patient walked away. Moments later, he heard his name called by one of the nurses.

"Dr. Pollard, we're receiving a telemetry strip from the field. It looks like the paramedics are bringing in a sixty-one-year-old man with a possible acute myocardial infarction. Also there is a very serious ventricular arrhythmia."

The pace was picking up. Things were getting back to normal in the Emergency Department.

CHAPTER 12

George rushed out of the Emergency Department. He felt uncomfortable in a medical environment and wanted to end the experience as fast as possible. No doubt, he probably had a kidney stone. That first episode at Fred's house was all too similar. Two kidney stones were double bad luck. How could anyone tolerate such pain if the stone was stuck for days? Maybe, thought George, he should get those damn tests done.

Gail was waiting at the kitchen table when he got home. She glanced up from her coffee and felt reassured. By his calm expression, she was certain he was pain free.

"What happened?" she asked.

"The doctor said I had a kidney stone. Lucky for me, though, they didn't have to do anything. The pain is gone."

"A kidney stone? What the heck..."

"Yeah."

"Hmm. I can tell that you feel better. I called your work today and spoke to the foreman. It's Andy Simpson, right?"

George nodded yes.

"I told him that you went to the hospital because of the pain."

He looked relieved. "Yeah, good idea. Thanks for telling him," said George

"It wasn't my idea. You told me to do it."

"I did?" he said, looking startled.

"Don't you remember?"

For several uncomfortable moments, he stared back at her with a blank expression.

"Must have forgotten," George mumbled. "That pain was all I could think about."

Gail countered with, "You've been forgetting a lot. When are you going to realize you're not yourself? I don't know who you are anymore. Look at what's happening to you. Stomach pains, kidney stones, forgetfulness, you're angry all the time; you're even fighting with people. Please! Take those tests that Dr. Crowell ordered. I can't understand why you don't do it."

He felt backed into a corner. "You're right. I'll go, but now I'm going to work."

"Work? When I spoke to Andy, he figured you wouldn't be back today."

"I got lots of work. Gotta go now." He brushed her cheek with a quick kiss and dashed out the door. She watched him leave, thinking he appeared calmer than earlier. She considered speaking with Dr. Crowell since George did not get angry when she approached the subject of his following through with the prescribed tests.

Andy looked up with surprise when George walked in. "Your wife called and said you went to the hospital. We didn't expect you today. Everything okay?"

"Yeah. I'm okay. The doctor thinks I passed a kidney stone."

"Man, that hurts." Having had a kidney stone himself, Andy knew.

"Worse pain I ever had."

"Sure you're okay?" said Andy.

"Sure. I'm fine."

"Why not work on the lighter stuff today?" suggested Andy. "Take care of the trim, and let the other guys do the rest."

"No, no. I don't have any more pain and can do my regular work. In fact, when I finish today's work, I'll start the trim."

Andy eyed him with suspicion, but kept quiet. George knew Andy was watching him and he went to great lengths to avoid Andy and his coworkers. Not only had his relationship with coworkers changed, but also everyone was on guard not to provoke him.

He felt anxious even though he was not suffering recurrent pain. He would be involved with some task and then suddenly forget what he was doing and how he got there. Such confusion compounded his anxiety. During periods of clarity, he recognized his faulty thinking, but at other times, he reverted to paranoia.

CHAPTER 13

Meanwhile, Gail was busy researching the subject of brain tumors. She got good news and bad news. The good news was that George did not complain of headaches, a major symptom. Yet he did have an episode of vomiting, which could also be symptomatic of a brain tumor. Still, she suspected his ulcer might have triggered the vomiting. Her paramount concern was his mental change, an initial symptom in twenty five percent of all brain tumor cases. The findings included personality changes, confusion, disorientation, behavior changes, and complete psychosis. She convinced herself of her need to confront him now. She needed to make certain he got the MRI. She telephoned Dr. Crowell's office. He was away for a week at a post-graduate course, but his nurse lost no time scheduling the MRI and providing Gail with full instructions.

That evening when she mentioned having scheduled his MRI, George flew into a rage. He picked up a nearby stack of books and slammed them on the floor. "What? Who told you to do that?" he shouted. Such an unexpected display of anger at this time caught Gail off-guard, and she started to cry. "You promised," she choked through her sobs.

George had enough presence of mind to realize that Gail was displaying raw emotion in a way that she had not done before. He realized the need to placate her, and calmed himself down.

"Okay, I'll go, but it's a waste of time."

Gail made the appointment.

He was unhappy, but he convinced himself to get it over with.

Four days later, when he anxiously arrived at the hospital, the hospital technologist explained the procedure for the MRI to him and asked if he was claustrophobic. When he assured her he was not, she assisted him in lying down on the table and covered his eyes with a cloth to help him relax. Then she guided him into the tunnel. Seconds later, he slithered off the table and landed on the floor. As he was panting and hyperventilating, the worried technologist rushed to his side.

"Don't be afraid, it happens sometimes."

George was trembling. "It felt like I was buried inside a casket."

"I won't use a cloth over your eyes," she said. "When you enter the tunnel look towards your feet, so you'll see outside the tunnel and know you're safe and not surrounded by it on all sides."

He fought the urge to leave, but controlled himself. When the technologist gave him an injection of contrast material to 'light up' a possible abnormality, his ordeal was soon over and he was free to go.

"How was it?" asked Gail.

"A piece of cake," he reported with a smile.

The following two days were nerve-wracking for Gail while she waited for the test results. The news was good. His MRI was perfect. There was not a single abnormality.

"Now are you satisfied?" he said. "My brain, like everything else, works just fine."

Gail let out an audible sigh. "Better get to work," she told him.

CHAPTER 14

George tried his best on his job, but problems continued to plague him. One afternoon he experienced a recurrence of the ulcer-like symptoms. He had stopped his medication after thinking the pain was gone, so after work he drove to the local drugstore for a bottle of antacids.

This evening he didn't come home from work on time. Gail became anxious and after two hours passed she telephoned the construction site, but nobody answered. She assumed the worst. His job was a thirty-minute drive from home, and many hospitals were located along the way. She called the two nearest ones, but they told her that George Gilmer was neither an inpatient nor had he come through the Emergency Department. Just as she was considering calling the police the telephone rang.

"Hello, Mrs. Gilmer?"

"Yes, who is this please?" she asked.

"I'm a police officer from Roby Avenue police station."

"Oh, my God. What happened?"

"Your husband was caught breaking into a car parked in front of a drugstore. He smashed the window on the driver's side, got in and drove away. A pedestrian noted the make of the car and the license plate number and called the police. We had a patrol car pick him up. He didn't answer questions, so the officer called for help and we brought him into the station. He wasn't cooperating and was acting funny. It took us a while to find out that the car your husband broke into was his own. He smashed the window to get inside after realizing that he had locked the keys in the car. We've got him calmed down now and he's okay. But I got to tell you, he came real close to jail time."

Gail forced herself to remain calm. "Will he be able to come home now?" she said in a controlled tone of voice.

"Yeah, we were worried about drugs or alcohol, but he snapped out of it fast so that couldn't be the problem. Right now he's fine."

"Thank you, officer." Relieved, she hung up the receiver. She had not asked to speak to George for fear he would say something wrong in front of the police. She waited for him to arrive and within twenty minutes he was back home.

Gail remained noncommittal while observing his familiar blank stare and lack of communication. After ten seconds of silence, she spoke. "You might be angry with me, but I need to tell you that you're a very sick man. You broke your car window and almost wound up behind bars. What could you possibly have been thinking?"

"I had to get into the car. My keys were there."

Gail countered. "But the police said you didn't know what you were doing and they thought you were drugged, or maybe even drunk."

"They're all exaggerating", said George with a brush of his hand in the air.

"Forget it, George. Nothing's changed. You're sick. You forget a lot. You're nervous and irritable, and I'm even getting scared to live with you. You've got to take Dr. Crowell's advice and go see a psychiatrist, and also get the blood tests he ordered. You didn't do those yet."

"Maybe you're the one who needs the shrink," George answered sarcastically.

"You're right, I am going nuts," she sobbed, "but you're driving me there. You have no idea what this has done to me. Your MRI may have been normal, but something is happening to your brain. Can't you see it? We can't go on like this."

He felt impacted by Gail's tears. Despite his altered mind-set, there appeared some glimmer of recognition regarding his fragile situation, both at home and work.

"Yeah," he said. "I'll go. But it's just another waste of money."

She kept still, fearing that any further discussion might cause him to change his mind.

She telephoned Dr. Crowell's office the next morning and spoke to his nurse. Realizing the urgency, the nurse arranged for George to see a psychiatrist right away. The psychiatrist's schedule was booked months in advance, but he agreed to meet George in the hospital where he made patient rounds.

Gail and George met Dr. Louis Clementi at the hospital clinic. He was everyone's vision of a psychiatrist—tall, with a gray beard, glasses, a slight Italian accent and a navy blue suit with a light blue shirt and striped tie. Gail thought he resembled an Italian reincarnation of Sigmund Freud. The doctor's calm presence put them at ease. They entered a small examining room in the outpatient department.

"I'm pleased to meet you both," said the doctor. "I hope I can help."

Gail related the entire story, beginning with George's failure to get the prescribed tests. The doctor took notes while keeping a watchful eye on his patient. He observed George's fidgeting, anxiety, inattentiveness, and above all, his facial expressions and body language. Then he suggested to Gail that she step out of the room so he could interview her husband in private. The doctor spent the necessary time questioning George before inviting Gail back in. Then, he sat and faced the two of them.

"I don't like to make a firm diagnosis after one visit." he offered. "For the record, however, here's what I think. First, the normal MRI is good news. Your concern about a brain tumor, Mrs. Gilmer, was a good one in light of your husband's symptoms, and we're happy that was not the problem, but other conditions can cause such symptoms, even with a normal MRI brain scan. As you know, I see only patients with emotional or mental problems, so I end up with a particular psychiatric diagnosis. Mr. Gilmer has many different symptoms of anxiety, perhaps paranoia, agitation, restlessness, and even amnesia. Yet, I'm beginning to focus my attention on a medical diagnosis rather than a psychiatric one. Many medical problems can affect the brain; that list is endless."

George listened, squirming in his chair. He tried to concentrate on what the doctor was saying, but he was flooded with a barrage of simultaneous thoughts.

"To tell you the truth I have practiced psychiatry for nearly thirty years and don't deal with anything purely medical. Nevertheless, not every patient fits into some tight little psychiatric pocket. Mr. Gilmer is a perfect example of this. If there is a moral to this story, it would be that procrastination in getting a full medical work-up can be very dangerous. You must get the tests that Dr. Crowell ordered. You should see him very soon. I will send your doctor a full report." Clementi paused long enough to make certain that he had made himself clear. Then he said, "Have you any further questions?"

"Is there anything he can take in the meantime to help him relax?" asked Gail.

"He could, but I'm reluctant to prescribe anything without first establishing a specific diagnosis. I don't want either of you to expect some simple cure that you can obtain from a bottle. This is urgent. You must complete the medical investigation. That is priority number one." He paused to look at George. "I cannot stress this enough, Mr. Gilmer. There are plenty of unusual medical problems that can cause your symptoms."

Gail could only hope that the appointment with Dr. Clementi might get George to move forward. "Dr. Crowell is out-of-town," she said, "but we have his order for the tests so we can go ahead and get them." Gail glanced over at George, and then she turned her attention back to the doctor.

"Good," replied the doctor.

George didn't say anything until they left the clinic. "I told you I wasn't nuts," he said. "Today was a waste of time. Everyone's just passing the buck."

Gail was unfazed by his remarks. "If you get the tests and something curable is found, it will be worth it. No more stalling."

"I'll do it, don't worry."

"George, I'll be staying home this weekend. I'm not going to visit my mother."

"No way. You and the kids looked forward to this trip for a long time."

"It doesn't matter. I'll feel better staying home."

"No," he insisted.

She felt threatened by his tone, enough to force her to drop the subject.

Neither spoke much at dinner. That was a good sign to Gail, since by his very silence George offered no opposition. She felt hopeful.

Nevertheless, his silence betrayed a storm in his brain, a gathering force, fueled by a chaotic internal chemistry that would soon explode and alter their lives. When Gail left home the next morning for her mother's house, George headed to the neighborhood drugstore for more antacids as his symptoms were returning with a vengeance.

CHAPTER 15

George Gilmer and family lived in a typical middle-class, blue-collar area of Chicago. There were many such neighborhoods, most of them with an ethnic majority, but George's area included people of all ethnic origins. Most of the residences were small homes built seventy to ninety years ago. They had well-kept small front lawns and larger back yards. Intermingled with all the homes was an occasional three or four story apartment building with many permanent and some transient residents. Two of the transient residents were Larry Benson and Philip Matt. They lived about six blocks apart and approximately one-half mile from George. They were drinking friends.

Both men enjoyed the Friday night fish fry at Traficante's Bar and Grill located on one of the main streets that coursed through the neighborhood. Philip was a frequent patron there and he first met Larry six months earlier at the bar. Larry was six foot five inches of solid muscle with pitch-black hair, a prominent square jaw and a face that said, 'be careful.' He worked as a truck driver for a local bakery. Whenever he and Philip entered the grill together, owner Joe Traficante would bellow, "Here come Mutt and Jeff." Traficante, an older man, had to explain who Mutt and Jeff was—old time comic strip characters.

Philip was five foot seven inches with light brown hair and blue eyes. He was slender and frail appearing, in stark contrast to his friend, Larry.

Larry and Philip enjoyed their Friday evening fish fry and two-beer ritual. Traficante had joined them for a beer since it was later than usual and the place was almost empty. The three of them engaged in small talk while watching the Chicago Bulls play basketball on TV.

Afterwards, Larry and Philip left together and went separate ways to their respective apartments.

It was after ten in the evening. Philip Matt was walking alone down one of the dark, deserted side streets. This neighborhood was perfect for him and his wife. It was handy for work and close to recreation and extensive shopping. There were several homes available for sale within half a mile of the apartment they lived in, and they had their eyes on one of them.

Then, as he turned the corner, Phillip saw what appeared to be a man crawling along the sidewalk. As he moved closer, he could see that the man was in distress, his head bowed, staring at the ground, swaying from side to side. He was wearing what appeared to be a plastic hood. It covered his ears and his forehead to the level of his eyes. Why would anyone wear a hood like that on a nice night like tonight? Philip thought. He rushed to the fallen man's side.

"What's wrong, buddy?" asked Philip. He stooped to assist, but at that moment, the stranger sprang to his feet, lunged forward with a knife, and aimed for his victim's chest. Philip's hands flew in the air as he tried to shield himself, but too late, he felt a stabbing pain in his chest as he crashed to the ground by a sweeping action of the stranger's left leg. He screamed. Then he felt three more sharp pains in rapid succession—one on his hand and two in his chest. The dim light of the bungalows faded from Philip's eyes. He felt his heart thump in his chest as complete darkness engulfed him. The stranger disappeared into the evening shadows.

CHAPTER 16

Leo Carlin was rising from his living room chair. The news was over and it was time to go to bed. He looked out of the front room picture window, but the light from the lamp obscured his vision. He turned off the light and caught a glimpse of a man dressed in dark clothes running north down Iowa Street. He would never have seen him had he not had cataract surgery five months ago, but now his vision was excellent. He then turned his gaze to a man lying on the sidewalk. He could see a dim outline in the dark, but the man's spasmodic movements made him more visible. He's shaking: convulsions, he thought. He needs help. As he rushed toward the door he called to his wife, "Sylvia, call 911. There's a man on the sidewalk in front of the house."

When he reached the stranger's side, he was no longer having seizures. He was unconscious with his mouth open and his eyes closed. There was blood on his jacket on the left side of his chest. Stabbed, he thought, and right in front of the house. He put his ear to the victim's chest. He wasn't sure he could hear anything. His wife called from the porch. "What is it?" Carlin turned to look at her, his eyes opened wide. He shook his head. "He's been stabbed. It looks like he's dead. Did you call the paramedics?"

"Yeah. They're coming right away."

Within minutes the paramedic ambulance came down Iowa Street. Carlin was on the curb waving them on. Two men leaped out of the ambulance and ran to their patient. "Step back into your yard," they said to Carlin. "This is a crime scene. Keep away and don't touch anything. Don't let anyone walk here. We're calling the police. They'll be here soon."

They placed the victim on a cart, and left for the Emergency Department of Covenant Hospital. They reported his clinical status to the ED via telemetry, and at the same time notified the police.

Within a few minutes, two squad cars drove up. The Carlins were waiting on their front porch. "The man was right over there," Leo pointed. The officers got the witnesses names and address and the story of what occurred through Carlin's eyes. They wrote everything down. The area was yellow taped and a drawing was made of the area while awaiting the arrival of the crime-scene analysts.

This was an easy crime scene for the first responders. There was no chance of fingerprint lifting, but there was blood identified on the sidewalk, and they took specimens. They identified one footprint next to the sidewalk in a partial grassy area between the sidewalk and the street. A portion of the print, dug into the soft ground "Looks like about a size eleven." said one of the analysts. "Notice how the toe area is dug deeper into the dirt. This guy wasn't just standing here whoever he was. This must have been his back leg while he was doing the dirty deed. The front leg would have been on the sidewalk right about here. Let's check. We'll have to get the victim's foot size and check his shoes. But I'll bet money this print wasn't his." They completed their work and left for headquarters. They would return in the morning.

CHAPTER 17

Alan Forman had been a paramedic for more than ten years and knew this victim was close to death. The patient did not respond to verbal or sensory stimulation. He was comatose. His pupils were equal, but not dilated. The victim's pulse rate was too rapid for an accurate count. His blood pressure was not audible. Forman began cardiopulmonary resuscitation. He placed electrocardiogram leads on his patient's chest, and the tracing was sent via telemetry to the Emergency Department at Covenant. There the nurse on call picked up the tracing, noted the rapid rhythm and immediately notified Dr. Pollard.

Pollard lost no time contacting the ambulance. "What do you have?" he asked. He noted that the tracing indicated a regular heart rate of 160 per minute.

"A young guy in complete shock," replied Forman. "It appears he was stabbed in the left chest. Pulse very rapid and thready and veins are collapsed, but I believe I've got a good venipuncture. Saline going at rapid rate. He'll need a central line, but my best guess is that the knife wounds entered his heart. Two of the wounds are at the fifth intercostal space medial to the midclavicular line, and the third wound is lateral to the first two. I think he's got a chest full of blood."

"Any blood pressure?" asked Pollard.

"Only by palpation. You can't hear anything. The systolic is about sixty as best as I can tell, but I'm not certain."

"Are you close to the hospital?"

"We're pulling in."

The ambulance arrived at Covenant, and they wheeled the victim into the ED. Dr. Pollard and his team of two residents and three nurses were ready. They rapidly placed a central line, drew blood for routine tests, type and cross match and inserted a Foley catheter. Universal donor blood was on the way. Then they inserted an endo-tracheal tube, started mechanical ventilation and inserted a chest tube that confirmed the presence of blood. While all this was in process, the electrocardiogram changed, signaling that the patient had gone into ventricular fibrillation, a rapid and fatal fluttering of the heart. With this abnormal rhythm, there is no regular cardiac beat to propel the blood through the circulatory system. With no blood circulating, a person has no blood pressure, cells receive no blood and oxygen, and unless reversed, death would be imminent.

"Code 99, code 99" resounded from the ED intercom. The hovering medical team started direct current defibrillation. They infused one hundred milligrams of lidocaine and a resident began to administer external cardiac compression. When the cross-matched blood arrived, they instantly transfused the patient. Two medics and two nurses circled his cart, all with specific duties, but the ventricular fibrillation became a flat line, indicative of no cardiac electrical activity. As a last ditch measure, Dr. Pollard injected adrenaline directly into his heart.

Philip Matt remained unresponsive to all measures and Pollard declared him dead twenty-seven minutes after arriving at the hospital's Emergency Department. One more statistic for the F.B.I., and another average day around the Chicago Metropolitan area, thought Pollard. The physician team separated and left for the care of other patients. The nurses removed all tubes from the victim's body, cleaned him up, covered him, and transferred his body to the morgue. When no family was present, Dr. Pollard moved right onto the next case. Because the stabbing had been a clear-cut homicide, the hospital reported it to the authorities.

"Thanks, everyone, for your hard work," said Pollard, looking tired and drained. "The bleeding was just too massive, and the injuries too great."

He would never get used to witnessing victims of violence—but it was over. He told himself that now it was time to concentrate on the living. He knew the next patient deserved his full attention, and he needed to shift gears and get to work.

Pollard entered the next room, where he saw a young girl lying on her side with her eyes closed. Sitting beside her was the child's mother, looking very worried as she clung to her daughter's hand beneath the covers. After diagnosing tonsillitis, getting a throat culture, and prescribing penicillin, the mother was reassured and Pollard moved on to his next case.

Suddenly, as he was examining an elderly patient, he heard a scream from the next room. Because these sounds were common in the ED, he continued with the task-at-hand. However, the screaming did not stop so he went to the source and witnessed Dr. Carly Godwin come crashing through the curtain that enclosed the entrance of the adjacent room. She landed on the floor. She was lying prone on her back as Pollard rushed to her side.

He knelt down beside her. "Are you okay, Carly?"

She looked stunned. Shaking her head in acknowledgment, she pulled herself up to a seated position. Before replying, she paused to check the bridge of her nose with two fingers. "Yes, I think I'm okay," she said.

"Let's look," he said. "No it doesn't look fractured."

"Well, at least I'm happy about that. My looks don't need any more asymmetry."

"Any other injury, Carly?"

"No, Dr. Pollard. Just a fist in my face is all."

"Here, let me help you." He extended his hand to help her get up, and assisted her to the nurse's station in the center of the rectangular ED, where both sat down. Pollard, at six feet and three inches was a foot taller than his astonished resident. Carly put her disheveled blond hair in place with both hands. Her dark eyes still registered the shock of her encounter.

Dr. Pollard asked, "What happened?"

Carly said, "I was examining a man who I thought was having a psychotic episode. The police brought him in after they found him wandering the streets. He wouldn't respond to their questions. He resisted them, and his behavior was so bizarre that they brought him here rather than take him to the lockup. They had no idea if he was drunk, drugged, or sick. I ordered some haldol, and we were trying to restrain him when he reached out and swung at me. Lucky for me I managed to see it coming and I was able to move away from the punch so I didn't get the full force of the blow."

"That's your tennis training giving you those lightening like reflexes," chuckled Pollard.

Carly laughed. "If I had your tennis reflexes he wouldn't have gotten near my nose," she countered. You know, this is the first time a patient ever hit me."

"Join the club. I hope it's also the last. It's one of the occupational hazards of being an emergency medicine physician. Thank God it's rare."

"Perhaps you should add some Tae Kwan Do training to your curriculum, Dr. Pollard," smiled Carly.

"If I do, within six months I'm sure you'll be a black belt," he laughed. Meanwhile, the patient had quieted down. The haldol injection was taking effect.

"Have you ever seen this patient before?" asked Pollard.

"No, this is the first time."

He nodded his head. "Seeing psychotic young men come into the ED isn't a daily occurrence. Tell me what else you know about him."

"Well, like I said, the police brought him in. They found him wandering the streets. Even from a distance, they could see that his walk was abnormal. He fell down once and had trouble getting up, and when they spoke to him, he became violent, so they cuffed him. They thought he was under the influence of something, so they put him in the paddy wagon and brought him here. He would be quiet for short periods, but when someone tried to touch him he became violent. I never saw anything quite like this. I don't think he knew if he was an animal, a vegetable, or a mineral. He was a danger to himself and the staff so I ordered restraints, and believe me it was a job getting them on."

"Did you detect an odor of alcohol on his breath?"

"None that I could tell."

"Any chance of drugs playing a part?"

"That's a possibility. I'll order a drug screen."

"Is the patient in restraints now?"

"He should be. We were putting them on right before round one of my boxing match." Carly glanced into the patient's room. "Yes, they're on now."

"Well, he's quiet and we all have a lot of work to do. Finish your examination and come up with a differential diagnosis. When I come back, we'll take a few minutes to discuss your findings and recommendations."

Dr. Pollard returned to his elderly congestive heart failure patient. He telephoned her physician to discuss strategy, issued written orders and had her admitted.

Meanwhile, Carly returned to examine her patient. The room was quiet, and just one nurse was present. "The haldol quieted him down. He's sleeping now," reported the nurse.

"Good. I'll examine him, but let's order a full blood profile, a CBC, a drug screen, and a serum amylase. Also, might as well get a portable x-ray of the chest and an EKG while he's here. I'm sure he'll be admitted." Carly continued her evaluation.

There are limits to a physician examination when attempting to work-up a sedated patient. Nevertheless, Carly knew Pollard would quiz her. Under such scrutiny, any resident would feel pressured to be careful not to miss anything. She could not take a history, but she could do a careful physical examination. Based on what she knew, or didn't know of the patient's history, the partial physical exam, and the lack of laboratory data, she was prepared to run her mentor's gauntlet.

Pollard was completing the workup of a patient with a classical acute cholecystitis when Carly approached him. He motioned her to sit down while he finished analyzing the ultrasound. It revealed the presence of gallstones, confirming his diagnosis. Then he turned his attention to the young doctor.

"First," said Carly, "my patient's under the effect of haldol, so any examination is limited. He's young, and has no obvious clinical findings on neurological examination. His general physical exam is also normal. Heart and lungs are okay, the abdomen is negative, and there's no patient response to epigastric palpation. I mention that because of the possibility of pancreatitis that could present this way. There is no alcohol-like odor to his breath, the integument is normal, genitalia and rectal exam were negative, no testicular masses present, and the funduscopic exam was difficult although I could see an edge of the optic disc and there was no papilledema. Ear, nose, and throat are also normal. In short, the physical examination was not diagnostic. All I have to show is a definite altered mental state."

"That was very thorough, Carly. So, what do you think? What's your differential diagnosis?" asked Pollard.

"I have three thoughts. The first is a severe schizophrenic episode, second, a drug overdose, and third, an organic psychosis. If it's an organic psychosis, then the possibilities are endless since, as I recall, the causes of organic psychoses go on and on."

"Good thinking, Carly. I agree with your differential diagnosis. We won't talk about organic psychoses now, because that's a subject for a whole textbook. Let's go visit him." He stood up, and she led him to the patient's room. She walked over to his bedside, followed by Pollard, who stopped short in his tracks. He smiled, but just for an instant. He then became very serious as he turned to face his resident.

"You look surprised, Dr. Pollard. What's the matter?"

"Nothing other than the fact that I'm quite sure I know his diagnosis."

"Now wait a minute. Are you trying to tell me that you took one look at this patient from ten feet away and you know his diagnosis?"

"Sure," he said.

Everyone knew about Dr. Pollard's legendary ability to diagnose, but this was too much. Carly felt inadequate. "Wow," she groaned. "Okay. I give up." She stared at Pollard in disbelief. "What did you see from ten feet away?" she asked.

"Nothing."

"Nothing?"

"That's correct. I only saw a man lying on a bed, someone covered with a sheet from the neck down. What else could I have seen?"

Carly now felt like the victim of a cat and mouse game with the good doctor in control. She scrutinized the patient again. All he saw is his face, she thought as she stepped a little closer, just enough to peer into her patient's face. "He looks normal," she said, still mystified.

"I agree,"

"I feel like a ball of yarn, and you're playing with me like a cat. What are you driving at?"

He laughed. He was enjoying himself. "You're right, I couldn't resist. But this is too serious to fool around with any longer. The truth is I am the cat. But the reason I'm convinced of the diagnosis is that I've seen this patient in the Emergency Department before. If I remember correctly his name is George Gilmer, and he was here with a syndrome of severe flank and abdominal pain, and microscopic hematuria. What is that?"

Her jaw dropped. "A kidney stone?" she replied still puzzled.

Still, he was not finished. "Right," he replied. "Now, what's the diagnosis? You have presenting symptoms and findings from today, and also the history that you did not have earlier, a kidney stone. Can you put it together with his other symptoms and come up with a diagnosis?"

"Hmm, uh…no." She looked skeptical. She realized it was now a new ball game, and that Pollard had the whole case figured out. No surprise, she thought. It happens all the time.

"What have you ordered in the way of studies?" asked Pollard.

"Full blood profile, CBC, serum amylase, drug screen, EKG and Chest x-ray."

"Good thinking. Those are all appropriate considering your differential diagnosis, but I'm interested to know if you're in a hurry to get any of these tests."

"Maybe the electrolytes?" she replied.

"Good idea. Add stat to the electrolyte order since abnormal electrolytes, such as sodium, can cause an altered mental state, and that's an urgent situation. We need this information fast. But, considering the patient's age, and in the absence of any physical findings, an electrolyte abnormality would be a last choice. So far you've come up with three possible diagnoses. All of them make sense, but remember this important clinical axiom: If you can explain all the symptoms, physical findings, and historical information with one diagnosis, do so. But can you do this?"

Carly thought for a while and shook her head. "Nope," she said.

"Would you like a hint?"

"I could use all the help I can get." She smiled. "Could I use one of my lifelines?"

He roared with laughter. "No lifelines allowed in the ED, doctor. But, here's a hint: Stones, bones, abdominal groans, and mental moans." He was grilling his resident hard, and he knew it.

Her eyes opened wide. She slapped her forehead. "My God. Hyperparathyroidism. I've never seen a case."

"It's a rare diagnosis. But if that's what he has, his case is very unusual."

"You mean cases as severe as this?"

"Yes. Most cases, thank goodness, are much milder."

"I sure hope so."

"How will you determine if he has hyperparathyroidism?"

"I would get a serum calcium level," she suggested.

"Yes, stat. Since you drew a full profile, which includes serum calcium, call the lab and have them do the calcium on an urgent basis. That will give us the results in about an hour. If the calcium is elevated, we can assume that the patient has hypercalcemia, the most likely cause of which is hyperparathyroidism. As you know, there are many causes of an elevated serum calcium level. We'll talk about that later."

"I'll let you know when I receive the results," she promised.

"All right, but what will you do about the patient in the meantime?"

"I'll start an IV and write further haldol orders if necessary. I'll also monitor his vital signs every fifteen minutes."

"Good thinking," smiled Dr. Pollard.

This was his favorite way of teaching: at the bedside. The problem is that it's a luxury not always available due to heavy patient volume and the necessity to keep working. However, this was important when an unusual case presented itself. The residents appreciated his approach as well because they had to think on their feet. A lesson learned in this manner was a lesson retained.

Carly understood that what one reads in textbooks is readily forgotten. On the other hand, what you learn at the bedside you remember. It is not likely that she would ever forget what she had learned today. While this type of learning could be intimidating, Pollard's residents were mature enough to welcome the intellectual challenge.

The hospital processed George's blood on an urgent basis or 'stat.' Results of these tests are telephoned to the ordering physician the moment completed.

While Carly was busy examining another patient, a phone call interrupted her. It was the laboratory informing her of the patient's test results.

"Yes?" she answered.

"The serum calcium on George Gilmer is 13.8," reported the laboratory supervisor.

"Thank you, 13.8 right?" Carly repeated, double-checking the laboratory findings.

"That's right, doctor."

Pollard's right on target again, she thought. She sought him out for advice and consultation. "You got it right," she said. "Mr. Gilmer's serum calcium is 13.8, so it seems as if your diagnosis of hyperparathyroidism is accurate. What do we do now?" Carly asked.

"First, we start 0.9 sodium chloride intravenously and administer 80 milligrams of lasix IV. Since he is under the influence of haldol and his illness has rendered him psychotic, I would insert a Foley catheter and keep him restrained for the time being. The purpose of this therapy is so that the sodium chloride will expand his extracellular volume, and this will enhance calcium excretion in the urine, and the lasix will cause a vigorous diuresis, which will help eliminate calcium from the body. We have to lower his serum calcium as fast as possible since it is having such deleterious effects. Also I would order serum calcium levels at least every twelve hours so we can follow the progress of our therapy. As a routine, also get a parathormone level. That will confirm the diagnosis of hyperparathyroidism."

"Right away."

"That result will take a week or so, as it has to be sent out to a reference lab," said Dr. Pollard, "and when you're finished with the stat therapy, get him admitted and then come back. We've got more to talk about."

After George's therapy had begun, Carly returned to find Pollard. They went to his office to talk.

She sat across his desk, behind which was a built in bookcase filled with two shelves of medical texts in all specialties reflecting the broad range of knowledge required of emergency medicine specialists. On a third shelf was a long row of emergency medicine journals. On the desk was a picture of Dr. Pollard's wife and six children. On a side desk was a computer. "Let's put our brains in gear," he said. "Have some orange juice. Let's refresh. What's your diagnosis now?"

"Hyperparathyroidism."

"Has that been established yet?"

"I hope so. We've been treating him for it."

"Have we been treating him for hyperparathyroidism?"

"Okay, doctor. I'm the ball of yarn again, and I'm not following you."

Her candor humored him. "I have little doubt that your patient, Mr. Gilmer, has hyperparathyroidism. However, right now we are treating an elevated calcium level that can be very hazardous to his health, so we don't have the time and luxury to wait for a final diagnosis. Right now our diagnosis is hypercalcemia. Remember to keep your diagnosis at the level of your current state of knowledge. I'm certain you'll agree that all we know for certain is that Gilmer has an elevated level of calcium."

"Yes, that we do know for certain."

"Let's think," Pollard continued. "What else causes an elevated calcium level?"

"Well, I once had a patient who developed it from taking a thiazide diuretic," Carly said.

"That can happen. Nevertheless, we know from Mr. Gilmer's last visit that he was not taking any medication. Granted, how reliable is that information?"

"Malignancy can cause elevated calcium levels," said Carly, her interest was now piqued.

"Right again, Carly. Malignancy, with the spread of cancer to bone, such as carcinoma from many primary sites; leukemia, lymphomas, and myeloma. Also, malignancies that do not involve bone but still elevate calcium through the elaboration of a parathormone like substance. Anything else?"

"That's about all I can think of."

"Other considerations would include hyperthyroidism, vitamin D intoxication, milk alkali syndrome from drinking too much milk or taking too many antacids, sarcoidosis, and an underactive thyroid gland for some unknown reason. These are only rare possibilities."

Carly broke in. "Milk alkali syndrome?"

"Yes, why?" asked Dr, Pollard

"Something's ringing a bell," she said, now unable to control her excitement. "When we were trying to identify him, we found a bottle of antacids in his pocket."

"Ah hah. Now you understand why one has to work at the current level of his, or her, knowledge. We have a new possibility. Could this man be a heavy antacid consumer or a milk drinker? Could he have developed an elevated level of calcium due to excess ingestion? Or, is the underlying pathology his hyperparathyroidism that can also cause an ulcer, which may be why he was taking an antacid? The plot is thickening."

"Yes," Carly said with wide opened eyes reflecting her admiration for Pollard's way of thinking and depth of knowledge.

"What kind of antacid is it?" asked Pollard

"Tums."

"What do you know about Tums?"

"Zero," she admitted.

"It's a calcium-based antacid, so Tums could have some relevance here. It is possible to take enough antacids to cause hypercalcemia, or taking the antacid might have further elevated what may have been his already elevated calcium level from hyperparathyroidism. Either of these scenarios could have pushed him into a psychotic state."

"Never a dull moment," Carly replied nodding in disbelief.

"Anyhow, nothing really is changing in terms of our therapy, but we must establish the diagnosis of hyperparathyroidism. Be sure that a parathormone level is ordered. That'll tell us if his parathyroid gland is making too much hormone."

"Already done."

"Great. Send the patient to the medical floor, and be sure to brief the medical residents. Chances are they have never seen anything like this."

"I bet they haven't," said Carly, shaking her head.

Pollard quickly added, "Also it wouldn't hurt to call a psychiatric consultation. They may have something to add, and besides, it will be an educational experience for them. This case explains how a medical problem can manifest itself as a psychiatric illness."

"Good idea."

"By the way, Carly, you found Tums in his pockets. Did you find anything else, a wallet perhaps?"

"Yes, he has a wallet in his pocket. I left it there."

"Good, let's look at it."

Carly reached into George's back pocket, retrieved the wallet and handed it to Pollard.

Pollard examined the contents, and found a folded prescription. "Look at this," he said. This is Dr. Crowell's prescription. He's seen this patient before and ordered these tests on him. It looks like he was working Mr. Gilmer up. I'm going to call Crowell now and see what we can learn."

CHAPTER 18

"I brought you here to celebrate our anniversary," said Burt Crowell to his date Eve Worthy.

"Anniversary?" she responded looking at him cross eyed.

"Yes, our one month anniversary. We had our first date here one month ago."

"I see. How romantic," said Eve. "Well, you picked a fine place. This restaurant has wonderful ambience and the food is great."

"There's another reason I like to come here. It's close to the hospital, and I'm on call tonight."

"With two of you in practice, you take call pretty often, don't you?"

"Well, you'd think every other night, but for a special financial consideration, I agreed to more. I don't mind it. I'm young and still have the resident mentality in me when I was working so many hours. Anyhow the faster I learn the ropes, the better I like it, and the more I keep busy the easier it is on my mind."

"Good idea. I feel the same way. How's your mentor, Dr. Wagner?"

"He's a great boss. I'm learning a lot from him. He's already making plans for his retirement and assures me he'll be out of my way in about six months. It'll be all mine then.

"Do you think you'll be able to handle it?"

"I do. If it becomes a little overwhelming, I've got a guy picked out to come join me, but we'll see—or maybe you'd consider going to medical school? It would be worth the wait."

"Ha, ha, funny man. No thank you. I love my life as a nurse."

"My luck."

"Well, good luck to you," said Eve. Solo practice today is not easy. Find an associate as soon as you can."

"I will. Thanks for the advice. How do you like Covenant?" asked Burt.

"I like it," she nodded. "I thought it wouldn't be as busy as Illinois General, but I learned that wasn't the case. They already put me on the hospital-wide Quality Committee because of my experience at Illinois General. They thought maybe I could make a contribution"

"That's great. Maybe you could teach me a few things, or better yet, maybe I could lobby to get on your committee and we can practice some more togetherness." He smiled.

"You are devious, aren't you?"

"Ha ha, yeah, just kidding. I won't be a full attending physician for another year, so I couldn't serve on that committee anyhow."

"Well, if you ever do get the chance, take it. There's so much to learn about hospital-wide safety. It's a very complicated issue."

"I can imagine."

"By the way, what do you think about George Gilmer?" asked Eve

"George Gilmer. Yes, thanks for the referral. I presume you know him."

"I'm very good friends with his wife. She called to ask me for a referral to a doctor."

"Oh they never mentioned that to me."

"His wife was worried about his strange behavior. Her husband doesn't seem to believe in doctors."

Burt nodded yes and said, "I'm getting that message. I ordered tests and he didn't get them yet,"

"I know."

"You know?"

"His wife calls me often. We've even had lunch together. She told me all about him. So you can tell me what you think. I wouldn't say anything, of course, and maybe I could help."

"Well, what about confidentiality issues? Can I really speak with you about a patient?"

"Probably not, but I can tell you all I know about him. His wife has no hesitation in confiding to me about everything, and I have some thoughts about him that I'd like to share with you."

"Okay, I understand, but let me tell you what I think first."

"That's a deal."

"He had abdominal pain characteristic of peptic ulcer disease, so I did a complete physical and ordered tests including helicobacter pylori studies. He never got them. I chastised him on a second visit. He was developing some other symptoms of a mental nature, so I stressed the urgency. By then I was starting to worry about things like a brain tumor or a psychiatric emergency or even hyperparathyroidism."

"I guess, as the saying goes, great minds think alike. Those were my thoughts too," said Eve. "Have you seen hyperparathyroidism before?"

"Yes, I have. Once as a resident, I had a man who had a slightly elevated calcium level, but he was completely asymptomatic. I thought about the possibility of hyperparathyroid disease, and asked an endocrinologist about it. He told me if the patient was asymptomatic, even if he had a slight calcium elevation, nothing need be done. Yes, he could even have a small adenoma of the parathyroid glands, but with this level of calcium, he didn't need surgery, and watchful waiting could be appropriate. I explained this all to the patient back then. He asked me if he could have this adenoma? I suppose it's possible, I said. Then he wanted to know how he could find out. A nuclear medicine test, I told him. To make a long story short, he insisted on the test, and sure enough there was an adenoma present. Even though he wasn't having symptoms he wanted it out. So out it came, courtesy of a happy surgeon. Anyhow, I should be hearing about Mr. Gilmer's tests any day now."

"I wish him luck. Whoops, there's our food."

"Are you sure you don't want a drink? Don't worry about me not having any since I'm on call."

"I'm fine thanks."

As they ate, Burt thought of the last month since he had known Eve. He liked what he had seen on the medical floor. She was efficient and compassionate. His partner was out of town, so he had been too busy to date her again, but he enjoyed lunch with her a few times in the Covenant cafeteria, and he found himself looking for her every day. In his mind, at least, he was getting more and more interested. He hoped the feeling was mutual. At the end of the meal, his cell phone rang. "Excuse me, Eve, my cell. Hello, this is Dr. Crowell."

"Hello, Burt, it's Jason in emergency."

"What can I do for you, Jason?"

"Your patient, George Gilmer is here."

He waved his hand at Eve, pointed to his phone and quietly mouthed the word—"listen".

"What's wrong with Gilmer, Jason?" He emphasized Gilmer and nodded at Eve.

"He was admitted in a complete psychotic state. He punched out one of my residents, Carly Godwin."

"George Gilmer punched out a resident? Jeez. Little Carly? How is she? How's Gilmer?"

"The resident's fine. We're admitting Gilmer now and we have a diagnosis. He's still out of it."

"Did you do a serum calcium?" he said looking at Eve.

"Yep, 13.8. Good thinking, Burt."

"Thirteen point eight calcium," he said, looking at Eve and raising his left thumb in the air. "Is he getting fluids?"

"Yes, plus lasix."

"Okay, great, I'll be there in fifteen minutes. Thanks." He put the phone back in his pocket. "Come on, Eve. I need your help with George. Damn, I was hoping to show you my etchings tonight."

"Oh, sorry about that," joked Eve.

CHAPTER 19

They started George's treatment and transported him to the floor in restraints. When Burt arrived, he performed a careful examination of his patient who was undergoing an extensive diuresis. Eve stood by to assist. The only additional medical finding uncovered was a superficial laceration on the right palm of his hand that had bled, but shallow enough not to require stitches. I wonder how that got there, thought Burt.

The floor nurses, alerted to the patient's pre-medication behavior, remained vigilant. While the patient was in the ED, an electrocardiogram and a portable chest x-ray were normal. They drew more blood and changed the Foley bag because the diuresis caused by the lasix filled it to capacity. It was now time for watchful waiting.

Several hours passed, and George began to stir. He was confused and disoriented, but no longer violent. As he returned to consciousness, they reduced the lasix and removed the restraints.

Within one day, George was more alert. When he understood commands and was rational, Burt removed his Foley catheter and stopped the IV fluids and asked George how he got that cut on his hand.

George responded, "No clue, doctor."

Follow-up serum calcium tests showed much improvement, and within forty-eight hours, the patient was responsive and asking for a telephone to call his wife.

He telephoned home several times, but received no answer. Then he remembered. Gail and the children had left for the weekend to visit his mother-in-law. He would call there now.

"It's you," shrilled his mother-in-law when she heard his voice. "Where have you been? Gail's been calling and she's worried sick. She left the kids here a few hours ago and drove home. She should be there by now. God, where are you, George?"

"I'm in the hospital, but I'm okay."

"Hospital? What happened?"

"I only remember being home, and the next thing I knew I was here at Covenant hospital. They've been doing a lot of tests. The doctor said he should have all the results by tomorrow morning. Don't worry. I'll call Gail at home."

"Thank God you're okay. Have her call me," said his mother-in-law.

"Sure, talk to you soon."

Gail was crying by the time he reached her. She had been frantic. George told her everything he could, and she said she'll be there soon. As soon as he hung up the receiver, Burt walked in to examine him. "How are you doing?" said Burt.

He managed a rare smile at Burt. "Better," he answered

"Do you remember what happened, George?"

"No, doctor, nothing. I guess I'm in a fog. I don't know how I got here."

"Well, you were brought to the hospital unconscious and we did manage to get the tests I ordered, so we have a diagnosis now."

"Are you sure?"

"Ninety-nine percent sure. Let me explain it to you. You have a gland in your neck called the parathyroid, which is imbedded in the thyroid gland," he said, pointing to George's neck. "There are four of them. We think that your parathyroid gland is overactive. It makes a hormone that controls the calcium in your body, so when it gets overactive the calcium level becomes too high. That explains why you got so sick and didn't know what you were doing. Too much calcium affects your brain, and that's the bad news. It also explains all the other symptoms you've been having; the ulcer, the confusion, the kidney stones. An overactive parathyroid gland can cause all of them. The good news is that a small tumor of the parathyroid more often than not is the cause, and it's an easy job to remove that tumor. If it comes out, you're cured. Right now we're ninety-nine percent certain that's what you have. Meanwhile, we're waiting another test called the parathormone level. This one is a very unusual test that we had to send to a special lab, so it will take about a week or so for the results. It tells us if your parathyroid gland is making too much of its hormone that controls calcium. Also we need to take a nuclear medicine test that will pinpoint the exact location of this tumor so surgery will be easier."

George shook his head. "Oh, boy, I get the message. But, since this is all going to take time, can I go home?"

"I rather you stayed here," said Dr. Crowell firmly.

"Why," asked George with a serious expression on his face

"Past experience tells me you won't get the test as an out-patient," said Dr. Crowell firmly but calmly.

"I swear I will. It's just one more test to find this tumor, right?" said George

"Right. But as fast as your calcium seems to go up, it might be dangerous for you to leave. You have to understand that if you don't get this taken care of it can kill you. And I'm not kidding."

The slow careful enunciation of Burt's calm voice removed all thoughts of resistance from George's mind. "I hear you, doctor," he said, feeling calmer then he had in months in spite of the bad news.

"I'm going to arrange the test appointment for you. We'll get it done as soon as possible because we don't want your calcium to get too high again. If the test shows the tumor, you'll be scheduled for surgery right away."

"Can you find out when the test can be scheduled?"

Burt called the Nuclear Medicine Department, stressed the urgency of the condition and got an appointment for Tuesday—in four days. George saw no sense in waiting in the hospital, and Gail, who had arrived, told Burt that she would watch her husband "like a hawk."

With that assurance, Dr. Crowell discharged him with the understanding he would return for the test with his wife.

Gail and George clung to one another as the doctor brought her up to date on George's condition. His briefing relieved her. Her dream of a simple, easy, and correctable diagnosis had come to pass, or, as the good doctor put it, the diagnosis was a ninety-nine percent certainty. They still needed the parathormone blood test result to return and to do some imaging studies to eliminate all doubt and localize the tumor. Gail thanked Dr. Crowell. She hugged Eve.

George obtained a hospital discharge that day and Dr. Crowell handed him appointment slips for follow up testing. Then he was careful to document the instructions in George's chart.

CHAPTER 20

The police investigation of Philip Matt's murder swung into action. Criminologists evaluated the body. They took blood samples from the victim's shirt and hands, fingerprints and scrapings under the victim's nails. They scrutinized the crime area in front of Leo Carlin's house, confirming the size eleven footprint. The victim wore a size nine. In addition, there was no certainty that this was the exact spot of the murder as they found several drops of blood ten yards from the body to the north recognizing that it might be blood spatter from the murder site or some dripping off the murder weapon. In addition, Leo Carlin told the police that he heard a scream and within seconds after that he looked out the window, caught a glimpse of a man running north and saw the man on the ground in front of his house. Therefore, it seemed that the victim fell where the murderer stabbed him. Carlin wore a size eleven shoe, but no one thought for a minute that this frail and skinny eighty-year old veteran could have committed the murder. They placed Carlin on the back burner for a time.

The chief pathologist, Dr. Frank Morelli, performed an autopsy the next day.

The Chicago police department assigned the case to detective Richard Galinski, a lifetime resident of the area. Galinski was of medium height with dark brown, somewhat sparse hair, and appeared much younger than his mid-fifties. His stellar performance over the years resulted in his advancement to homicide in spite of his baby face.

Galinski arrived at the morgue to confer with Dr. Frank Morelli. The pathologist was standing over the body lying on a metal slab and was working on the official postmortem. Dressed in his blood stained lab coat, he turned to greet his visitor, now gowned, gloved and masked.

"Hi, detective. I'd know you anyplace, even under that mask."

"Hi, Frank. We got to stop meeting like this."

"Yeah, that would be nice, but not much chance."

"So what was the cause of death?" asked Galinski.

Morelli became very serious as he contemplated his response. He looked up from behind his thick reading glasses. His face was grim. "This poor young man didn't stand a chance," he replied. "There were four knife wounds. The first penetrated the heart and cut the left anterior descending branch of the left coronary artery. The second also penetrated the heart about one inch from the first, and the third missed the heart but entered the lung and caused considerable damage. The fourth wound was a superficial laceration on the right hand, probably because of a defensive posturing by the victim. The wounds were narrow, more like a pocketknife than a hunting blade. I would say whoever did this had some knowledge of anatomy. There was massive hemorrhage. No one could survive such an insult. Here, take a look." He showed Galinski the laceration on the right hand of the victim, and then he freed the heart from its connections, held it in his hands, and showed him the cardiac stab wounds.

Uunperturbed, Galinski looked at the lacerated heart. In his right hand, he rotated two small antique marbles; good luck pieces that were the vital clues to the solution of his first murder case, kept as a permanent souvenir used when he was deep in thought. "Well," he said, "that seems to be enough to do him in. Was there anything else?"

"No, he was a healthy young man. It's such a shame."

"We may wrap this case up soon. We've got a strong suspect and what looks like the murder weapon," said Galinski while his marbles clicked in his hand.

"That was fast work," said Morelli.

During a routine gang roundup for another incident, the police found one young black man named Ronald Jones possessing a knife. It was a large red pocketknife with bloodstains on the blade. Jones insisted it was not his, and that he had found it on the street. When asked where, he identified a site that turned out to be very close to the murder site.

The criminologists evaluated the knife for evidence and discovered two types of blood. The first, B-negative, was the same blood type as

Philip's. A second blood type was A-positive. So it appeared that the victim's blood was on the knife, but also the blood of some unknown person. In addition, they discovered two sets of fingerprints on the knife. The first matched the strong suspect, and the second was unidentified. Further blood analysis on the shirt of the victim also identified the same two blood types, B-negative and A-positive. Although this was strong evidence, the unknown blood type did not match that of the strong suspect, Ronald Jones. His was O-positive. Therefore, since no one could disprove that the strong suspect, Jones, did not find the knife, he took and passed a lie detector test and was released from custody. Had they been able to match the second set of fingerprints and the unidentified blood on the victim and knife to a single person that would provide strong evidence of the murderer. Still pending for complete absolute identification was blood DNA analysis, and Detective Galinski lost no time in his relentless pursuit of the investigation.

CHAPTER 21

When wallet cards found in the dead man's wallet identified Philip Matt, Galinski visited the victim's wife to give her the bad news. In the meantime when Philip had not returned home his wife filed a missing person's report, so she was not surprised when a police officer, accompanied by Galinski, showed up at her door.

When they rang the bell and she saw them standing there she started talking right away. "I'm sure you're here about my husband. He still hasn't come home. I don't understand it. He never did anything like this before." Then she thought to ask, "Did you find out anything?"

Galinski said, "May we come in, Mrs. Matt?"

"Oh, yes, please. Sorry, come in."

"Please sit down, Mrs. Matt."

She stared at them. "Why, why do I have to sit down? Oh my God, You got bad news. That's why you want me to sit down. That's right, isn't it?"

"I'm afraid so Mrs. Matt." Galinski told her what had happened. She collapsed in a chair, her hands over her eyes.

Then, after regaining her composure, she told him that Philip had dinner at Traficante's Bar and Grill on the night of the murder. Traficante would be Galinski's next call.

"Did your husband have any enemies, Ms. Matt?"

She shook her head. "No way. Not a chance."

"Do you know a man named Leo Carlin? He lives about two blocks from here."

"Carlin? No, I don't."

"Did your husband ever mention his name?"

She shook her head. "No, never. Why?"

"He's the man who called the paramedics when your husband was assaulted. It happened right in front of his house."

Galinski and the other officer stayed in her apartment asking more questions. Ms. Matt called her parents and they said they would be right over. Galinski asked for and received a picture of Philip Matt. He waited for the parents, and spoke with them for a few minutes as the three family members tried to console each other over the bad news. His next stop would be Traficante's Bar and Grill.

CHAPTER 22

The bar and grill was a popular local watering hole, established twenty-five years in the same location. As you entered the square space, there was a long bar on the left. On the right were about a dozen neat tables and a row of booths along the wall.

Galinski approached a man standing behind the bar. He introduced himself. Galinski flashed his identification.

"Sure. What can I do for you, detective?"

"Are you Mr. Traficante?"

"Yes, I am."

"I believe this man was a customer of yours," he said, showing Traficante the picture of Philip Matt.

"Sure, that's Philip Matt. What do you mean—was a customer?"

"He's been murdered. We're investigating the case."

The glass that Traficante was cleaning fell from his hand and shattered on the floor. "Oh shit, murdered? When? What happened?"

"It looked like he was mugged, stabbed to death. It happened a couple blocks from here last Friday night."

Traficante looked stunned. "Philip was here. He came nearly every Friday for my wife's fish fry. God, I can't believe it!"

"Was he here alone?" asked Galinski.

"No. He met a friend of his here."

"Do you know who that friend was?"

"Sure. Larry Benson. He eats here too."

"Do you know where Mr. Benson lives?"

"Yeah, three blocks south in the corner apartment building."

"Not the same one where Philip lived?" asked Detective Galinski

"No. Philip lived about four blocks away in a different corner apartment building. We only have two apartment buildings in this neighborhood. Most people living here own their own homes."

"What else do you know about Larry Benson?"

"I've known him for about five or six months. He's a big guy and drives a truck for Sid Rosen's Bakery."

"Have you seen him since the Friday night of the murder?" asked Galinski.

"No," was the prompt reply.

"Is Benson married?"

"No. I'm sure he's single."

"Have you seen Philip here with anyone else?"

"Yeah, sure. He's been here with other people, and also with his wife."

"Do you know these other people?" asked Galinski

"As best I can remember, only a few have come in with him, and they've all been from the neighborhood." Traficanti shook his head sadly.

"Any strangers come with him?"

"None that I can remember. The last night I saw Philip in here, I sat with him and Benson awhile. They were here late and most of the dinner crowd was gone, so I had the time while my wife worked the bar."

"What were you talking about?" continued Galinski.

"Mostly we were talking about basketball. We were watching the Bulls play ball."

"Did Phillip and Benson both leave together?"

"Yes, they did."

Do you know anything else about this Benson guy?

Traficante thought a while. "No, not much."

"Have these two guys lived here all their lives?" The questions from Detective Galinski were coming in rapid fire.

"Philip moved here within the last year. I think he came from Kansas City."

"What did he do for a living?"

"He worked as a printer."

"What about Benson? Is he a Chicagoan? Has he lived here all his life?"

"As far as I know he's from Chicago, but he moved to this neighborhood about six months ago. I think I remember him saying it was closer to Sid Rosen's Bakery here."

"Did you ever hear about any antagonism between these two guys?

"No way. They seemed like real good buddies."

"One more thing. Think about other people who may have been here with Philip. Ask around. In a few days, I'll have an officer come in here and see what you might have remembered. Thanks. We appreciate your cooperation. We'll keep in touch."

Traficante shook his head. "We're not used to such things in this neighborhood. This is awful. I still can't believe it."

CHAPTER 23

The following day, Galinski and a crime technician visited Benson's apartment building. They came with a search warrant. When no one answered the doorbell, Galinski got a key from the landlord and entered the flat. The landlord had no knowledge of his tenant's current whereabouts. He reported that he always received his rent payments on time and considered Benson a decent tenant. He described him as quiet and never received complaints about Benson from other building residents.

Neither Galinski nor his crime technician could find gross signs of blood anywhere in the apartment. There was nothing in the bathroom or medicine cabinet. The crime technician also dusted the apartment for fingerprints. The predominant prints found all over the apartment, on the drinking glasses, counter tops, and doorknobs belonged, no doubt, to Larry Benson. Analysis of the fingerprints would soon determine that none matched the unknown prints on the knife, and none matched the victim. The fibers collected did not match the victim. There was no trace of Philip Matt ever being in the apartment. It appeared that Benson, a prime suspect and the last known person to see Philip Matt alive, had disappeared. Why, they wondered? This in itself was suspicious. Had he fled the scene shortly after the murder?

The two principle suspects, the man who found the knife and Larry Benson, entered the persons-of-interest classification. What there was of fingerprint evidence could not incriminate either one of them. This case would require all the skill Galinski could muster from his thirty years of total police experience. He twirled the marbles in his pocket and told the landlord to call him if Benson should return.

CHAPTER 24

Back at Covenant, Dr. Crowell knew it was time for George's nuclear medicine test to be completed. The test would pinpoint the suspected parathyroid tumor, known as an adenoma. He was eager to examine it since he had never analyzed a positive diagnostic test for parathyroid adenoma. Everyone was certain the test would be positive.

In past years, if a doctor suspected a parathyroid adenoma he or she surgically explored the neck. Knowledgeable parathyroid surgeons could identify and cure parathyroid disease in over ninety percent of cases on a neck exploration in those days. Nowadays there are more sophisticated diagnostic tests available to localize the lesion increasing the odds of cure and simplifying the surgery. Still, hyperparathyroidism is a complex disease. At times there is no adenoma found, which could then mean that all the glands, although normal in appearance, are overactive. Removing them would mean no parathyroid gland activity, and, as a result, no parathyroid hormone production causing calcium levels to plummet resulting in dire consequences. To complicate matters further, a parathyroid adenoma may reside in locations other than the neck in aberrant parathyroid tissue. Scientists have developed several different nuclear medicine and ultrasound tests to localize the adenoma. Today's surgeons armed with this benefit of exact localization of the tumor can operate with more confidence.

Dr. Crowell went to Nuclear Medicine to review George's results, but the director informed him that the patient had never shown up for the test.

"Shit!" he exclaimed. After phoning George's home and getting no answer, he went up to the medical floor to tell Eve. "Can you believe what George did?" He never took the test. That really pisses me off."

"Cool it, Burt. It's not your fault. At the time, you discharged him he was fine and not receiving intensive service, so you had no choice. He received informed consent and instructions and you documented it all. If he'd gotten the tests you would have had the answer. Patients must assume some responsibility for their care."

"I know what you're saying, but how could anyone be so—never mind." Between his teeth he whispered—"son-of-a-bitch."

Eve shook her head. "You did all you could."

"I'll phone his house every day and send him a letter," replied Burt.

"Keep trying. I would dictate a brief addendum to his chart saying that he failed to show up for the tests. Also, document the fact that you're trying to reach him by phone and letter. Copy the letter for your files, and that's all you can do."

"Damn, I'm lucky to know a hot-shot medico-legal consultant like you. Would you care to go out with me again one of these nights? I got a lot more I need to learn, you know."

"Yeah, I bet you do."

CHAPTER 25

That same afternoon, Covenant's Medical Record department received a telephone call from a Dr. Irving at Sheridan Hospital's emergency room.

"I'd like some information about a former patient of yours," requested Dr. Irving.

"Would you like us to send you the information?" replied the health record analyst.

"No. I need it stat. The patient is in our emergency room."

"Please give me the patient's name, sir. I'll need to get the records and call you back. It will just be a few minutes."

"Please hurry," said Irving. "It's urgent. The patient's name is George Gilmer...GILMER."

"Sure." Five minutes later, she had located George's chart and had Dr. Irving back on the telephone. "What can I help you with, doctor?"

"Is there a discharge diagnosis?"

"Yes, it's hyperparathyroidism."

Pause..."Who was the attending physician?"

"Dr. Burt Crowell."

"Could you reach him for me, please?"

"Yes. I'll connect you to the operator, and she'll know where we can find him."

When the operator reached Crowell, it was obvious from his tone of voice that he was excited about the phone call. Crowell called Dr. Irving who said, "Your patient was admitted here at Sheridan Hospital after an automobile accident. He had no obvious head injuries, but he was incoherent and could not respond to questions. We ordered an emergency CT scan of the head. It was negative. We learned who he was by his wallet identification, and inside the wallet was an appointment slip for nuclear medicine tests at your hospital. That's when I called medical records and discovered the discharge diagnosis of hyperparathyroidism. I've ordered a stat serum calcium for him."

"Thanks doctor," replied Crowell. "When he was a patient here he had a psychosis and he also had a prior emergency visit for a kidney stone. He was popping antacids for abdominal pain, and that could have been an ulcer. So, the whole thing fits. A classical, but very severe case of hyperparathyroidism."

"That is amazing. Anything else?" said Irving.

"Yes, the patient's calcium level was 13.8, but he responded to IV saline and lasix, and his calcium returned to very near normal. He never got the nuclear medicine study and an ultrasound as an outpatient. If we found the adenoma, we'd schedule the surgery, but he never kept the test appointment. I can't believe how fast his calcium must have come up again."

"Quite a story."

"We would be happy to take him back when you're comfortable about sending him," offered Crowell.

"I'll start saline and IV lasix and transfer him right out," said Irving. When the serum calcium comes back we'll let you know."

George was a direct admission and arrived on the floor, where Dr. Crowell was waiting to examine him. The result of the serum calcium was 13.2, so his condition had deteriorated within a very short time. This meant that the adenoma, if present, was very active and pouring out parathormone at a rapid rate. Burt had learned that only three percent of these tumors were malignant, but since this one was so aggressive, the possibility could not be discarded.

Gail had been home when she learned of George's transfer to Covenant and rushed to the hospital. George went to the grocery store, but when he did not return she was starting to panic. Dr. Crowell allayed her fears, reassuring her that her husband should do well despite his not being rational. He based this on George's history of prior therapy. They would not let him leave until they made a final resolution of his problem.

As George's calcium lowered, he regained his senses. He took an ultrasound, and a 99mtc scintography in the Nuclear Medicine department. Both tests confirmed what everybody was hoping for. An adenoma existed in the parathyroid gland located on the inferior pole of the right thyroid lobe. Gail was relieved. She felt certain their nightmare would soon be over.

After the patient was clear headed enough to comprehend, Dr. Crowell discussed the case with him.

"Remember me?" I'm Dr. Crowell."

"Yeah, I remember." said George.

Dr. Crowell was relieved to hear George talk. He sounded more rational. He was less agitated. His facial expression was no longer as tense as it had been.

"You were in an automobile accident, and the ambulance took you to another hospital," continued Burt. "Your injuries were minor, but you were confused. One of their doctors identified you as a patient of ours by an appointment slip found in your wallet. That's when the ambulance transferred you back here. All the tests we wanted you to get before are done now, and we know for sure that you have that tumor we suspected and we're going to take it out very soon."

"When?" asked George.

"Tomorrow," Crowell replied. "How come you didn't keep your appointment for the test?"

George stared and shook his head.

"Never mind. Your calcium must have jumped up too fast and affected your brain. The fact that it did that means we can't wait any longer. You need to get fixed now."

"Does my wife know? asked George."

"Yes."

George smiled. "The fog in my brain has cleared up. Thanks for all the good work. I guess I've been lucky."

"Your wife said she's not taking you back until that tumor is out."

"Yes, sir," he grinned.

"Glad that's settled. Dr. Boyd will be your surgeon, and he'll stop by later to meet you," said Dr. Crowell.

Dr. Boyd arrived during Gail's afternoon visit. After examining George, he explained his findings to both of them. "I looked at your tests, and there is no doubt you've got the tumor. The good news is that removing it will cure you. You're young, and other then the tumor you're very healthy and should do well. You'll need to sign a consent form before I operate."

George read the consent form, and then handed it to Gail. "Scary stuff. He turned to the surgeon. "Might as well go ahead and do your thing."

"You'll have to sign the consent form authorizing the surgery. Take note of three magic words: benefits, risks, and alternatives. First the benefits are simple. The surgery will cure you. Speaking of alternatives, in your case there are none other than the surgery. If you do nothing it will threaten your life as I'm sure you've already learned. Then there's always that three to five percent chance the tumor could be malignant, which is another reason in favor of surgery. The risks are no different from any other operation. They include infection, bleeding, and, in this type of case, damaging a nerve that could affect your voice. The chance of any of these things happening is less than one percent. Your chance of dying from the procedure is almost nonexistent. So, finish reading the form and I'll get a nurse to witness the signature, then I'll sign it too. After that, you're ready to go. You are scheduled for surgery at 10:00 o'clock tomorrow morning."

George signed the form, resigned to the fact that surgery was his only option.

Gail returned to the hospital early the next morning and stayed until they wheeled him to the operating room. She had every confidence he would do well. Now that she understood his medical problem, she was amazed at the difference in him since his calcium level had approached the normal range. She had no idea how susceptible the human mind was to any alterations of normal body factors. She was grateful to the doctors for identifying his problem in time. She could not blame him for procrastinating, not after she had discovered that his mind, altered by the elevated calcium caused by the parathyroid tumor, rendered him incapable of rational thought.

The next morning, they took a nervous George into surgery. His wife and children were all there—a great relief for George.

Dr. Boyd exposed the posterior thyroid capsule. Pre-armed by the nuclear medicine study, it was a simple matter to explore, expose and do a resection of the tumor. Following two hours in the recovery room and a final examination by the anesthesiologist, they transferred George to his room where Gail was waiting. His postoperative calcium levels needed monitoring several times daily to be certain they returned to normal. Afterwards, he would settle down to a few days of a restful recovery, examinations and blood studies. A large protective bandage covered both the incision and a drain in his neck.

CHAPTER 26

While George was recuperating, Detective Galinski's laser-like police work was bearing fruit. The DNA analysis was still a work in progress, and he was waiting for the final report. The FBI traced the fingerprints on the knife to a former Chicagoan employed for summer work by the Chicago Park District nearly fifteen years earlier. It was S.O.P. for all employees to undergo fingerprinting before they started work. Although four people with the same name resided in Chicago, they could trace a suspect to George's address. They eliminated the three other suspects.

When George was seventeen years old, he took a summer job with the Chicago Park District. Since his fingerprints were on record, Galinski was able to determine that his prints matched up with those on the murder weapon. George Gilmer was now the principal murder suspect. Still listed in the telephone book at the same address that the Park District had on record, Galinski had no trouble locating him. "It looks like this case is solved," he thought. Next, he made an anonymous call and spoke with Gail.

"Hello, is George Gilmer there?" Galinski asked.

"No, he's in the hospital," answered Gail

"Oh, I didn't know."

"Who is calling please?"

"Just a friend from work," lied Galinski

"We told George's foreman about his hospitalization," offered Gail.

"I'm sorry. I didn't know because I've been off work for a week. What hospital is he in? I'd like to send him a get well card. I hope it's nothing serious."

"No, it's nothing too serious, he's at Covenant."

"Thank you." Galinski hung up to avoid further questions. He now had his suspect's exact location nailed down.

We've got him, a triumphant Galinski thought. He's at Covenant. I don't know why he's there or when he might go home, so we better move fast. I'll check it out.

Galinski and two officers arrived at the hospital and went to the administration office where they identified themselves. The hospital administrator provided them with George's room number and the name of his attending physician. Then the administrator paged Dr. Crowell, instructing him to report to the administrative suite on an urgent matter.

Burt arrived with a worried look on his face. The administrator said, "Hello, Dr. Crowell, these men want to talk to you."

Burt turned and looked at Galinski who was approaching him with hand extended.

"Thanks for your promptness, doctor. My name is Detective Richard Galinski, and these two men are my associates. We want to talk to you about a patient."

"What can I do for you, detective?" said Burt relieved that he was not being summoned on some personal matter.

"Do you have a patient named George Gilmer?"

"Yes sir, I do."

"What's he hospitalized for?"

"He just had surgery for a parathyroid tumor."

Detective Galinski had no idea what type of surgery it was, but he proceeded. "How long is he going to be here?"

"About two or three more days, if all goes well that is."

"We need to speak with him as soon as possible. When would be a good time?"

"Tomorrow morning would be okay," he replied, becoming suspicious about the detective's line of questioning. "What's this all about?"

"It's part of an ongoing investigation. That's all I can tell you now. Are you sure we can't see him now?"

"Not wise, he just came out of surgery. He's groggy and in pain."

"Okay, then tomorrow it is." Galinski knew it would be ill advised to read someone his Miranda rights in no condition to receive the news. "What would be a good time to come?"

"I get there at eight in the morning," said Burt wondering what this was all about, but knowing better than to ask.

"Will Gilmer be alert and able to talk and understand things by morning?" asked Galinski

"Oh, yes."

"Good. Then we'll be here at ten minutes to eight. Meanwhile, I'll leave two men here as guards. Don't say anything about our visit to anyone. Here's my phone number. If there's any change in the patient's condition, or if circumstances change for whatever reason, I'm counting on you to get in touch with me. It's very important." He gave Burt his card.

"Yes, sure, detective," replied Burt, eyeing him with concern.

Through the hospital administrator, Galinski arranged for the stationing of two police guards outside George's room. He briefed the unit's nursing director.

After more than twenty years of detective work, he would be making his first hospital arrest. He was sure he had followed proper procedure because he first checked with the police department's legal division.

The next morning, as had been prearranged, Galinski and his staff were already on the floor when Burt arrived.

"Good morning, Dr. Crowell, may we see your patient?" asked Galinski

"Sure. First I need to examine him to see how he's doing."

"Go ahead, but please remember not to say anything," said Galinski.

"Can't you tell me what this is all about?" asked Dr. Crowell.

"Not until after you finish examining your patient."

The seriousness, with which Galinski delivered this statement, sent Crowell a message that no further questions would be welcome until after George's interrogation. "Okay," said Dr. Crowell who now was certain that George might be in some sort of trouble. He rushed inside to see him.

"How are you feeling this morning?" Crowell asked.

"Okay," said George.

"Are you in any pain?"

"Not much."

"Great. Let's check you over." He paused to scan the chart. The vital signs were normal, temperature was 98.8 and urine output was good. He also noted with satisfaction that the surgical dressing had very little drainage. The patient's voice was normal. The incision looked good. His heart tones sounded normal, and his lungs were clear. He appeared alert and comfortable.

"You're doing well. Everything is coming along even better than expected. We'll be checking your blood twice a day for the next few days to make sure your calcium level has returned to normal and that it stays where it belongs."

"I do feel good. I don't have that tense feeling anymore. I know that my cure is the result of you good doctors and God."

"In that order?" said Crowell.

George laughed, but the pain that his laugh exacerbated shortened the laugh, although the thought that he could now appreciate a joke sustained him. "How long will I have to be in the hospital?" he whispered.

"Probably two or three days; the surgeon will be checking your wound and making sure that everything's okay. Be patient. It took you a long time to get here, and within a few days you'll be back home. We only need a couple more days to be sure that you have a permanent cure. The blood tests will tell us for certain."

"Yes, sir."

Crowell forced himself to maintain a calm presence for George's sake. Still, he agonized over the need to inform him about the detective camped outside his door.

"George, there's a man out there who wants to speak with you. He's a policeman, but I don't know anything about why he's here."

George looked puzzled. "I don't remember a thing about my accident."

Burt bowed his head. With a final sigh of resignation, he patted George on the shoulder, turned and walked out of the room. Once outside, he faced Detective Galinski and confronted him for information. "Now can you tell me what this is all about, detective?"

"We are going to arrest your patient for suspicion of murder," he replied. Without further explanation, he marched into George's room, leaving Burt standing stunned and perplexed.

"George Gilmer?" asked Galinski.

"That's me,"

"I'm Detective Richard Galinski. You're under arrest for the murder of Philip Matt." George's face turned white. For several seconds, a blank stare was all that he could muster. "There must be some mistake. You're in the wrong room. I've never heard of a Philip Matt."

"You have the right to remain silent. Anything that you say can be held against you in a court of law. You have the right to the presence of an attorney, or one will be appointed for you prior to any questioning."

George was pumping adrenaline, fighting to comprehend what he had just heard. Was this a joke? Or some mistake? Either way, he was not amused. Whatever postoperative discomfort he had been experiencing vanished.

"I don't know this man you say I killed. I never killed a soul!" It felt like a nightmare from which he could not awaken. Am I dreaming?

"You'll stay here until the doctors say you can leave. You'll be in our custody," said Galinski as he turned and left George's room leaving his two officers to guard the new prisoner. George was experiencing a recurrent brainstorm, only this time his calcium level was normal.

Burt witnessed the proceedings in stunned disbelief. The detective swore him to secrecy until he spoke to George. However, he no longer felt constrained to remain silent. If he did not confide in someone soon, he feared he might explode. The logical people would be Dr. Pollard and Eve.

CHAPTER 27

When Burt confronted Pollard in the Emergency Department, residents and medical students surrounded him.

"Do you have a minute? I have shocking news," whispered Crowell.

"Sure, what is it?" asked Pollard.

"I need to speak with you in private, if you don't mind."

As soon as they secured an empty room, he began. "Do you remember George Gilmer?"

"Yeah sure. Why?"

"He's just been arrested for the murder of a man named Philip Matt."

Pollard's forehead creased and he shook his head. "Oh, damn. We declared Matt dead right here, and by me, when he failed resuscitation after the paramedics brought him in. He had three fatal knife wounds in the chest. Don't tell me they're hanging it on Gilmer?"

"Yes, and I can't believe it," said Crowell.

A reflective Pollard said, "You know, George was admitted in a psychotic state on the same day that Philip was killed."

"What else should I know?" said a stunned Dr. Crowell.

"He was violent and out of control when he came in. Remember, he assaulted my resident, Carly Godwin."

"What you're saying is that Philip Matt could have been killed by a man in the throes of an organic psychosis who had no recollection of anything?"

"You got it. If Gilmer did commit the crime, he doesn't have a clue. That was obvious at the time."

"The poor guy is in for it now," Crowell said.

Pollard said, "Well, if Gilmer did this while in a psychotic state, the attorneys who argue the case may also go psychotic. By the way, you can count on all of us as witnesses. So, from this point forward our lips are sealed, and I mean tight. Say zero to zero."

"Right. Thanks Jason, I appreciate the advice." He found himself shaking and thought of Eve, the good friend of Gilmer's wife—and his friend as well. He would inform her very soon. He went to the medical floor where he found Eve charting surrounded by other nurses. He wrote a note on his prescription pad and when she was free, he handed it to her. The note said: I have something important to tell you. I need a drink and you will too. Call me after work.

Gail was devastated. Yet, after recovering from the initial shock, she demonstrated complete support for her husband. She knew that he was incapable of violence when in a normal state. Nevertheless, she could not overlook the nagging suspicion that he, in his changed mental state, had become a different person. She knew that George never for one moment suspected her of having any doubts because she suppressed them from him. He only witnessed her overwhelming love and support. She had other concerns, too. She worried about their livelihood. With George unable to work how would she and the children live? Besides, how could they afford an attorney?

George shared Gail's anxiety as she searched for a way out. Once George settled down from the initial shock, he was able to speak to his wife in a more rational manner. He said, "I'm going to have to lean on you for a lot of support. We'll get through this. Why is this happening to me? To us. What's God doing here? Is there a master plan for us? I have to think like that or I'll go nuts."

She wiped her eyes and looked at him. She tried hard to force a smile. "No matter what happens, I'll always be here for you. We'll figure it out together."

Several days later George's calcium level had returned to normal and he was discharged, but not free. Handcuffed, with his neck bandaged, they drove a confused and distraught George to Chicago's central lockup.

CHAPTER 28

As per Burt's written instructions, Eve did call him when she finished work. He picked her up and told her they were going to the same restaurant, only this time they would sit at the bar. When they arrived, Burt ordered a Bombay Sapphire on the rocks. What'll you have?" he asked Eve.

"The same, please." She looked at Burt and wondered when he would divulge the reason for the note, but Burt just stared back with a serious expression on his face.

"Well, I can't stand it anymore. You got me here under this cloak and dagger scenario. So what's all the mystery?"

"George Gilmer has been arrested for murder."

As Eve sat in stunned silence, George told her the entire story, at the end of which all she could stammer was, "Poor George…poor Gail… poor family. What are they going to do? I have to help Gail. She's been so good to me ever since we met."

"I'm sure she's going to need all the help she can get. This'll take a long time and I'll do everything I can to testify on his behalf."

"I can't believe it. There's no mistake?"

"That was one serious detective. That's all I can say."

Eve sighed and Burt stared ahead. They both sat speechless for a time.

"If there was ever a case for an insanity defense, this is it," said Eve.

George took a large swallow of his drink. "Yep, there it goes again— the legal eagle in action. Damn, but you are multitalented. What a lucky break for me that I met you," said George through glazed eyes.

"I bet you say that to all the girls."

"Only you, Eve. You're it for meee, don't you seee, a girl like you, brings harmoneee."

"Well, listen to that; the poet laureate of Covenant. I'm impressed. Is that you, or is it the Bombay Sapphire?"

"It's all me, baby. I think I'm drunk. Not from the Bombay, but from George. Maybe I'm suffering from hyperparathyroidism. Perhaps I have to change the subject of George to you, so I can get my mind off this bombshell I received this eve. Indulge me, please."

"Yes, I understand your brain fog, but am I seeing a different side of Burt tonight?"

"You're seeing a Burt who is dizzy from today's events and is trying to tell you that he thinks you're great, and is very interested in you. And the mere fact that I'm so concerned over my patient, George, and I would still have you on my mind, says something."

"What are your intentions, Keats."

He laughed. My intentions...my dear lady...is to have—he held up his drink—a meaningful...overnight relationship." He tried to keep a straight face and not smile, but he succeeded in only pursing his lips.

Eve quickly picked up on this attempt at humor (at least, that's what she hoped) and said, "Not only a poet, but a stand-up comic too? I'm impressed. Did that spontaneously pop into your brain, or did you read that someplace?"

"Spontaneity is my hallmark, but I suspect that underlying that spontaneity there is a hidden desire I have when I look at you that bubbles up to the surface in spite of my efforts to suppress it.

"You have such an honest way of communicating. I like honest."

"Do you like me?"

"Have I turned you down on any dates? I'm here, aren't I? Let's take it slow, Casanova. We've both been through the wringer not too long ago and we need to be snails and not rabbits."

"Well put, my love. Slow is good."

"It looks like this is your terms of endearment night," said Eve.

"Every night with you would induce me to use such terminology. I can't help it. I want to be with you. I'm falling in love with your brain."

"That's all, just my brain?"

"The brain is you. After all, what you are is what your brain has made you. The rest of your body, as good as it looks, is there for one principle purpose: feed your brain and keep it alive and well. Well, perhaps that was somewhat of an understatement. The rest of your body does indeed have some important uses." He held up his glass.

"A scientist, a poet, and now a philosopher. I am impressed."

Burt said, "I'm glad. Changing the subject before I go nuts thinking of George, and speaking of brain, what do you know about interior decorating?"

"I love it. I took one course as an elective in college when I got my B.S. in nursing."

"Would you like a moonlighting job?"

"Hmm, sounds like I'm being offered something in the pro bono area."

"That depends upon how you define pro bono. In this case there would be no monetary remuneration, but I would pay off in gratitude, devotion, free meals, drinks and—more."

"Sounds like an offer no girl could refuse. What do you have in mind?"

"I need help decorating my condo. It's seventy percent empty. I need to keep busy to keep my mind off George"

"Good thinking. That sounds like a challenge."

"Are you up for it?"

"I'd love to. It should be fun."

"I'll take you there now and show you the layout."

"Only if I'm going with Mr. Snail."

"It's a deal. Let's shake on it."

CHAPTER 29

Since George's fingerprints matched those on the murder weapon, there was no longer any question about George being the principle suspect. Detective Galinski now concentrated on him, turning his attention away from Larry Benson. As far as he was concerned, he had the killer. George's blood type and fingerprints matched those on the murder weapon and DNA studies were underway for further verification.

Since the issues surrounding Benson was unfinished business, Galinski was stunned when Benson's landlord phoned to inform him that his tenant was back. Benson had apparently been vacationing out of town.

"I'll be right over."

One thing for certain, thought Galinski. Benson is either innocent or insane. Why would a guilty man return to the scene of the crime? Anyhow, it looks like Gilmer's the man and I'm probably wasting my time.

Galinski and a police officer knocked on Benson's door. A man with huge shoulders and rugged features opened the door to greet them. He had small, dark eyes framed by bushy brows, a strong chin, and large lips. His uncombed hair was black. The top of his head almost hit the doorframe. His massive body obscured any vision into the room. Galinski had to extend his neck to look into his face.

"Are you Larry Benson?"

"Yeah, and who are you?"

"I'm Detective Richard Galinski. We're from the Chicago police department. We'd like to speak to you inside."

Benson stared at both men and shrugged his shoulders. "Sure, come in." He escorted them into a sparsely furnished living room. A small sofa faced a portable TV on a metal stand. The sofa, designed for two, would have no room if Benson sat down in it.

"Sit there," said Benson pointing to the sofa, "and I'll pull up a chair." When his visitors looked comfortable, he said, "What's this all about?"

Galinski came right to the point. "Philip Matt is dead" He chose the word dead rather than murdered or killed.

"What?" Benson's body slumped forward, his eyes opened wide. He stared at Galinski as if not believing what he had heard.

"Yes, he's dead," said Galinski again.

"What happened?" asked Benson, slumping back in his seat.

"He was murdered." Galinski omitted any details wanting to hear what reaction it would elicit in Benson.

"I don't believe it. Damn, he was such a nice guy. What the hell's this all about?"

"We're here to talk to you because you were the last person to see Philip Matt alive."

Benson stood up and walked over to look out the window. "The last time I saw Phil," he reflected, "it was a Friday night. We were both at Traficante's Bar and Grill."

"Go on. We already checked that out. What happened after you left Traficante's?"

"We both left the same time. We live in different directions, so he went one way and I went the other."

"And you never saw him again."

"No," never. "In fact the next morning I left town and I just got back. That was the last I ever saw him, about two weeks ago. Who did this? You got anybody?"

"We have a suspect. But, since you were the last one to see him alive, we need to find out what you know."

"That won't take long. How was he killed?"

"He was knifed."

"You're wasting your time with me. You said you got someone. Who is it?"

"We've got the murder weapon and the suspect's fingerprints and blood type on the knife. That's all I can tell you."

"So what do you want from me?"

"We want your cooperation, Mr. Benson. We hope you won't mind letting us take your fingerprints and draw blood for typing and DNA analysis."

"But you say you've already got the guy."

"Yes, but don't forget you're the last one to see him alive. You're a loose end that we need to check out. If we can do that, and clear you, we can concentrate on the suspect and forget about you."

Benson walked back to his chair and sat facing Galinski. "I got nothing to hide. If you want my fingerprints and blood, help yourself."

"Good thinking, Benson. Let's go down to the station and get it over with."

Benson's fingerprints and blood type failed to match the prints and blood on the knife. During the initial screening, Galinski also sent Benson's blood sample for DNA analysis to the police lab. He sent Benson's photo, prints, and his current and previous home address out on the nation-wide police wire. One week later, the DNA would come back a non-match.

Galinski could concentrate on George Gilmer and he eliminated Benson as a suspect.

CHAPTER 30

George was at Chicago's central prison awaiting his arraignment. The brainstorm that had captured his mind returned. Only this time it was secondary to sheer terror over his plight. He was now lucid and felt tormented that his interrogators ignored his protestations of innocence. Soon he realized that nothing he could say would have an impact, and his only recourse was to remain silent until the nightmare played itself out. At least Gail believed in him. Nevertheless, his financial resources would dwindle and could not cover legal fees. If only they captured the real killer within a day or two, he would be free to go home. As nighttime loomed, his mind raced so fast that he could not sleep.

By morning, he felt fatigued and demoralized when they brought him to the courthouse. The clerk instructed him to fill out a financial form and then handed the information to Judge Kaufman. The form revealed that he was a homeowner with a mortgage, was financing a car, had a checking account of three thousand dollars and had no investments or other assets. He met his payments, but had no extra funds to hire an attorney and now faced bankruptcy.

He stood before Judge Kaufman feeling intimidated by his authority. He could only see his black robe, narrow shoulders, serious face, and almost completely bald head. He knew that his fate rested in Kaufman's hands and he felt powerless to sway him.

"Mr. Gilmer," began the judge, "we are here to determine your need for a court appointed attorney, or perhaps you have already hired one to defend you?"

"No sir, I have no lawyer."

"Then we'll provide you with one."

George panicked. "This is crazy. There must be some mistake. I didn't kill anybody."

Without raising his voice a single decibel, the judge replied, "I did not ask you that, Mr. Gilmer. You'll have plenty of time to discuss that with an attorney. We'll pay attention to those details later."

George, traumatized by the succession of events, vowed to do everything in his power to remain calm. When the guards returned him to his cell, he pondered his fate. Raised religious, he would have to tap into whatever faith he could muster.

CHAPTER 31

The court appointed attorney assigned was Paul Stuart, four years out of law school when he took the case. Becoming an attorney had been his childhood ambition, and he passed the bar after attending night school. Evening classes permitted him to work during the daytime enabling him to be self-supporting.

Stuart grew up on Chicago's south side with middle-class black parents. His father was an auto mechanic and his mother a teacher's aide. The Stuarts had struggled to put their son through college, but it was his decision to attend night school so he could work during the day to ease their financial burden.

Stuart was five foot ten inches, of medium build, with black hair and light brown skin color. After graduation from law school, he became a public defender. Although his salary was meager, the compensations more than made up the financial deficit. Most important was the challenge and invaluable experience he obtained. He married a court reporter, and they moved to an apartment downtown to be close to work

He was concerned when he first reviewed his new client's case. It was a first and it would force him to do research in an unfamiliar area. He had no experience with a medical case and knew he would have to hit the books or the internet. They had the murder weapon with George's fingerprints and blood type, and George's blood type on the victim's shirt. If the blood DNA on the knife and on the shirt matched George's, the prosecution would have an insurmountable advantage. The red herring was the medical implication, but nothing was comprehensible at this time. He would interview the suspect the next morning.

Stuart arrived at the central prison and was ushered into a meeting room with two-way glass. A table with two chairs stood in the center of the room. Moments later two guards escorted their prisoner inside.

"Mr. Gilmer, I'm Paul Stuart. The court appointed me your lawyer. I've gone over your case and I want to hear your story. I'm here to learn everything I can from your perspective."

George observed this newcomer now charged with his life. He took note of the serious-looking and well-dressed young man who was making direct eye contact with him. He was wearing a dark blue suit with a red tie and a white dress shirt. This attorney looked too green, he thought, but he had no alternatives. Yet he felt comforted by the young man's confident manner.

George answered. "I can tell you everything I know in five seconds. I don't know anything about this murder. I never heard of the victim, and I didn't kill him. That's it."

"That's pretty clear cut and to the point. Tell me what you know about your illness. May I call you George?"

"Sure." He complied with the young lawyer's request, explaining the details as he understood them. "The doctors told me my brain was affected by the tumor in my neck. Most things I don't remember. They took the tumor out and I'm cured."

"I'll be checking your medical records to learn all about it. I need to understand everything about this tumor since it's important for your defense. I'll be talking to your doctors as soon as I can make arrangements."

"Thank you. I appreciate any help you can give me."

Attorney Stuart continued. "Do you own a red pocket knife?"

The suddenness of this change of subject surprised George. "Yes, why?"

"Do you know where it is?"

"I remember seeing it in the top drawer of my bedroom dresser."

"Do you remember the last time you carried it with you?"

"No, I don't."

"The police have the murder weapon in custody. It's a red pocketknife. The bad news is that the knife has your fingerprints and blood type on it. Has anyone checked to see if your knife is still where you say it is?"

"Nobody asked me," said George his pulse-rate accelerating

"Then I'll need your permission to check the knife out. I need to figure out a way to do it."

"My wife is coming soon. I'll ask her to get it."

Stuart shook his head no and said, "If she does the searching alone we can be accused of manufacturing evidence. For instance, who's to say the knife she comes up with is not one she just purchased to try to help you. What I'll do is tell the arresting officer and ask him to send someone to go with her back home after she leaves here. If he witnesses your wife finding the knife, we lay down some smoke and damage the prosecution's case. If not, you're no worse off. When is she coming?"

"Eleven o'clock." George felt a sudden wave of relief. He was getting some help at last.

"I'll make all the arrangements. Meanwhile don't speak with your wife before she gets here."

"I won't," he said, so fatigued that his reply was almost inaudible.

"I'll visit you as often as I can and keep you posted on the latest." He then told the guards to make sure George did not have access to a phone.

"Thanks," a relaxed George murmured as he eased back into his seat.

Stuart notified Galinski about the knife search, and after Gail had visited George, he dispatched an officer to accompany her home. When they arrived at the house, she couldn't locate his pocketknife anywhere. With the officer watching her, she explored every square inch including her husband's workshop and toolbox.

The accompanying officer reported to Galinski, who then advised Stuart. Little doubt now remained about the ownership of the murder weapon—George.

George returned to court with his attorney. Several others were also present; people whom he had never met. Assistant District Attorney, Doris Donaldson, began the proceedings. She made an excellent appearance in a dark green suit with a tan blouse and matching scarf. Her red hair and green eyes matched her apparel. She was slim and stood five feet and three inches in height. She wore a minimum of makeup and pearl earrings as the only accessory.

"Your Honor," said Donaldson, "the defendant, George Gilmer, is accused of first degree murder. A young man knifed and killed, stabbed three times in the chest with a knife that had the defendant's blood and fingerprints on it. The defendant's hand, cut during the struggle, deposited blood on the victim's shirt. Mr. Gilmer is a danger to society and must not post bond. I plead that the court detains the accused until trial. If you release him, he is certain to flee."

Stuart was next to address the Court. "The prosecutor's demands are outrageous, your Honor. Attorney Daniel's requests are for serial killers. My client has no prior record, nor any desire to flee. His only wish is to clear his name and prove his innocence."

George listened, but heard little as the unfamiliar process created havoc with his psyche.

"Anything else to add from either of you?" asked Judge Kaufman. Neither attorney had any further statement.

"As is typical," said the Judge, "the prosecutors want the moon and the stars, and the defense likewise. I'm setting bond at one-half million dollars." He spoke with finality. George knew that his fate was sealed. He felt helpless when the bailiff returned him to his cell. Since ten percent of one-half million dollars equaled fifty thousand, he knew that bond might as well have been set at one billion. He had no choice but to remain locked up.

CHAPTER 32

Stuart visited the office of the public defender to confer with his mentor, James Kantor. At this stage of investigation, both agreed on three points. First, interview George in detail and second to interview his wife since George's medical condition might prevent him from understanding and recollecting details. Lastly, he would study the medical records to determine all possible implications of the case. He embarked upon this three-pronged course of action.

He interviewed Gail for a full hour. She reported on her husband's illness from the earliest signs to his developing a full-blown syndrome and final surgical cure. With her permission, he taped her interview for later analysis.

The next time he questioned George, the difference between his and Gail's interpretations amazed him. It was evident the illness had caused this patient to forget the sequence of events. No wonder he was so confused. He could not mask his depression and he broke down and cried.

"I know how you feel," said attorney Stuart. "We're getting plenty of information that I think will help you. I'll be studying your record and learn everything I can."

George regarded his young lawyer with appreciation. This was a guy who cared. He reached into his pocket for a handkerchief and wiped his eyes. "I have to rely on a professional like you. If it wasn't for my wife and kids I might crack. When I was in bed last night, I came up with the idea that maybe a lie detector test would help me. What do you think? Can I take one?"

"Lie detector? That's not so simple. The court won't allow its use as evidence in a court of law because it's not one-hundred percent reliable like other types of testing or documents or weapons or actual witnesses. We couldn't submit the results of a lie detector test as evidence unless the prosecution, the judge and the defense agreed. It's a risky move and one I'll need to think about."

George was paying close attention to Stuart's arguments. "I'll be glad to take the risk. I might rot in here, or get death for something I didn't do. I'm not afraid of the test." When he finished speaking, his face seemed to brighten. He had grasped one more straw in his fight to stay alive.

"I hear you loud and clear. Let me first talk to my boss before getting back to you with an answer. I promise to be quick," said Stuart.

"Sure," he sighed, "but, I'm counting on you. I've got nothing to lose."

"I won't let you down," said Stuart in as reassuring a voice as possible.

CHAPTER 33

Stuart reviewed all hospital and emergency records, taking copious notes with the aid of a medical dictionary at his side. He wrote down the following key words: kidney stone, ulcer, hyperparathyroidism, parathyroid adenoma, hypercalcemia, psychosis, amnesia, Dr. Jason Pollard and Dr. Carly Godwin—Emergency Medicine, Dr. Crowell—Internal Medicine, Dr. Boyd—surgeon, and one other doctor whose name he could not read but who filled out a form labeled 'consultation'. He had plenty of work ahead. George's doctors could fill him in with crucial evidence for the defense. Also important was the victim. He studied the emergency room record, noting that the date of the murder and emergency room visit were the same. He would need a clear understanding of the malady that affected his client in order to conduct intelligent interviews with the doctors. This was of paramount importance in preparation for his client's defense.

After consulting with Kantor, he arranged for George to take the lie detector test. He advised George to remain patient throughout the procedure, even though some early questions might sound irrelevant. The initial questioning would help to develop a solid baseline of responses. They measure these responses later when comparing any differences when and if they would pose pertinent and pointed questions. George understood this since he had read up on polygraph tests.

George's demeanor had changed after Stuarts' briefing. He appeared confident and relieved, and he passed the exam. As soon as Stuart heard the results, he relayed them to George. Though George knew they could disallow it as evidence, the results still gave him a psychological boost. Coupled with this good news, bad news was still around the corner, but Stuart didn't have the heart to tell George before discussing the matter with his boss Kantor at the public defender's office.

CHAPTER 34

"Even you'll have trouble with this one," said Stuart to Kantor sitting behind his desk with his jacket off and his white shirt sleeves rolled up. Approaching fifty years of age, Kantor was a man who inherited money that allowed him to pursue his passion of legal defense. Five feet and nine inches, prematurely graying hair and a muscular appearance honed by years of a swimming and weight lifting habit gave him an appearance of being younger than his age in spite of his early gray hair.

"What have you got?" asked Kantor.

"I've combed the hospital records, and I'll tell you that was no easy task. I needed a crash course in psychiatry and endocrinology. Science was not exactly my favorite subject. What I know is that the evidence against my client is overwhelming. How do we get around this? The murder weapon belongs to my client. His fingerprints are on it. His blood is on it. His blood is on the victim. That's for starters. I'll have to conjure up Clarence Darrow for this one. On the other hand, who needs Darrow when I've got Kantor?"

Kantor laughed. "I agree that your client's in trouble," he said.

"Yes, but the good news is that he passed the polygraph test with flying colors."

"The plot thickens," said Kantor.

Stuart continued. "They brought George and the victim into the same hospital at the same time. George was psychotic; he had no recollection of anything that day."

"Did they bring them in together in the same ambulance?"

"No, two separate ambulance runs."

Kantor was deep in thought. He stroked his chin. "Okay. The whole case sounds like grounds for an insanity defense."

"There's more. From my examination of the record, he was psychotic due to a medical condition caused by a tumor of one of his endocrine glands. His doctors diagnosed the problem, operated, and removed the tumor, and that cured the patient. His mind is clear, he feels fine, and he's in jail."

"What endocrine gland?"

"The parathyroid."

"That is fascinating. You better interview all the doctors because we'll need them as witnesses. This is certainly not a run-of-the-mill crime. What's your next step?"

"I was considering questioning the doctors, but first I want to take that crash course in endocrinology. I need a better background to understand what they're talking about."

"Good. Keep me posted, and don't hesitate to come to me with any problems. This is a fantastic case. I've got lots of ideas, so keep me involved. Besides, I like the work you're doing. Remember what Disraeli said."

"Here we go again. You got me. What did Disraeli say?"

"Justice is truth in action."

"That's good. In other words, keep the action going and find the truth. Thanks. I intend to wrap myself around this one. I'll be in touch."

CHAPTER 35

In school, Stuart took only the minimum requirements in science and math. He hated those subjects. They were difficult and he didn't enjoy rote memory. "Too much black and white," he would say. He preferred the gray of the law, the fascination of argument, the difference of opinion, and the search for justification. Still, he would need to readjust his mind set for this case. A proper defense would depend on his understanding of basic medical and pathophysiological principles. It would be difficult, but he loved a good challenge. No two cases were ever the same, and each one added to his reservoir of knowledge. "Like exercising my body adds to my store of muscle," he liked to tell his wife.

Stuart knew nothing about the functioning of the parathyroid glands, except that this gland was one of many comprising the endocrine system. He needed to brush up on basic physiology. After one week of study, he felt better qualified to interview the medical team.

He could no longer withhold information of the DNA results. It was time to level with George. The blood on the knife was his. However, his client's calm reaction to the news that the DNA results identified him surprised Stuart.

"You know," said George, "I half expected that news. I've had lots of time to think in here. The only thing going for me is the lie detector test, but I can't use it. They tell me I went nuts the day of the killing, and I can't remember anything that happened. Did I kill the guy when I was out of my head? The way I feel now, I sure couldn't do it. But if they find me guilty I could be facing the death penalty, and if that happens I'll go to my grave screaming I didn't do it!"

Stuart nodded with compassion. "I can't even imagine what you must be going through. You know I'm on your side and I'll do everything possible. James Kantor has taken an interest in your case. It means you've got the best legal mind in the state on your team. He's a brilliant defense lawyer with twenty-three years of experience in the Public Defender's office, and I give him a report every step of the way. I'll be interviewing all of your doctors. I promise to let you know what's happening all the time."

"How long will this take before the trial?"

"We never know for certain. A lot depends on what we come up with, but sometimes it can take up to one year." He eyed his client as he saw George slump back in his chair looking very depressed.

Stuart planned to interview each doctor obtaining as much detail as possible. This would require many trips to the hospital.

First on his list was Jason Pollard who gave him a crash course in parathyroid physiology. He was an excellent teacher and reminded him of Kantor. Pollard supplied him with details of George's first visit to the emergency room, when he first suspected a kidney stone. Stuart also learned more about George's second visit to the ER when admitted in a psychotic state. Pollard told him, "It was the second visit after he had developed other symptoms, especially the psychosis that I had enough information to come up with a diagnosis of hyperparathyroidism. This was the worst case I have ever seen."

Carly Godwin described her first meeting with her aggressive patient when, in his psychotic state, he knocked her down. She had the highest praise for Pollard, crediting him for coming up with the right diagnosis. "That was the first case of hyperparathyroidism I had ever come across. And from what I understand, I'll probably never see another one like this if I practice for fifty more years."

Dr. Burt Crowell reported his anxiety over George's failure to follow up with the necessary investigative tests. He described the systematic thinking that led to the diagnosis. "A rare disease like this is always on your mind, but you need a lot of information both of a clinical and laboratory nature before you can come up with a diagnosis. It took a while, but there was no doubt once we got the calcium test that pointed us in the right direction. If only the patient would have gotten the test the first time I ordered it, he could have prevented all this. What a case."

Dr. Boyd described the surgical procedure, stressing with virtual certainty that George would enjoy a permanent cure. "The surgical cure was simple," he said. "With all the localizing studies we have today, if there is an adenoma that shows up on the test, we can go right to the site, cut it out and cure the patient."

At Sheridan Hospital, Stuart interviewed Dr. Irving who described the automobile accident, his surprise at learning of the diagnosis, and George's transfer back to Covenant. "It was lucky that the patient had his appointment slip for the nuclear medicine test in his pocket. With that, I knew to call Covenant and find out about the hyperparathyroid diagnosis. There would have been no way for me to make that diagnosis of an auto accident victim without any past history information."

One by one, each doctor questioned shed new light on the case. A common thread in all their testimonies was that nobody could hold George accountable for his actions on the day of the murder. It was simple: his brain, awash in pathological levels of calcium from the excess produced by the parathyroid adenoma, made him not responsible for his actions.

This exhaustive testimony confirmed the insanity plea for the defense. Now it was time for Stuart to confer again with Kantor.

Meanwhile, prosecutor Donaldson felt satisfied with the evidence and expected to wind up the case. To have such overwhelming evidence against a suspect was unusual. Clear-cut blood, DNA and fingerprint evidence, not to mention the murder weapon, made this a no-brainer. The red herring was the medical evidence and its effect on the jury. She and her team expected an insanity defense, and understood it was the defendant's only hope. She also anticipated it would not take long to convince the jury of the suspect's overwhelming guilt. The prosecution might only require two witnesses to confirm that the blood and fingerprints on the knife belonged to the defendant. In her estimation, the facts were indisputable: George Gilmer committed the murder of Philip Matt. The question of his mental state remained the only unknown variable at this time.

Stuart was equally confident of his client's innocence. His extensive research led to only one direction—an insanity defense. He convinced himself that they had an open-and-shut case, and his only problems rested with his lack of experience. Since he had never pleaded an insanity defense, it was off to the books again. Even more important, he needed to pick the brain of his mentor—Kantor.

CHAPTER 36

"I need some help about some defense issues," Stuart told Kantor.

"Shoot," said Kantor. "Have a seat."

"The prosecution has a pile of evidence against George, and I feel we've got justifiable reasons for an insanity defense. The problem is I'm new to the game with this kind of plea."

"Good thinking. I believe I know what's on your mind, but let's hear."

Stuart spoke with confidence. "If he committed this murder, then he was psychotic and didn't know what he was doing. As one doctor put it, 'he had no idea if he was animal, vegetable, or mineral.' He was in a state of temporary insanity, triggered by some unusual medical condition that they identified and cured late because of an uncooperative patient. If he murdered this guy, he has no recollection. He even passed a lie detector test. Weird as it may sound, only a different brain could have murdered Philip Matt. Not his normal brain, but, as another doctor put it, a brain bathed in pathologic levels of calcium. This is a reportable case."

"I agree with your line of reasoning. In my twenty-three years working in defense, I never have seen such a case. So let's discuss the insanity defense and have a look at some basic principles to see if it fits. First, do you believe that based on what you know about this case, the mental factor could excuse your client from criminal liability or negate his culpability even if he were the murderer?"

"For sure."

"Do you also believe he would pass the 'wild beast test?'"

"If that means he acted like a wild beast, the answer is yes. But if you're talking about some specific legal principle, you got me."

"Well, I'm reaching down into ancient legal history, but it has relevance here. This oldie states that to be found not guilty and escape punishment, the accused must have been void of any comprehension when the crime was committed. In other words, his actions compared with that of a wild beast. You have to be a raving maniac for this rule to excuse you. Not what you call modern-day psychiatric terminology, but I'm sure you get the point."

"Yes, I get it. He would pass the wild beast test, but I think you are referring to a psychiatric problem. The problem here was not psychiatric, but was due to a medical problem that mimicked a psychiatric illness."

Kantor nodded his head. "That's good news for you. If George had only a psychiatric illness, chances are you would have both psychiatrists for the defense and for the plaintiff at odds with each other. That would complicate a decision here. You can always get two psychiatrists to come up with opposite decisions. However, when a proven medical condition causes the psychiatric condition, then it ensures that the psychiatrists will agree."

"Right, I got it."

"By the way, was your client seen by a psychiatrist?"

"Yes. During his first hospitalization, a psychiatric consultant saw the patient and wrote up a consultation report that I couldn't read, but I did identify him as a Dr. Lim. Then another psychiatrist, a Dr. Clementi saw him as an outpatient before this all happened. I spoke with them both. They claimed the suspect had a condition known as 'organic psychosis,' an illness due to the high levels of calcium that stemmed from the tumor in his parathyroid gland, and that he was not responsible for his actions."

"Sounds like your defense strategy is solid. Here's another one for you. Your client would also pass the McNaughton rule. This is another mid-nineteenth century oldie that is similar to what we discussed. It states that to be found not guilty, or to be excused from any responsibility, it must be proved that the accused party was so lacking in reasoning power from disease of the mind when the act was committed, that he could not comprehend what he was doing, or, if he did know it, he had no idea that it was wrong."

"Man, you're better than a library. Everything you said applies to this case and could be included under the category: 'disease of the mind.' It's a medical condition that affects the mind in the same way as a psychiatric illness, although by a different mechanism," said Stuart.

Kantor quickly added, "There I might disagree with you because most, if not all, psychiatric illnesses have a medical or chemical basis. What counts is the ultimate effect on the brain despite the cause. In your case, there's no doubt as to the cause of your client's problem. Here we are dealing with a known medical condition, known effects, and the likelihood of psychiatrists disagreeing is remote. So much for the lecture; it's back to Lexis-Nexis for you."

"I know, and thanks again for the help."

"Be sure and get back to me after you have a clear direction for your defense."

"Yes. I hope soon."

Stuart reviewed case histories on the insanity defense. When it came to specifics about hyperparathyroidism, he found nothing in the legal literature that was similar to his client's case. They bore a close relationship to his client, but his case was stronger than any others he reviewed. The insanity defense was a certain winner. 'Certain' was a word that many attorneys later regretted using. Nevertheless, George's case had just one option: a plea of insanity. He fit the legal definition, and it would be a bona fide, legitimate, and an appropriate ticket to freedom for his client. Convinced, he telephoned Kantor to arrange for another appointment.

When he arrived, Kantor could see a confident look on his junior attorney's face. "Well," said Kantor. "The way you're bouncing in here, it looks as like you've got this case all wrapped up."

"I do feel good about it," he admitted.

"I like what you've done. It's clear and concise. I'm not surprised you couldn't find anything in the legal literature like your client's case, but I wonder if any reports exist in the medical literature. It's not something I know much about, but this case is so unusual that I'll bet it might be a reportable one for physicians, too."

"That's a good idea, and one I didn't think about. Thanks, I'll get on it right away."

"Have you worked out a strategy for your next steps?"

"I was thinking of talking to Doris Donaldson, the attorney for the prosecution."

"Do it soon," said Kantor. "First, I would get an opinion about your client's current mental health. We know how he was at the time of the murder. That's clear from both medical records and the doctors' testimony. These doctors can testify as expert witnesses to your client's medical condition and his state of mental health now, but they aren't true experts since they aren't psychiatrists. We need the official stamp of approval that his recovery is so complete that he's incapable of repeating the act that they accuse him of. He must be presented as normal as you and me."

"Oh, no, poor guy."

"Yeah, you're right. I guess that was a bad analogy," laughed Kantor.

"Do you have a psychiatrist in mind?" asked Stuart.

"I do. His name is Peter Geary, Chief of Psychiatry at Midwest Medical Center. I'm familiar with his work and have used him as a witness several times. He's board certified in both psychiatry and neurology, and he speaks with authority based on years of experience as a practicing psychiatrist. He teaches and he's an author too. I know he'll be fascinated with this case and want to help. He'd be the one to search the medical literature for anything similar that resembles your case. I'll call him. We're not close friends, but we've worked together and have mutual respect for each other's work. I'll tell him to expect your call. Get back to me in a few days. I'll let you know if I've reached him and when you should call. I'll also give him the basics about your client and you'll fill in the details when you see him. Oh, and by the way, don't forget to bring along copies of all medical records."

Stuart left the meeting convinced of victory.

CHAPTER 37

Eve had been in touch with Gail and offered her help. Gail made an appointment to see Stuart to discuss George's case and took Eve with her.

Eve said, "I'm sure this has been an emotional and financial strain on you and your family. Please, Gail, you can always count on me for help, and never hesitate to ask. Burt said that he would see to it that his office would always accept your insurance payment in full and never take a co-pay or any balance for either one of you."

Gail broke into tears. She hugged Eve and said, "I don't know what to say. I'll never forget this, Eve."

They arrived at Stuart's office. They sat down in front of his desk. Gail asked, "What's happening with my husband, Mr. Stuart?"

Stuart spoke about the plans for George's defense, stressing that an insanity defense should be a winning strategy.

"What a relief." Gail answered. "I thank you with all my heart."

"Have you spoken with all his doctors?" asked Eve.

"Yes I did. They all agreed that George could not have been responsible for his actions at the time of the murder, if indeed he did it. Don't forget, he's innocent until proven guilty in our system. The only criticism they had was his failure to get the tests they ordered, but they did agree that his mind could have been affected by the tumors and be responsible. This is all helpful in his defense."

"I'm so grateful," said Gail. My husband has confidence in you, Mr. Stuart. You've relieved my mind. I can't thank you enough."

"Not at all, Mrs. Gilmer. I want you to know that another lawyer, James Kantor, who heads up the public defender's office, is helping me.

He's very interested in your husband's case and is working with me to plan the strategy for his defense."

"That's great, sir. Thank you so much."

On the way home, Gail said to Eve, "What do you think?"

Eve responded promptly and firmly. "I think your husband's in good hands. I like that guy. He was sincere and came across as being very dedicated to his profession and his clients."

"Yes, I felt the same way, only It doesn't stop me from worrying."

"I understand. How is your financial situation, Gail?"

"We're getting by with some help from my parents. George's parents are both dead. His father was killed in an automobile accident when George was a toddler, and his mother died of ovarian cancer."

"Again, Gail, if there's anything I can do to help you, please don't hesitate to ask."

"I love you, Eve. I hope Dr. Crowell knows what a good person you are."

CHAPTER 38

There was another victim in this case, and that was Alice Matt, the victim's wife of six months. It was clear to her, once she became familiar with the facts of her husband's murder, if the doctors diagnosed the crazy murderer in time her husband would be alive today. Not long after her husband's murder, she sought out Hugh Adams, a famous malpractice attorney with offices on Michigan Avenue, downtown Chicago. He subpoenaed the hospital records and learned the facts about Philip Matt and George Gilmer. Alice's husband, Phillip, had neither an estate nor life insurance. Someone had to pay. Hospitals and doctors have many deep pockets, and that can serve in place of careful estate planning.

Adam's reputation for ruthlessness and chicanery amazed even his fellow attorneys. When Alice Matt visited his office and related the story behind her husband's death, he leapt into action. The records confirmed that there indeed was a cause of action here. Adams also learned that the defendant was now in jail for murder and that the evidence against him was solid. So here was a wrongful death suit with a twist; a suit not against the medical establishment for the death of one of their patients, but for the death of a man killed by one of their patients. There were many deep pockets available: numerous physicians and two hospitals. Never mind that an insanity defense was a likely winner in this case, for the crucial point was the delay in diagnosis that made it possible for George Gilmer's condition to deteriorate leading to its horrible outcome.

Attorney Adams didn't hesitate to go to work. "Sue 'em all, sort it out later," was his guiding legal principle number one. He sued every physician who had anything to do with Philip Matt and Covenant and Sheridan Hospital. The doctors who took care of Donald were in for the experience of their lives. Hugh Adams would always sue for about ten times more than it was possible for them to obtain from their malpractice carriers. This would force the doctors to either hire their own attorney to protect them beyond their insurance limits, or forget it and just pray. The expense usually forced them to choose prayer. "Gotta give 'em something to think about," said Attorney Adams, espousing legal principle number two. And think about it they did. Alice Matt was delighted. Hugh Adams exuded confidence that gave her strength. In just two days, she had the money spent in her mind.

Never settle for a big prize when it could be bigger. Hugh Adams realized there was another victim in this case. She was the wife of the killer. Through no fault of her own, she was now without the comfort and consortium of a husband. Her source of financial support ended, and she and her children were suffering. She was just as much of a victim as Alice Matt, and he could represent them both. If only the doctors had been more diligent. A two-pronged plaintiff attack against the medical establishment in this case would enhance the possibility of a blockbuster award. His office would approach Gail Gilmer. With this in mind, he called Gail advising her of the suit filed against the physicians and the hospitals on behalf of the victim's wife, and inviting her participation because the doctors failed to diagnose her husband in time to prevent him from murdering an innocent victim. Gail was stunned. All she could think of was Dr. Crowell and her good friend Eve. She blurted out, "Oh my God, I can't talk now. I have to go."

"Call me tomorrow, Mrs. Gilmer. Don't forget my name—Hugh Adams."

That evening, Gail called Eve and told her of the conversation she had with Attorney Adams.

Eve was not surprised. "What are you going to do?" she asked.

"Nothing, of course. I'm so amazed, I can hardly speak."

"Well don't be. This type of thing happens all the time. Are you sure you're going to do nothing?"

"I'm 100 percent sure. I love you, Eve, and your doctor friend is a thorough and compassionate man. I could no more sue him than sue my own mother."

"If it was me being asked, I would go and talk to the lawyer just for the experience and the pleasure of listening and when it was all over say an emphatic no thank you and walk out. I would view it all as just another bit of education."

"What an interesting idea," said Gail. Maybe I should do that and then I could tell you all about it."

"Gail, I wasn't suggesting that."

"I know, but…"

"But what?"

"I'll do it for you and Dr. Crowell, Eve. It'll be an adventure. I feel like a spy. Maybe I'll find something out to help Dr. Crowell. I will do it. Yes."

"But, Gail, I don't know if that's wise."

"Hey, a no is a no, and I'll learn something just as you said. Do you want to come with?"

A surprised Eve stammered, "I better not."

"Why?"

"I'm sure a lawyer would only want to talk to the client and not someone who wasn't involved with the case."

"I guess that's right. I'll talk to you later, Eve. I'll keep you posted."

CHAPTER 39

The next day, Gail called attorney Adams and made an appointment to see him. She arrived downtown and was ushered into an enormous office larger than her living room and dining room combined. There were floor to ceiling windows on the thirty-fourth floor, which overlooked Lake Shore Drive and Lake Michigan. Two walls were floor to ceiling bookshelves filled with neatly placed volumes. A third wall had numerous diplomas and a large, framed drawing of a cow with a man pulling the cow's tail, and another man pulling on the cow's ears. An attorney, dressed in nineteenth century legal regalia, was sitting on a stool milking the cow. The caption under the picture: *"The Law Suit."* In a corner of the room was a beautiful table surrounded by four chairs. The floor appeared to be of solid oak, partially covered by a square-shaped oriental rug.

Gail saw two large, cloth-upholstered chairs placed before a massive wooden desk. On the other side was Hugh Adams, who rose when Gail entered the room. "Good morning, Mrs. Gilmer. My name is Hugh Adams. Please have a seat." Adams was a middle aged, balding, overweight man of medium height wearing half-reading glasses.

'Thank you, sir."

"Thank you for coming, Mrs. Gilmer. I will get right to the point. We are filing a lawsuit on behalf of the victim's wife, Alice Matt. Her allegation is that her husband would be alive today had your husband been diagnosed in time. We recognize that your husband may not have been responsible for his actions, but that is irrelevant. The fact is that he is the only suspect, and the evidence against him is strong."

"You've convicted him already, and he hasn't even been to trial yet," Gail stated appearing depressed.

"You're right, Mrs. Gilmer. There is the presumption of innocence until proven guilty. That is the way we operate in this country, but as I have already stated, your husband remains the only suspect. I want you to know that I believe he is innocent, but for reasons of insanity. I've studied the case inside out. Please, don't misunderstand me. Insanity is a legal term, and what he did was without his knowledge because of his distorted mind. The fact is your husband's in jail and will be there for a long time; meanwhile, disrupting both your life and the life of your children. We have spent a great deal of time evaluating the merits of this case, and we are preparing to file. We believe we have a good case against the doctors involved in your husband's care. You and your children are entitled to compensation due to doctors' negligence and the disruption to your family life, not to mention your pain and suffering."

"You would sue Doctor Crowell?" asked Gail.

"He's one of the doctors, so of course we would."

"But he did his very best to find out what was wrong with my husband. He ordered tests, but my husband refused to get them.

"That may be, but these details may or may not be relevant. It is for a jury to sort out. For instance, we don't know what he ordered. He could have ordered tests that would have established the diagnosis, or even tests that were unrelated to the diagnosis. We determine these details as part of our investigation of the facts. But these issues should not concern you; they are legal technicalities best left in our hands. Emotion has no place in these matters. Who's emotional about your suffering children? We are. Moreover, we intend to get you compensation for what you've been through. God knows with an unemployed husband, you and your family must be suffering. We have years of experience in these matters, and we don't lose cases."

Gail sat facing the desk, but was staring past Adams. A flock of birds that flew past the window had disrupted her focus of attention. She followed them as they soared into the distance. As she sat watching, Adams words faded and she began to lose her concentration. She found herself doing this quite often. Gail did not attempt to respond.

Adams tried again. "Don't forget, Mrs. Gilmer, this does not cost you a penny. We advance all costs and at settlement, or judgment, we recoup our expenses plus one third. You get the remainder, which will be substantial, I assure you."

Gail remained in her seat, her expression unchanged. After many silent seconds, she rose from her chair and with tears in her eyes, she turned and walked to the door. Without looking back she said, "Goodbye. No thank you, sir."

Attorney Adams stared after her. He had never before witnessed this reaction. Too emotional now, he thought. Better let her go. We'll pursue this later.

However, a temporary disappointment would not stop his firm's forward progress in any way. They subpoenaed the medical records and staff nurse attorneys scrutinized them word by word looking for any possible lead, any written statement that would expose the mind-set of the treating physicians, any clues that might suggest a delay or a failure to investigate, and any evidence that might suggest that hyperparathyroidism was not part of the physician's initial thinking.

CHAPTER 40

A process server appeared in Burt's office and handed him his "gift" witnessed by three patients sitting in the waiting room. His records were also subpoenaed and evaluated. Doctors Pollard, Godwin, Boyd, Irving, Albert, Covenant and Sheridan Hospitals received theirs as well. Never mind that some of these defendants were only involved as consultants and had no direct responsibility for George's care. Legal principle number one necessitated such measures. The multimillion-dollar price invoked legal principle number two: economic loss plus pain and suffering and loss of consortium. The physicians sued gave the subpoenas to their malpractice carrier, the Illinois State Medical Society, as this was the only company available. Previous carriers had fled the state due to excessive defense costs and financial loss thus necessitating the formation of a medical society-sponsored malpractice carrier. Each defendant's attorney came from a major downtown law firm. It was every man or woman for him or herself. The instructions given were, "say nothing to anyone, and don't speak with anyone other than your attorney. Remember that anything you say may come back to haunt you. Speak with no other doctors involved in the case. Don't worry, leave the details to us, but since the suit is more than your insurance limits we need to recommend that you hire your own attorney because we can only protect you for the limits of your policy. Consider this case as 'one of the risks of doing business.' Suppress the anguish, as there is no other choice. Learn how to compartmentalize. Your patients deserve your full attention."

Of course, the physicians could not afford the expense of a private attorney. The cost of five years or more for defense before the case would come to trial would exceed their incomes over that same period. The malpractice lawyers assigned would be their sole defense. Any judgment exceeding those limits would mean bankruptcy.

The physicians met with their defense attorneys, and the details of their interaction with George Gilmer discussed in exquisite detail. The doctors were educated as to how to comport themselves in the depositions to come. "Don't volunteer information; just answer the question and don't embellish your answer." It was a game of cat and mouse. "Be aware that the same question may be disguised in many different ways. The goal is to confuse you and hope that you make inconsistent statements."

In the meantime, Detective Galinski was occupying himself with other cases.

CHAPTER 41

Peter Geary had a distinguished career at Midwest Medical Center. He was sixty-four-years-old with one-year left to serve as Chief of Psychiatry. Midwest had a mandatory retirement age of sixty-five for any department chairperson. One could stay on in another capacity, but only if the individual and the administration agreed. In Geary's case, the administration had requested that he remain. He would continue in a teaching role, be involved in research, and consult on select patients. Geary had a national reputation and he published in psychiatry and neurology literature. Most psychiatrists practice by virtue of their psychiatric residency, but Geary had a unique advantage. He was board certified in two specialties: psychiatry and neurology. This gave him an edge. He had a broad understanding of neurology, and an exquisite up-to-date knowledge of brain chemistry and psychopharmacology. As a world authority on brain chemistry, Kantor had selected him for his unique ability in evaluating and explaining an organic psychosis defense.

Geary was fascinated when he learned about the facts of Gilmer's case. Though he had witnessed hyperparathyroidism lead to full-blown psychoses, never had he seen it lead to murder, or so the legal community believed.

Attorney Stuart brought George up to date after speaking with Geary. "We're bringing in a famous psychiatrist to check you out, George. He'll help us to determine if you were or were not responsible for your actions at the time of the crime and testify about your present mental state. We're sure he will agree with all the other doctors who saw you and say you're perfectly normal now, so cooperate with him."

"I will," sighed George. "But what about the other doctors who took care of me? Are they going to testify?"

"They've all promised to testify for you."

"So, nothing has changed," he said. "To get me off, they have to say I'm insane, right?"

"Only insane at the time the murder was committed. If we attempt to fight the evidence against you, we'll lose."

"I could get the ultimate penalty. I still can't believe I could murder anyone, even if I was insane."

"The insanity defense is the only way to go. It is clear and simple and a winner. That's what's important. Look at it this way. Have you ever heard about people possessed by the devil who then undergo exorcism by a priest?"

"Sure, but I don't believe in it."

"Well, for the sake of discussion, let us assume that it can happen."

"What are you getting at?"

"Your case got me interested in this subject, so I read a lot about it. Okay, picture this, and I'm not saying that you committed this crime, but let's assume a demon entered your brain and took it over so that you ceased to exist. It turned you off or kicked you out, whatever. The demon was in full control and replaced your brain and your mind. It controlled your entire body. This demon took a knife, and using your arms and body, he killed someone. You didn't do it. You weren't functioning any more. The demon was the killer. After the murder, the demon left your mind and body and you took back control. You would never know that the demon and your body had joined to commit some murder. Are you, guilty? Hell, no. It was the demon. Is it fair to put you to death for murder? No way. In your case, the demon was the tumor. The priests who performed the exorcism were the doctors who made the diagnosis and the surgeon who cut the demon out. That's what an insanity defense is all about. It's fair, and it'll free you. I still don't believe you did this, but as long as you're being accused, that's the way we have to think."

George listened for a few seconds. He did not want to miss a point. "So," he replied, "if I win, I'm free to go, but I've got a record. I'll be innocent due to insanity. Is that right?"

"Yes, but better than the alternative."

"Then I put myself in your hands, Mr. Stuart. You're the pro. I keep thinking that the reason for all of this will get clear to me some day."

"Thanks, George. The famous psychiatrist I mentioned is Dr. Peter Geary. You'll hear from him soon."

Follow-up calcium levels after the surgery, combined with his clinical findings and behavior, confirmed a complete cure. The brainstorm that had plagued George was long past. His mental state was excellent although, as expected, he felt depressed. Gail's frequent visits helped sustain him.

CHAPTER 42

Stuart reported to Kantor.

"Good work," Kantor said. "We need to wait for Geary's report. It'll be thorough I'm sure. Any judge will accept his conclusions without a doubt. This will be the final word. Peter Geary is the ultimate in second opinions. Have you spoken to the prosecution yet?"

"Not in any great detail, but I'm ready to now."

"Bring Doris Donaldson up to date. I'm sure they'll get their own psychiatrist in. I'm also sure the psychiatrists will accept all facts of the case. He was insane, and now he's normal. We're going to make legal and psychiatric history on this case. Can you imagine? Two psychiatrists in agreement," exclaimed Kantor.

"We'll write it up, and then have a new legal principle like the McNaughton rule. We'll call it the 'Gilmer Principle,' and all future attorneys will invoke it if, and when, the future brings together two psychiatrists who can ever reach agreement," laughed Stuart.

"You got that right," said Kantor. "Well, get to the prosecution as soon as possible. Keep me posted. You and I may write this one up. You get top billing," he added.

"Quite an honor," proclaimed Stuart, as they both laughed.

"Now go talk to Doris Donaldson," said Kantor.

CHAPTER 43

Doris Donaldson had been with the prosecutor's office for nine years since graduating from law school. She had dealt with Stuart on several previous cases so they were on a first-name basis. Stuart sat at Donaldson's desk, waiting for her to enter. He poured two cups of coffee.

"How are you?" Donaldson said, as she entered the room. "I think we've got a lot to talk about today."

"Right. I'm sure you understand that we'll use the insanity defense.

"Yes, no doubt," nodded Donaldson, sipping her coffee.

"Peter Geary is our expert witness. He'll decide on my client's mental state at the time of the crime and his current state of mental health," reported Stuart.

"Our psychiatric consultant is Betty Carey," said Donaldson.

"I recently spoke to James Kantor who came up with an amazing scenario." said Stuart.

"What about?"

"He's certain that both psychiatrists will find themselves in agreement. George Gilmer was insane at the time of the murder, but now he is normal and rational."

"Whoa, psychiatrists in agreement? The judge will be flabbergasted."

"This brings us to the principle of an honest offense," continued Stuart.

"What do you mean?"

"According to one of my law professors, the best defense is an honest offense. Of course, this presumes that the prosecutor has a high ethical standard and is searching for justice. That's why I'm glad to have you on this case. I know you won't conceal facts like some people we know."

"Thanks, but are you trying to butter me up for something?" laughed Donaldson.

Stuart joined the laughter and said, "When the psychiatrists complete their reports we'll move for an innocent plea by reason of insanity and spare the defendant a senseless trial."

"It may come to that," she said, "but hold it a moment. I'm not there just yet. I've got lots to do before we get to that stage."

"I know, I'm just planting a small seed, and I have no doubt that the seed I plant today, and which you'll help me water, will grow into a beautiful flower of justice," he said with an angelic look on his face.

"How poetic. Now, get out of here. I have too much work to do."

"Bye," said Stuart, with a flirtatious wink as he got up to leave her office. He felt satisfied with the meeting. Now he would give Donaldson time to reflect, though he was certain she would see it his way.

CHAPTER 44

The more Dr. Geary studied George's records, the more fascinated he became. He arranged for a meeting with Doctor Lim so he could brief him. They both agreed that the history, clinical examination, and laboratory facts pointed to a strong insanity defense. It was clear that George was not responsible for his actions. Geary searched his records. He discovered that after more than thirty-four years of experience in academic medicine he could only uncover five cases of psychoses due to parathyroid adenomas. A literature search revealed that psychoses occurred with calcium levels between twelve and twenty-two. George's level of 13.8 was consistent. Now Geary was ready to meet with George.

Since in any psychiatric interview the purpose is to establish a doctor-patient relationship, the initial interview is most relevant. Geary assumed that if Gilmer were normal, then he would need to probe for any hint of some lingering psychiatric pathology. In addition, if Gilmer was responsible for the murder and any doubt still existed about his mental state, then he owed it to society to be thorough and cautious. He would insist on a setting for George's interview that was quiet, comfortable, and conducive to open and uninterrupted discussion.

He used a room with a desk, two chairs and an examining table. A one-way mirror allowed interior viewing, but the room's occupants could not see out. George had been there less than five minutes when Geary arrived.

"Good morning, Mr. Gilmer. I'm Dr. Geary, and I'm here to examine you."

"Sure. Good to meet you, doctor."

"I've studied your records and I spoke with some of the physicians who took care of you. I need to take a full history and perform a complete medical examination."

"Okay. I'm ready."

"Tell me, please, what led to your imprisonment? I'm interested in your own interpretation of what happened."

George was composed as he repeated the entire story.

Dr. Leary listening intently responded compassionately when George finished. "I can only imagine what you're going through. I'm impressed by the calm way you tell your story."

"I have to keep thinking that everything happens for a reason and that one day all of it will make sense."

Geary probed further, exploring the medical history from childhood on. He questioned him about family, medical, occupational, and social history while noting his words, any facial expressions, his gestures, and his body language. A good psychiatric interviewer could receive a wealth of valuable information from such subtle body movements. George's speech, appearance, behavior, thought processes, thought content, affect, memory, and cognitive ability appeared perfectly normal. Next, he did a complete neurological examination: Motor and sensory examinations were normal; cranial nerves were intact; reflexes were equal and normal; no evidence of pathological reflexes; coordination, gait, and stance were all normal. In short, the patient was medically, neurologically, and psychiatrically intact.

"I'm finished, Mr. Gilmer. I will tell you that I'm pleased with the results, and I'll send a written report to your attorneys in about two days."

"Thanks for your help," said George. The two men shook hands.

"I wish you the best of luck," said Geary. "I'll be available to your legal team for as long as it takes to complete your case."

George bowed his head, grateful for the doctor's professional analysis. "Thanks again, sir."

"My pleasure, Mr. Gilmer. Good-bye." He knocked on the door to signal the end of their meeting.

That evening he dictated an eleven-page report that included past social and medical history, physical examination, George's mental state at the time of the murder, the current status of George's mental health, and all available information related to the psychosis of patients with hyperparathyroidism. Most important, the conclusion stated that George Gilmer was insane at the time of the murder, and therefore not responsible for his actions. His report ended with the equally firm conclusion that George was cured, was psychiatrically normal and no longer posed any threats whatever to society.

Dr. Joyce Carey evaluated George and arrived at the same conclusion as Dr. Geary. She reported her findings to Doris Donaldson. Prosecution and defense were cooperating as one, and legal strategists were planning their next move.

CHAPTER 45

Because the evidence against George was indisputable and because there was no shortage of murders to investigate, Detective Galinski busied himself with other cases. He was preoccupied with another matter when Donaldson's office called to inform him about the latest status of George's prosecution. More than twenty years investigating murders had given him a sixth sense about these matters. Nevertheless, this case left him baffled.

Richard Galinski's father and grandfather were both detectives. He grew up living and breathing police work. Once he met eligibility requirements for the police force, he applied. Five years later, and after a stellar, award-winning record of routine police work, he became a member of the homicide division, earning fame investigating numerous high profile murders.

When Galinski met George during the hospital arrest, he sensed that George was a sincere religious person whose faith fueled him with the strength to withstand the humiliation of a first-degree murder charge. He believed that George was telling the truth. He once read that when a man was hypnotized they would never follow a command that went against their code of ethics. He wondered if the same thing would apply to a man victimized by a medically caused psychosis. He kept these thoughts to himself because he understood that this type of situation was different from a hypnotic state. He viewed the lie detector test as an ego booster for the defendant, but was sure the court would never allow it.

The murder victim Philip Matt's fingerprint report had not yet come back. Since criminal records are confirmed based on fingerprints, the missing report could yield valuable clues and at times provide information that could throw a new slant on the case.

When he first phoned the FBI to check on the delay, the agent in charge promised to investigate and let him know. After one week passed with no word, he called again. He was surprised to learn that the FBI office wanted to meet with him, but would need to call him back. Never before had he experienced any delay obtaining routine information. When the FBI did call, they requested that he report to their Chicago office with a picture of Philip Matt and copies of his fingerprints. Although taken aback, he complied without question.

Seated behind the desk in the director's office was a gray-haired, middle aged man with a weathered face and a toothy smile. The director's handshake made Galinski wince.

"Good morning, detective. Please sit down. I'm agent Alfred Marshall."

"Pleased to meet you. I'm Richard Galinski." He passed his card to the agent.

"Yes, I know. We've got your picture on file. Sorry for all these precautions, detective." He paused for a smile. "In your line of work I know you understand."

"Sure, but why all the cloak and dagger stuff?"

"We needed to be certain you were who you said you were when you phoned the FBI. We also needed to be certain that the prints and photograph belonged to Philip Matt."

"You can count on it. I'm Richard Galinski, all right. I also will vouch for the validity of the picture and prints."

"I have no doubt, detective. Let's see the evidence, please. It'll just take a few minutes to check a few matters, and I'll be right back." Marshall carried the prints and photograph into the next room and returned in two minutes. Galinski could not help but notice the somber expression on the agent's face as he sat down.

"Let me show you the results. Look here. Here's your photo of Philip Matt, and here's the one we took of him two years ago...'

Galinski interrupted. "How come you got a picture of him from two years ago?"

"Hold that question. It'll soon come clear."

"These two pictures of Matt are the same person. Now, here's a third one. We took this a few months before the two-year-old photo..."

"How come? How did you know him then?" Galinski interrupted.

"Let me continue, detective, and you'll see soon enough. Notice the difference in the pictures. His nose is bigger, no mustache, a different hairdo, and yet I'm certain that all three pictures, based on precise anthropomorphic measurements, are of the same man. Now look. Here are the fingerprints you brought, and here's our copy of the prints. They match too. We have no doubt that Philip is dead."

Galinski, flabbergasted by Marshall's remarks, said, "I agree. I haven't seen a dead guy get off the autopsy table yet—especially when the pathologist is holding his heart in his hands."

Marshall laughed. "Yes, but we needed to be certain, detective. We assume full responsibility for notifying his family."

"His wife already knows. I spoke with her myself," said Galinski, unable to figure out what Marshall was driving at.

"He has another family."

"Oh?" Galinski leaned forward in his seat so as not to miss a word, put his hands in his pocket and rolled his two marbles frantically. "I wasn't aware of that. His wife never said anything to me, and as far as we know she's the only living relative."

"She didn't tell you because she doesn't know either."

"What?" asked a startled Galinski. How could a wife not know about her husband's family? This is getting weirder by the minute."

"This wife did not know about her husband's family because," said Marshall, "the victim was not Philip Matt."

Galinski leaned forward in his chair, stared ahead his mouth hanging open, his eyes staring at Marshall. Then he fell back against the back of the chair, threw up his hands and waited for amplification of this bombshell.

Marshall continued, "The murder victim was in the witness protection program under the assumed name of Philip Matt. His real name was Thomas Brown." He paused for effect. Galinski was shaking his head, his features the picture of confusion. Marshall continued, "Brown was part of an illegal organized crime drug gang in Detroit, and he turned state's evidence against them. After his testimony, his life wasn't worth a nickel.

He got a nose job, grew a mustache for a time, changed his hairstyle, and disappeared into the witness protection program. He did well for about two years, although maybe they caught up with him."

Galinski's mind was racing. This put a new wrinkle on the case. He shook his head in disbelief and said, "I've got to do some rethinking now. I thought we had already wrapped this case up. The evidence against our lead suspect, George Gilmer, seemed complete, though I never was 100-percent comfortable with what we had on him. Now it looks like we'll need to dig deeper. Never a dull day in this business, right? Thanks for the news, Mr. Marshall, you just put a hell of a new wrinkle on this case."

"I believe you, detective; you've got your work cut out for you now. We'll help in any way possible. If anything turns up, we'll get back to you right away. Thanks for coming in."

While driving back to the office, he reminisced. His grandfather and father investigated organized crime when Galinski was a youngster. When he was old enough to understand, his father told him about their work. Back then, organized crime was a powerful force. Though the days of bootlegging and Al Capone were history, Chicago maintained its image as a gangster city. He smiled. In London five years earlier, vacationing with his wife, their taxi driver asked where they came from. When the driver heard the word 'Chicago,' he said, "Now I don't know if you're gonna pay me or shoot me."

He started to wonder if the Matt killing was a result of drug gang violence. Philip Matt, the former stool pigeon, Thomas Brown, would have been a prime candidate for a gang hit. However, none of this changed the fact that all evidence pointed to their principle suspect, George Gilmer, sitting in prison. Could the gang have hired Gilmer, or did he belong to them? Was it possible that the gang set Gilmer up? Might the entire plot have been a red herring, and Philip Matt was the victim of some insane medically induced rage of George's just as everyone was postulating? Could George have unwittingly completed the gang's dirty work? Did the gang even know that Philip Matt was really Thomas Brown?

Marshall had been unable to solve the puzzle before handing it over to Detective Galinski. "Okay, detective," said Marshall. "You try putting the pieces together."

CHAPTER 46

When Dr. Crowell received the malpractice subpoena, overcome with a mixture of anger and depression he swore, but only in his thoughts as he was within ear-shot of patients and office personnel. He called Eve to let her know. "I'm being sued by the wife of the murder victim," he said. "Son-of-a-bitch! I was always told that a malpractice suit was inevitable in a medical career, but damn, I just started."

Eve told him about her experience with Gail and the malpractice attorney's efforts to add her to the lawsuit, and Gail's refusal to be a part.

"And you kept it from me. That was thoughtful, Eve. I bet I have you to thank for Gail's refusal," he said.

"No, she thinks you're great, and she said she would no more sue you as sue her own mother."

"I'm still going to give you credit, sweet one. You're the best, and thinking of you helps wipe this shock from my mind." He paused. Then said, "by the way, the furnishings you picked out for my condo will arrive Saturday morning. You'll have to help me put it all together."

"That should be fun. I look forward to it. Now go ahead and try to put this suit behind you. You've got too much else to do."

Since it was determined that Dr. Crowell was George's physician, he would be the first one to be deposed. Both he and his attorney arrived at the office of Hugh Adams who was waiting in a large conference room. Seated at the end of the conference table, Crowell's outward appearance was calm, but inside was anger coupled with concern in spite of the fact that he had been well versed in deposition comportment for defendants. At the opposite and far end of the table, he could see his nemesis, Hugh Adams, seated next to a court reporter who was equipped to record every word with the help of a funny looking gadget on the table before her.

"Good morning, Doctor. My name is Hugh Adams. I will be asking you a series of questions, beginning with your full name, please."

"Burt Crowell."

"What is your specialty, please?"

"Internal medicine."

"For the record, doctor, what does this entail?"

"Do you mean what is the extent of my practice? What am I trained for?"

"Yes, tell me the extent of your practice."

"As an internist, I am trained to take care of adults. I treat medically, not surgically. My work is bound by my own training and experience."

"And where did you train?"

"Northwestern University."

"In an internal medicine residency, I presume?"

"Yes."

"Are you board certified in internal medicine?"

"Yes."

"Do you have any other board certifications?"

"No."

"Have you ever been sued for malpractice before?"

"No."

"Do you know George Gilmer?"

"Yes."

"Are you aware he is now in jail and accused of murder?"

"Yes."

"Did you diagnose him as having hyperparathyroidism?"

"Yes."

"Yes, I know he was diagnosed late into the game, but did you diagnose him as having hyperparathyroidism when you were seeing him in your office?"

"No, I suspected the possibility, but he never completed the investigation."

"I have a copy of your records which shows the visits with George Gilmer. Where can I find that suspicion of yours?"

"It may not be written down. With many patients there may be a large differential diagnosis and the average physician does not take the time to detail all of them in writing."

"What's a differential diagnosis, doctor?"

"It's a list of the possible diagnoses that each patient may have. From this list you try and pin down the single diagnosis, if possible."

"Tell us about the first time you saw George Gilmer in your office, doctor."

Burt looked at the record before responding. "He came into my office complaining of abdominal epigastric pain. I took a medical history and did a physical examination."

"Where's the epigastric area, doctor?"

Burt pointed.

"I'm sorry, doctor, the court reporter needs you to tell where it is so she can write it down."

"Yes, it's the center upper abdomen under the rib cage."

"Thank you, doctor, and what were your findings?"

"His exam was normal except for some minimal epigastric tenderness."

"How about his thyroid gland?"

"Normal, in that there was no enlargement or tenderness."

"Where does it say that?"

"Right here. EENT normal."

"Tell us what is EENT?"

"Eyes, ears, nose and throat. The thyroid gland is evaluated when you are examining this part of the patient's anatomy."

"Did you feel his parathyroid gland?"

"You can't feel those."

"What if it has a tumor?"

"You still can't feel it."

"Why not?"

Because the parathyroid glands are buried in the undersurface of the thyroid and they can't be felt."

"Are you sure?"

"Yes, I'm sure."

"What if the tumor gets very big?"

"In my experience, and from what I have ever learned, that does not happen. Now I have never done a world literature search, so I can't tell you if it has ever happened in medical history. However, this is irrelevant because George Gilmer had a tumor, which was not huge. Anyhow, even if it were possible for a parathyroid tumor to become very large, it would push the thyroid anteriorly, and on physical examination you would think the thyroid was enlarged."

"What diagnosis did you make at that first visit?"

"At the first visit I didn't have enough information to pinpoint a diagnosis. There were several possibilities, and I ordered tests to investigate those possibilities."

"And what were those possibilities?"

"Ulcer, perhaps due to helicobacter pylori, gastritis, hiatus hernia, gall bladder problems, and any problem related to the upper gastrointestinal tract."

Hugh Adams had a puzzled look on his face. "What is helicobacter pylori, doctor?"

"It is a bacteria known to cause ulcers. Ulcer has other causes also." answered Burt.

"Like hyperparathyroidism?" asked Adams

"Yes."

"How about hyperparathyroidism, doctor. Did you think of that at the initial exam?"

"At the initial examination? No. There are many different causes and sites of abdominal pain. You go about an investigation systematically. You rule out the most common causes and then zero in on other rarer possibilities."

"And what were the tests you ordered?"

"I ordered upper gastrointestinal imaging studies, and a complete blood work-up including stool and blood for helicobacter and urinalysis. The blood work-up, if he would have gotten it, would have diagnosed his hyperparathyroidism."

"Where does it say that?"

"Right here," said Burt, pointing to a specific area of the chart.

"What does W slash U mean, doctor?"

"W/U means work-up."

"Work-up is a very nonspecific term, don't you think? What does it mean?"

"It has different meanings in different cases. In this case, I gave Mr. Gilmer an order slip and asked that he make an appointment for an upper GI series, an upper abdominal ultrasound and blood work-up including a complete blood count and a blood profile and helicobcter and urinalysis. That was the initial work-up. I then would have wanted an upper gastrointestinal endoscopic examination if the preliminary tests I ordered failed to identify a diagnosis. He never got those tests."

"Do you have a copy of that order slip?"

"No, I don't. If he had gotten the tests, the results would be on the chart."

Adams had found his opening already. W/U was it. A nonspecific documentation tool that would leave some doubt about Doctor Crowell's thought processes the time he first saw George Gilmer. There was no evidence that the diagnosis of hyperparathyroidism was on his mind. Never mind that a calcium test was part of a blood profile that would have diagnosed the case had George performed the tests. The points to hammer home were: no diagnosis of hyperparathyroidism; no mention of a calcium test on the chart; no evidence that the doctor pursued George Gilmer to complete the investigation. Hugh Adams knew that the probability of a patient with abdominal pain, on the first doctor's visit, having hyperparathyroidism established as a diagnosis was close to nil from a probability point of view. But, these were concepts that would go over the heads of most juries, and this case had an enormous and emotional gut wrenching appeal for jurors. Although the practice of medicine is an evaluation of probabilities, in malpractice cases it has little relevance. With all these thoughts filed away in his cerebral cortex and on his legal pad, Hugh Adams went on with his questioning.

"Tell me again, doctor, what were your thoughts and possible diagnosis when you first saw George Gilmer?"

"The possibilities were that he could have had gastritis, or a peptic ulcer, or hiatus hernia, or gall bladder problem, or any other upper gastrointestinal area disease."

"Isn't peptic ulcer one of the manifestations of hyperparathyroidism?"

"Yes, it could be."

Another hammer's drive on the coffin nail, thought Hugh Adams. "Tell me, doctor, isn't pancreatitis also a manifestation of hyperparathyroidism?"

"Yes it could be because of elevated calcium."

"I don't see pancreatitis mentioned in the record. Were you thinking about it?"

"It is all part of the statement that an upper gastrointestinal work-up was being done. The pancreas is in the upper gastrointestinal area of one's anatomy."

"Is the word pancreatitis mentioned anyplace on the record?"

"No."

Getting better, thought Adams. Plenty of points made about the first office visit. Time to zero in on the second. "Did you see George Gilmer a second time?"

"Yes."

"And what was the purpose of the next visit?"

"This time he came in with his wife. She had urged him to visit me because she was worried about his mental state."

"In what way?"

"He was getting nervous, forgetful, and agitated."

"What did you think?"

"I wasn't exactly sure. Certainly it was possible that he was having some sort of mental breakdown. Also, I thought of the possibility of a neurological problem such as a brain tumor, but that wasn't the only possibility. Other and rarer possibilities always rear their ugly head."

"What did you do?"

"I recommended an MRI of the brain, and I also suggested a psychiatric consultation."

"What about the tests you ordered on the first visit?"

"I chastised him for not getting them when I ordered it and urged him to get them in the next day or two and gave him another slip to get the tests done. I told him to call back for the results."

"Why didn't you do the tests in your office?"

"I don't have an approved laboratory. I don't do any tests in my office. I send my patients to the hospital laboratories where I know that an approved, accredited facility performs the tests. One needs to be confident of results. Perhaps doctors in large clinics have approved laboratories, but no solo doctor's office has an approved laboratory facility on the premises that I ever heard of."

"Doctor, isn't it true that mental changes are one of the hallmarks of hyperparathyroidism?"

"Yes, it could be. That may well be one of the symptoms."

"On the second visit, did you think of the diagnosis of hyperparathyroidism?"

"Yes."

"But where is it written? How do you explain you're not making the diagnosis in this case when you had so many facts that would lead one to expect this diagnosis?"

"The diagnosis would have been made a long time ago had he only followed my instructions. It may not have been written down, but I can prove it was on my mind."

"Oh, how can you do that doctor?"

"I discussed his case with a nurse and we spoke about it."

"About what?"

"About the possibility of hyperparathyroidism being a part of the differential diagnosis."

"Who is this nurse?"

"A friend of mine who works at the same hospital as me."

"Was the nurse involved in the care of the patient?"

"No."

"Was the nurse a man or a woman?"

"A woman."

"Is she a close friend?"

"I object as irrelevant, the line of questioning being pursued by Mr. Adams," said Crowell's attorney.

Adams would let that one go. There would be time to check that all out. The jury would decide whether the doctor is telling the truth or not, but by that line of questioning he had left an opening for the defense. Damn, he thought. The nurse could testify to that and possibly confirm what Doctor Crowell said. I better hold off on this bit of information, but what was he doing talking to a nurse who wasn't involved in the patient's care? What about the confidentiality of that?

"What did you do next, doctor?"

"Again, I gave him a slip for the tests. I ordered the MRI and the blood tests, and he had his instructions to call back for results. He did get the MRI, and when he did phone, I was out of town. My nurse gave him the results of the MRI, which was normal, and she scheduled an appointment for Mr. Gilmer to see a psychiatrist."

"Did you ever get a calcium blood test?"

"That was part of the blood profile that I had ordered."

"Did he get it?"

"Apparently not."

"And, what did you do?"

"As I said, I was out of town."

"What did your nurse do about the lack of blood tests?"

"He only called for MRI results."

"Did you ever see George Gilmer again?"

"Yes, in the hospital."

"And that was after the murder took place," added Adams.

"Was that a question?"

"No, doctor." More ammunition, thought Adams. The interview was over. He had all the information he needed, his legal pad outlined with all the major "hanging points," as he called them.

Dr. Crowell left Adam's office. He could have returned to his office to see patients, but in thinking the deposition would last all day he had canceled his remaining office hours. He drove home after he met Eve and filled her in on the details of his first malpractice deposition ordeal.

CHAPTER 47

When Doctor Jason Pollard received his subpoena, he was very upset. His first thought was that the wife of Philip Matt was suing him for her husband's death. For what—failure to resuscitate? My God, he thought, they're suing me for failing to perform a Lazarus. Further reading of the subpoena revealed the tie in with George Gilmer. Then he realized that the lawsuit was about failure to diagnose George Gilmer therefore causing the death of Philip Matt when George supposedly murdered him. Nevertheless, this did not assuage his anger. Now it was a failure to diagnose suit, when he was the one who had made the diagnosis in the first place. So what, he thought? Since when does practicing good medicine have anything to do with preventing malpractice suits? With the expectations of patients and society today and the search for fault finding when there is an unexpected outcome, lawsuits become quite prevalent. It is the rare physician who can enjoy a career without becoming involved with the legal profession.

Some specialties are more vulnerable to lawsuits, and it comes as no surprise that emergency medicine is one of the leaders in this lottery. In this specialty, there is no firm doctor-patient relationship. Patients, once seen, get a referral to others for follow-up care. At Covenant, the volume of patients in the Emergency Department exceeds eighty thousand per year. The hospital has about sixty lawsuits filed against it each year and the Emergency Department accounts for almost half of the total.

When Pollard saw that Hugh Adams was the plaintiff's attorney, he knew he'd be in for a battle but was tired of being docile. Despite his attorney's appeals to 'say as little as possible, just give the facts and don't amplify beyond the direct answer to the question,' he was ready to launch a vigorous verbal defense. This meant a great deal of time reviewing the entire medical record, a necessary and time-consuming task in order to be prepared. In spite of the warning not to talk to anyone, Pollard assumed the role of psychologist/legal consultant to the two young physicians, Crowell and Godwin, sued so early in their medical careers.

Prior to the deposition, Pollard met with his attorney to discuss the procedure at length. Although Pollard had been through this before, he listened while his attorney discussed proper deposition comportment and strategy.

"Do you understand everything?" asked the Attorney.

"I sure do," answered Pollard.

The attorney, taken aback by the tone of Pollard's "I sure do" said, "Let's go. Be careful, please."

They arrived at Hugh Adam's office and were ushered into his conference room. Adams, with an entourage of two attorneys and a court reporter in tow, entered the room and sat down at the opposite end of the conference table.

"Good morning, Doctor Pollard. How are you today?" asked Attorney Adams.

"Can we just get down to business, Mr. Adams," said Pollard as his lawyer gulped.

"Doctor, we're just here to get the facts," said Adams in as gentle a tone as he could muster instantly recognizing that this doctor was loaded for bear.

"That's what I'm prepared to give you," replied Pollard. "Let's skip the preliminaries. My name is Jason Pollard. I'm a physician. I went to school at the University Of Illinois College Of Medicine, and after graduation, I took a residency in Emergency Medicine for three years. I was chief resident during my last year, and after completing the residency I stayed on as attending physician in the Emergency Medicine Department. Currently I am the director of the residency program in emergency medicine and I'm responsible for training the residents. In addition, I am chairman of the Emergency Medicine Performance Improvement Committee and my responsibilities are to monitor our performance, find new opportunities for improvement, and take the necessary steps to make sure that is accomplished. Anything else you wish to know about my curriculum vita?"

"I think that will do it. I have a copy here," replied Adams.

"Oh yes, and I saw both Philip Matt and George Gilmer."

This guy's trying to control this deposition, thought Adams. We'll see about that.

"Thank you, doctor. As you know, Philip Matt was murdered. You were the one who treated him, correct?"

"One of them," answered Pollard quickly.

"Was he potentially salvageable?" asked Adams.

"Not by mortals," replied Pollard. "The last time a patient like that was saved, his name was Lazarus and Jesus did it."

"Cool it," whispered Pollard's attorney.

"Calm down," he whispered back.

"I'll concede, doctor, that no one is likely to save a man who was stabbed in the heart and lungs and lost so much blood," returned Adams, dripping honey. "So, let's get on with our discussion of George Gilmer. This man is now in prison, accused of murdering Philip Matt."

"I'm aware of that, but the key word is accused," replied Pollard.

"We're not here to discuss the legalities involved, but the evidence against him is overwhelming, "said Adams.

"Innocent until proven guilty is my understanding of the law. But anyhow, I don't understand your point," remarked Pollard.

"The point is that Philip Matt would be alive today had George Gilmer been diagnosed in time," said Adams.

"Is that a question?" asked Pollard.

"No, a statement of fact," replied Adams.

"I want to get something on the record before we go on, Mr. Adams. I worked very hard on Mr. Matt. He was not salvageable. We attempted resuscitation and he didn't respond to anything. His death saddened me; we see too much violence where I work. You never get used to it."

"I appreciate that, but let me get right down to the crucial issue. Had George Gilmer been diagnosed in time and cured early, and you, as a physician, had the power to do that, but didn't, then I see a potential cause and effect relationship here, "exclaimed Adams.

"Well, no one's indicted me for murder yet. Are you disappointed?" suggested Pollard.

"Recess!" shouted Pollard's attorney.

"Sure, take five," said Adams while thinking, hmm, even his attorney is trying to cool him down.

In the adjacent room, Pollard's attorney confronted his client. "You're going overboard. What are you trying to do?"

"I'm in perfect control. Just let me handle this my way. No more interruptions, please. Trust me," said Pollard.

"You didn't tell me how you planned to handle this," said the attorney.

"I'll be fine. Just sit back and listen. I have to do this my way," replied Pollard. His attorney said, "Be careful with this guy. He's very shrewd." Then he shrugged as they walked back into the conference room.

"We were talking about the failure to diagnose George Gilmer," said Adams.

"What's that got to do with why I'm here?" asked Pollard.

"Everything."

"Then perhaps I have some misunderstanding of this process," replied Pollard.

"I believe you do," replied Adams.

"I thought I was here on a professional liability matter," stated Pollard.

"A malpractice case," said Adams.

"I prefer the term professional liability. Malpractice is the lawyer's terminology to brainwash a jury into thinking that someone performed malpractice who then has the burden of proving him or herself innocent. On the contrary, the burden is yours since you are making the accusation that I committed malpractice by not meeting the standard of care. I am here to defend myself from that malicious accusation, and I am awaiting your questions about my failure to meet that standard," responded Pollard.

This was a new experience for Adams. This physician was unhappy. This guy has been around the block he thought. Adams would try to use this mind-set to his advantage. "Doctor, did you see George Gilmer in the Emergency room?"

"Of course. You know I did."

"Just for the record, doctor."

"Shall I tell you about that meeting?" asked Pollard.

"I ask the questions," responded Adams.

"Go ahead," said Pollard.

"Where did you see George Gilmer first?"

"In the emergency room of Covenant hospital."

"And what was he there for?"

"He almost certainly had a kidney stone."

"Almost certainly?"

"Yes."

"Why not certainly?"

"Let me tell you why. When he came in, he complained of pain on the left side of his back and the lower left abdominal area. These facts in themselves are a classical description of a kidney stone, or left ureteral colic. So I did a medical history, physical examination, and a urinalysis. The urinalysis showed blood, further evidence consistent with the diagnosis. His symptoms abated and he did not want to stay for further tests. He was eager to go home. My full investigation met the standard of care."

"I didn't ask you that," said Adams.

"You didn't ask me what?"

"You know, doctor," replied Adams somewhat agitated.

"Oh, that I met the standard of care? You don't want me to say that? As you wish. I will not say that I met the standard of care anymore. I'll just let my up-front statement, saying that I met the standard of care, apply to any future statements that I have to make. May I continue?" asked Pollard.

Hugh, taken aback, was not happy with the way things were going. This guy was indeed controlling the deposition. Time to slow things down, Adam's thought. Better to disrupt his train of thought. "Let's take a break. Nature calls," Adams said."

When Adams returned, Pollard asked if he wanted him to continue. "Sure," said Adams.

Without skipping a beat, Pollard proceeded. "Since George Gilmer was now pain free and wanted to go home, I permitted him to do so, but, not before I ordered appropriate blood tests and an x-ray that he was to have on an outpatient basis, since he refused them at the time he was in the Emergency Department. I referred him to the on-call doctor since he told me he didn't have a physician and he didn't want to wait around for the tests. That concluded my first interaction with George Gilmer. Any more questions about this?"

"You say, he didn't have a physician?"

"Yes, that's what I said."

"What about doctor Crowell."

"Let me clear this up for you, sir. I asked him, as I ask every patient, if he had a doctor. He said, no. A mind reader, I ain't."

"Why didn't you diagnose hyperparathyroidism?" asked Adams deciding to get right to the point.

"That would have been done had he gone through with the tests I ordered."

Deciding to leave that subject, Adams asked, "Let's talk about the next Emergency Department visit when you saw Gilmer again," said Adams.

"Sure, what do you want to know?"

"I want to know what you diagnosed."

"I diagnosed hyperparathyroidism, as I'm sure you already know."

"How come you made the diagnosis then?"

"Because he exhibited psychotic behavior and I remembered him from his previous visit. Putting two and two together I came up with the diagnosis."

"Two plus two equals hyperparathyroidism? How come you didn't put two and two together on the first visit?"

"Because there was only one two, and if my math is correct, two plus zero equals two,"

Adams thought he would try to upset him. He said, "You failed to make a diagnosis and a man is dead."

"Ah, now we're getting to the point. Show me where I didn't meet the standard of care, Mr. Adams. Oops. I promised I wouldn't say that again, didn't I? Also, I think you're jumping the gun. Again, what if George Gilmer didn't do it?" asked Pollard.

"That's enough," retorted Adams.

"One never knows," replied Pollard. "I hope he did not do it. I would have a wonderful abuse of process suit against you."

"Are you threatening me?" asked Adams, sitting tall in his chair.

"I'm no threat to you, Mr. Adams. We're equal because, as best as I can tell from the way this deposition is going, you're no threat to me either. I am confident that I met the standard of care. Whoops." replied Pollard as he covered his mouth with his hand, feigning some slip of the tongue.

I give this guy credit, thought Adams. He's got balls. "I still want to know why you didn't diagnose him."

"The diagnosis was as close as a hypodermic needle stick. All he had to do was get the tests I ordered," replied Pollard.

"Why didn't you just draw the blood on him when he was there the first time?" continued Adams.

"Oh brother, now you want me to commit assault and battery on my patients!"

"Assault and battery?" repeated Adams with surprise.

"I told you that he was feeling much better and wanted to leave without taking any tests and not wait around for them. He said he'd do them later with the doctor I recommended for follow-up. That is why I ordered all tests as an outpatient. That is what he wanted. Had I done the tests without his permission, I would be committing assault and battery."

"And he didn't get them anyhow, right?"

"Right."

"Do you accept any blame for that failure on his part?" asked Adams."

"Not one bit. I make recommendations to every patient I see day after day, week after week, month after month, and year after year. When I make these recommendations, I desire that every patient follow my advice to the letter, but I know that a certain percentage will not. That's their choice, made after careful study of all the ramifications of the various options that are available. If they don't follow my advice, or the advice of any other physician, they may be making a mistake, or at times they may be showing good judgment. In my case, the reason I want them to follow my advice is because I have confidence in my professional judgment. When I am not as confident, my advice will be to see another physician and get another opinion. If you, sir, expect to recover a judgment against a physician every time some patient fails to follow his or her doctor's advice, which assumes the physician is at fault, then you will soon exceed the income of Bill Gates, and no physician will risk practicing medicine anymore."

He never took a breath through that entire monologue, thought Adams. "Another thing, doctor, when George Gilmer was hospitalized for the psychosis and the diagnosis was made, why was he discharged? Why wasn't he operated upon right then? Had he gone to surgery, a man would still be alive and we wouldn't be here today," said Adams.

"Here is my answer, Mr. Adams. First of all, once admitted to the main hospital he was no longer under my care. Emergency medicine physicians do not have admitting privileges. The patient had another physician for in-house care. I am sure you will speak with the other doctors, but I will answer the question and save you the trouble. Within forty-eight hours, George Gilmer was no longer psychotic. He was alert and rational because of therapy. The diagnosis of hyperparathyroidism almost certain, but he needed more studies to confirm the diagnosis and identify the precise site of the suspected tumor. We do this to assist the surgeon in localizing the lesion. In some cases, there is no surgically correctable etiology. Instead of a tumor causing the trouble, the normal glands become overactive and cause problems. In that case, no surgery is possible and the physician is committed to treating medically."

"I have a question at this point," said Adams." My understanding is that tumors cause this problem almost all the time. Why wasn't he just operated on, explored, the tumor removed, and the patient cured?"

"It's easy to, as we say, look back through a retrospectoscope. I'll grant you if we did that we would have found the tumor and cured the patient in this particular case. That's the way we used to do it in the old days before they had developed beautiful identifying imaging studies for localizing the problem. However, about ten percent of the time, in those days, they found nothing. That was considered standard of care then. Nowadays, that is not the standard of care. Had we done the surgery as you suggest, before any localizing studies, then we would not have met the standard of care by today's standards. Then you would be on my case like flies on honey. Sorry about using so many standards and about breaking my promise, but you gave me no choice. I hope that answers your question, but one more thing rears its ugly head when it comes to the question of why the discharge. He recovered. There was no justification to keep him. He no longer met the criteria of severity of illness or intensity of service to justify a hospital stay. At that point, continued care needed a less expensive environment such as an outpatient department. Government restrictions and our nation's insurance companies impose those rules on the medical and hospital community. Therefore, if you have a concern about that you will need to write to your senator or to the CEO of Cigna. Be that as it might be, the bottom line is that all of the doctors provided excellent care. All necessary diagnostic studies were either done or ordered to be done, and the diagnosis, including a precise localization of the tumor, was on the mark and the patient was cured."

Adams felt that any further discussion would not be productive. This was a far cry from the other physician he deposed. "We're finished. But off the record, you'd make a hell of a lawyer."

"Thanks for the compliment," smiled Pollard. "I like what I'm doing."

"Do you have any questions, council?" asked Adams.

"No," answered Pollard's attorney.

After Pollard and his attorney had left the room, Adams remained at the table while completing his notes. This deposition, as uncontrolled as it was, did not give him many points.

Adams had grudgingly given Pollard the ultimate compliment when he told his associates, "If this guy were in private practice, I'd use him myself. We'll stay away from him as much as possible. He is a hot head, but he won't buckle under fire. I've had cases like this before that involve the same principle, a late diagnosis and an untoward outcome. We win these by the 'you didn't do enough, you waited too long' approach. 'You should have looked harder for him. You should have called the police to find him. The man was a time bomb, and you allowed time for the fuse to be lit'. Plant this in the mind of the jurors by getting them to think that one of their loved ones is George Gilmer. We'll have no trouble getting experts to support this strategy. In these days of diminishing physician income, they're all around and I know just the one to use. You know, I'm looking forward to the opening arguments. That may win it for us right there. No one acted until it was too late. The price was an innocent man killed before he reached his full potential leaving a grieving widow who lost a young husband before they had the opportunity to raise their family. And the murderer; an innocent victim of the medical profession, all of whom were too busy to tend to their patient's desperate needs. There's a lot of patient dissatisfaction around today and jurors are patients."

Gilmer's wife and family needed to be part of this lawsuit, but Adams would work on that later. They still had plenty of time.

As Pollard and his attorney walked to the parking lot, his attorney commented, "I have to confess, you did good there, but you scared the hell out of me. As long as you keep your cool like you did, you'll make a good witness. You do feel that the best defense is a strong offense, don't you?" he questioned.

"In this case, yes. I think it might be, but who knows? Cook County juries are unpredictable. What will they really comprehend? Only time will tell. I think my reaction was more of a protest against the entire system. It's so easy to file these thousands of suits because of the contingency system. The cost is enormous raising expenses for everyone. All I can do is get back to work and wait the five or more years it will take before the case gets to court."

"I'll call you only if something important turns up or I need some help," his attorney replied, but don't hesitate to call me with any questions."

"Okay, thanks," said Dr. Pollard shrugging his shoulders

CHAPTER 48

Detective Galinski arrived back at the office and called Doris Donaldson who, by this time, had the report of her psychiatric consult attesting to the fact that Gilmer was insane during the time of the murder, but now was normal. Galinski told Donaldson the entire story—the Philip Matt, Thomas Brown connection, being careful to include all possible ramifications resulting from the puzzle unscrambling. She reminded herself of Attorney Michael Stuart's statement, "the best defense is sometimes an honest offense."

"Philip Matt in the witness protection program is really Thomas Brown? Whoa, this case has taken on the aspects of a fairy tale. Are you suggesting that George Gilmer is a drug gang hit man hired to take revenge on Thomas Brown?" asked Donaldson.

"That's one of the many possible scenarios. I can't conceive of it, but stranger things have happened. I prefer to believe that Gilmer is a carpenter who is married with two children, and he has never dealt with any drug gangs.

"It looks like your work is beginning all over again," said Donaldson.

"I'll keep you posted on any new developments," promised Galinski.

Donaldson replied, "What I'll do now is speak to Gilmer's attorney and fill him in with all these new facts. I know he's planning an insanity defense. That remained his only option until your bombshell today."

"Yes, let Gilmer's attorney know. I'll need permission to talk to Gilmer again, so let him know that I'll be getting in touch with him," said Galinski.

"Will do."

"Consider us in a holding pattern at this time, Doris. It would be a shame to have a guilty but insane verdict on his record if there are hidden facts we don't know about. I've got to start from the beginning again, and I'll need plenty of time to investigate. This case is now back on the front burner. I have lots of ideas."

"We'll hold until we hear from you. I'll try my best to keep the case from moving forward," she promised.

Donaldson called Stuart and related the entire Matt-Brown story. "So, Michael, we can't move forward on the Gilmer case yet. The police are back to work and need more time to investigate. Our job will be to get a delay to keep the case on hold. As long as there's the possibility of new evidence, we owe it to your client."

"I couldn't agree more, Doris.

"Galinski will be getting in touch with you. He needs to interrogate Gilmer again."

"Okay, what a case" replied Stuart, shaking his head.

CHAPTER 49

Galinski received permission to meet and talk to Gilmer at the prison. In the meantime, Stuart had prepared Gilmer for the meeting by informing him of the startling new developments. Stuart did his best to prepare his client for what he feared might be another ordeal that could delay his case and maybe provide an emotional setback.

After George heard Stuart, he said, "What does this mean?"

"It's possible, George, that it'll get the police looking in other directions, and this could delay your case because they have to concentrate on other things, but the good news is that it takes their focus off you now while they look for other possibilities, maybe even a search for the real murderer. We'll have to see what comes of it all. The detective should be here any minute. He's got some questions he has to ask you."

With eyebrows raised and a glimmer of hope entering his mind, George said, "Sounds good to me. I'll tell the detective whatever I can."

Galinski arrived and the two of them sat down at a table. Attorney Stuart said, "You two know each other, so why don't you just go ahead, detective, and do what you have to do. You'll get good cooperation from my client, I'm sure."

Galinski took out a legal pad from his brief case. He said to Gilmer, "I've got new information about your case that could be a big help to you. Up to now, we considered your case closed, but this new information your lawyer told you about means we are reopening your case. You know that Philip Matt whose real name was Thomas Brown fingered a drug gang in Detroit. They are all in the slammer now and Brown went into the witness protection program as Matt.

"This is worse than a crossword puzzle," said George."

"Ain't that the truth," countered Galinski. "We're starting all over again. Now that a drug gang is in the picture, we need to rethink this case since Matt was a prime target for revenge. Let me just come out with it. Have you ever been involved with a drug gang?"

Frustrated but realizing he had to offer full cooperation, George said, "I don't know anything about any drugs.

"Did you ever take any illegal drugs?"

"No way."

"Do you know anyone in the drug business?"

"Nobody."

"How about the people you work for? Are you aware of any drug connections?"

"Not a chance. They're one of the biggest builders in the country."

"Have you ever worked for anyone else that had any drug connection?"

"I do some private work for people on the side, but if they're into drugs they sure never told me anything about it."

Stuart said, "George, I agree that this is weird, but, don't forget what I told you, it could be good news because now there is a possibility of other suspects in this case. So keep it up."

"I will."

"Do you have a safety deposit box?" asked Galinski.

"No."

"We could check that, you know."

"Go ahead and check. I wouldn't have anything to put in there anyhow."

Galinski smiled and asked, "Have you ever lived in Detroit?"

"No."

"Have you ever lived anyplace besides Chicago?"

"No."

"Anybody in your family deal drugs?"

"Nobody," said George as his shoulders slumped forward and he bowed his head.

"Are you getting tired, Donald?" asked Stuart.

"No, but I have an idea."

"What's your idea?" asked Galinski.

"I know you're just doing your job and this could be a help for me, but I don't want you to waste your time. You could ask me questions about drugs and gangs until I'm fifty-years-old and you wouldn't get anywhere. So how about I take another lie detector test? This time you'd be asking me questions about my whole life. Things I know all about. The last time I took the test, you asked me questions about things I didn't know anything about. So if I take the test now and you ask me questions about things I should know, if I lie you'll know right away. Right?"

Galinski contemplated George's question. He could be right, he thought. "You'll need to talk to your lawyer about that," answered Galinski.

"How about it, Mr. Stuart?" asked Gilmer.

"We could arrange for it, George. Sounds like a good idea. You remember, it can't be used as evidence though," replied Stuart.

Galinski interjected. "Okay, I won't ask any more questions now. Get the test and I'll help frame the questions." He left feeling that Gilmer had made a good point. Any further questioning would be a waste of time. This still left him where he started the day—at square one. He mulled over the idea of interviewing the wife of Philip Matt to see what she knew of her husband's past life. For all I know, he thought, she could be in with some drug gang, and could have set her husband up. Nothing would surprise me anymore.

CHAPTER 50

Alice Matt had no problem with the Galinski interview. Anything she could do to complete the investigation would only accelerate the day that justice would be done and she would receive the green poultice from Hugh Adams.

Galinski arrived at her apartment. As he sat down, Alice poured each of them a cup of coffee.

"Do you have some news for me, detective?" she asked.

"There are some things I need to talk to you about."

"Any news about the suspect, detective?"

"He's still the only suspect, and there has been no change in the evidence."

"Did he confess?"

"No, he still insists he didn't do it."

"They all do, don't they?"

"I have some questions to ask you about your husband," Galinski continued without answering the question

"I already talked to the police and told them everything I know."

"I know you did, and you've been very cooperative, but I just need to close off some loose ends." Then before she could register any more protest he asked, "How long did you know your husband before you married him?"

"About six months."

"Where did you meet?"

"We met at Alexander's, a restaurant and bar."

"Yes, I'm familiar with the place. Was your husband born in Chicago?"

"No, he was born in Kansas City."

Galinski tried not to register surprise at this answer and continued. "When did he come to Chicago?"

"About two or three years ago."

"Why did he leave Kansas City?"

"He got a better job in Chicago. He was a printer. Say, what's this all about? Why do you need to know all this?"

He ignored the question again and continued. "Any family in Kansas City?"

"No. His mother and father are dead. He had no family in Kansas City. He had no brothers and sisters."

"Did he ever go back there in the time he was married to you?"

"No."

"What about to visit his folk's graves?"

"I asked him about that, but he said he had no reason to go. He doesn't remember his mother who died when he was young, and his father beat him, so he felt he didn't owe him anything."

"Did all this information you gave me come from your husband?"

"Yeah. Where else would I get it? She drummed her fingers on the tabletop. "I don't know where all these questions are leading. What's this all about, anyhow?"

"Okay, let me tell you what we know," said Galinski. We're doing more investigating now even though we have a prime suspect in custody. You know about that so I won't dwell on it. We just got some new evidence that is giving us reason to be extra careful and reopen the case. This is a bombshell, so be ready for some bad news."

Alice sat straight and squirmed in her seat. "What is it?" she asked.

"Philip Matt was not your husband's real name. His real name was Thomas Brown. There is no evidence that he was ever in Kansas City, but we know for sure he was in Detroit. He was a member of a Detroit drug gang, he turned state's evidence against them, and they landed in jail. He went into the witness protection program, changed his appearance, and resurfaced here in Chicago with a different identity."

Alice Matt jumped up from her chair, threw her hands up to her face, and wailed. "This can't be true."

"I know it sounds crazy, Mrs. Matt, but I wouldn't be here unless I had absolute proof. The FBI matched the fingerprints and the blood of Thomas Brown and Philip Matt. They also matched a photo of Philip Matt with a picture of Thomas Brown before he entered the witness protection program."

"Oh, my God." gasped Alice.

"So you see why I need to sort everything out. We can't help but wonder if some drug gang caught up with your husband."

"Then the Gilmer guy in jail who killed my husband is a drug gang member?"

"I'm pretty sure the answer is no, but we're looking into that possibility."

By now Phyllis was pacing back and forth.

"Could you take any more questions, Mrs. Matt?" asked Galinski.

"Please, I want to call my mother."

"Sure," said Galinski. "Go ahead."

Alice went into the bedroom, called her mother and Galinski could hear her crying as she spoke. After a few minutes, she returned to the kitchen. "My mother and father are coming right over. They only live about a mile away, so they'll be here in a few minutes."

"Do you want me to leave now?" asked Galinski.

"No, they want to see you and hear this from you. Right now they're pretty much in shock, just like I am."

When the parents arrived, Galinski repeated what he had just told their daughter. Then he spoke with Alice. "I came here to give you this information, but now that I've done that my real job begins. I have to ask these questions because we have a man in jail and the new information forces us to reopen the investigation. Remember this. Your husband was a hero. He alone is responsible for putting a large drug gang out of business in Detroit."

"Go ahead," Alice replied, without seeming to have listened to Galinski's explanation. "Ask all the questions you want. Check out anything you have to. I can assure you I don't know a damn thing about drug gangs, but my husband sure pulled the wool over my eyes."

"We'll check everything and keep you posted, Mrs. Matt."

She nodded her head, a dazed expression on her face.

It's been a long couple of days, thought Galinski. All I know for certain is that Philip Matt is really Thomas Brown. A journey of a mile starts with the first step. That's what I took today.

Donald Gilmer also took another step in the journey as he took and passed his second lie detector test.

CHAPTER 51

Galinski returned to the office and sat down to strategize his next steps. He needed to learn more about Alice Matt and see if everything she said was truthful. He made plans to tail her, look into her background and past history, check where she works, see what she does at night, and see who her friends are. Also, Galinski thought, Matt's parents might also merit some investigation, especially the father. What does he do for a living? He learned that he has a business in the neighborhood and that would have to be checked to be sure that it was not a front for an illegal enterprise.

Galinski then thought of the first suspect, Ronald Jones, the kid who found the knife but who he cleared. Ronald was a street-smart kid and might have some information that could be of assistance. He would make it his business to interrogate him again. Is there any connection in Chicago with the Detroit drug gang? Who out there might have some information? Does anybody know anything about a possible hit on Philip Matt? This type of information was the kind that stayed in the drug community's upper echelon, but sometimes made its way down to the street boys.

Also of importance would be to continue his relationship with the FBI and learn everything he could about Thomas Brown before he entered the witness protection program as Philip Matt.

Galinski cleared his schedule as much as possible for the next several weeks.

CHAPTER 52

Galinski called Agent Marshall who advised him that he had the Detroit FBI visit the Brown family to advise them about the death of their son. Also, Marshall told the Browns that a Detective Galinski from Chicago, who was investigating their son's murder, would want to get in touch with them. Galinski made all the necessary preparations to meet with the Brown family.

Before leaving town, he would bring Doris Donaldson up to date and he arranged to meet her in her office. "I'm moving fast, Doris. We're working on any possible drug gang connection to this murder. Please keep the Gilmer holding pattern as long as possible. I told Matt's wife and she seemed shocked by the news that her husband was involved with drugs and was in the witness protection program with an assumed name. She didn't know a thing about it. But, we're taking no chances. The wife and her parents will be under surveillance. I'm in contact with the FBI and will be going to Detroit to speak to the family of Brown-Matt. Get hold of George's defense attorney and clue him in, please. We need to keep him abreast of all developments on this case."

"I will. I appreciate everything, detective," responded Doris, respectfully.

Next Detective Galinski phoned Alice Matt. She agreed to speak with him and came to his office that day.

"I came as soon as you called, detective, but I hope you're not going to talk about this drug business."

"No, Mrs. Matt, I didn't get a chance to tell you everything at our last meeting. I have some more information to tell you about your husband."

"Is this another bombshell?" she asked with alarm.

"I'm afraid it is. I know your husband told you his mother and father were dead, but the truth is, they are not. They both live in Detroit."

Dead silence. "He lied to me," shrieked Alice after a moment's hesitation. "Kansas was a big lie. Everything about him was a lie."

"That's no surprise, Mrs. Matt. Don't forget that he was in the witness protection program. When you do that, you assume a different identity. You have to live a different life. You have to separate yourself from everything in the past, and you need to invent a new history. In your husband's case, it didn't work. He probably was the victim of drug revenge. But, all we have is this random killing and so far we have no drug connection. We just keep looking and that's why I must ask all these questions."

"I suppose I should meet his parents," suggested Alice. "After all, I was married to their son."

"You better let me tell them about you first. Don't forget, they never knew what happened to him, and so they don't know about you either."

"When are you going to meet them?"

"As soon as I can make the arrangements," said Galinski.

"Let me know when I could meet them, please," Alice said.

"Will do," said Galinski wondering where this tortuous path was leading.

CHAPTER 53

Alice left his office and called Hugh Adams. When she told him that she had urgent news, he agreed to see her later that afternoon.

"I can hardly believe what I have to tell you," said Alice, as she rushed into his office. "I got this news from the detective who's investigating my husband's murder." Then she began to relay the entire story to Hugh Adams. "What do you think?" she asked.

"Whoa…let me think for a minute…well, I don't think your case changes at all. The suit goes on since there is only one suspect. He did it. His blood and fingerprints are all over the knife and all over the victim," insisted Hugh.

"What if my husband's death was due to drug gangs?" inquired Alice.

"What did that detective tell you? Do they have any proof about that?"

"No. The guy in jail now, George Gilmer, is still the only suspect. The detective said that now, since they know who my husband is, they have to look into all possibilities."

"Do they think the suspect, Gilmer, is a drug gang member?" asked Adams.

"The detective says no, but he has to look into that too."

"Well, we still got a case," insisted Adams.

"But, what if the drug gang really did it?"

"If they did it, then we drop this suit like we were holding a hot potato," responded Adams. "But, as long as we have no information to the contrary, we go on with the case. I won't rush things though. I'll play it cool until this all sorts out."

"Okay, but it makes me nervous," said Alice.

"There is one thing, however," said Adams. "We should tell your husband's parents about the suit you filed. They have a right to file as well, or else be a part of your suit. After all, they are the mother and father," said Adams smiling.

"That means I would have to share the award?" inquired Alice.

"True, but it could mean the award will be that much higher," said Adams, trying hard to reassure his money-hungry client.

"Are you sure that's a good idea?"

"The more the better."

"Okay, I guess I have to leave such things to you. I better go now. But, what's the latest on the lawsuit?" asked Alice as she rose to leave Adam's office.

"We are finding some weak links in the defense that all works in favor of you," replied Adams. "If I learn anything more, I'll let you know."

Adams alerted his associates. The posture on the Philip Matt lawsuit would be to hold at this time, minimize expenses, and postpone any depositions while awaiting further information. He would make no effort to bring Mrs. Gilmer into the lawsuit, nor would he involve Mr. and Mrs. Brown until things sorted themselves out.

The prosecution and the defense were of one voice in the George Gilmer case. Both remained in a holding pattern, which at least gave George some glimmer of hope. For the first time since they apprehended him, there was a chance that someone else had committed this murder even though there appeared to be no evidence against anyone but him. It looked as if the worst case scenario might be a "guilty but insane" verdict. At least that meant no death penalty. Michael Stuart kept Gilmer's wife up-to-date, and they were coping. Detective Galinski was arranging to visit the Browns in Detroit.

CHAPTER 54

A disguised Detective Galinski was following Alice Matt all over Chicago. She was a full-time secretary at a downtown real estate office, arriving at work every morning at nine o'clock and leaving each evening at five. There were no breaks except for lunch at a nearby cafeteria, which she visited with the same two women every day. No one joined the three women at lunch, and Galinski did not notice anything unusual.

Each morning, Alice took the nearby elevated train two blocks from her apartment that delivered her to within one block of work. She took the same transportation home at night. She owned a car, registered in her late husband's name, and she used it in the evenings to shop or to visit her parents. On Friday nights, she drove to Alexander's Bar for a drink and dinner with her two woman friends.

Galinski followed the three women into Alexander's for a beer and the fish fry. No one met them there. The women enjoyed their fare, and when Alice left, she got into her car and drove home. In short, the tail was unproductive.

Evaluation of her past revealed that she was born in Chicago and attended grade school and high school in the same neighborhood where she now lives. After graduating high school, she took a job in the real estate office where she currently works. Her lifestyle was as far away from drug gangs as you can get.

Alice's father, Albert Ryder, managed a supermarket nearby which had all the earmarks of a strictly legitimate business. But, as luck would have it, two days into Galinski's surveillance he recognized two ex-convicts who entered the store. The two men made a purchase, and then stopped to speak with Alice's father. They all shook hands, but Galinski noticed that the father slipped one of them a white envelope as the two men clasped hands. After jotting down the license plate of the ex-con's car, he traced the ownership to Albert Guzmano. Although unfamiliar with Guzmano, he soon learned that he was a very wealthy and successful Chicago businessman with extensive real estate holdings in the form of strip shopping malls and large apartment complexes. In fact, his office was in the same shopping center as Alice's father's grocery store. Could this be a lead, wondered Galinski? What was that envelope Alice's father gave the ex-cons?

He would leave nothing to chance. A father-in-law would not be inclined to dispose of his son-in-law, but where drugs were concerned, anything goes. In this business, you had to be paranoid and assume the worst until proven otherwise. He would check out Guzmano and the two ex-cons. Did the father-in-law have contact with drugs? Or was everything noted a legitimate friendship and business activity? If Guzmano and the two ex-cons were involved with the drug trade, is this how they identified Philip Matt? What did George Gilmer have to do with this, if anything? So many questions, but very few answers.

Next, Galinski roamed the streets making contacts, but he was not receiving any leads worth following. He zeroed out wherever he went for information. The only positive gain was that his numerous contacts were on the lookout for news. So far, there was no brass ring.

Detective Galinski flew to Detroit. Before doing so, he managed to get information about Thomas Brown and the court case, which resulted in the drug ring's destruction. This was due to Brown's efforts. He couldn't help but develop a grudging respect for what Thomas Brown had accomplished, but maybe at the cost of his life. This brave kid purged Detroit of drugs. When he met Brown's parents, he learned that they had no idea as to their son's activities that led to the end of the drug gang in Detroit. Galinski brought them up to date. They cried, but were not surprised to learn about their son's death and agreed that they would like to meet their son's widow.

CHAPTER 55

Back at police headquarters, Galinski took notes on what he had learned: nothing yet on Alice Matt, but he would look into her father's contact with the two ex-cons and the lead to Guzmano. He arranged to meet with him, and went to his office in a strip mall.

Guzmano was a middle-aged man with pitch-black hair—probably dyed black, thought Galinski. His eyes were narrowly spaced. He was short and thin and was wearing a blue suit and a yellow tie with black diagonal stripes. You could see your face in his shined shoes. His office, furnished with wooden chairs and a wooden desk was simple and sparse with bare walls. He invited Galinski to take a seat.

"It's good to meet you, detective. If there's anything I can do to help you, rest assured I will."

"Thank you, Mr. Guzmano. As I told you, I'm investigating a murder and when I was in Mr. Ryder's grocery store here, I came across two men I recognized as ex-cons. Mr. Ryder gave them a white envelope. What can you tell me about Ryder, sir?"

Guzmano smiled and said, "I can explain that all to you, detective. I own this shopping center, and those two guys work for me. Ryder was giving them the rent."

"I see," said Galinski.

"Now you might ask why I have ex-cons working for me, and I'll come out and tell you. I'm an ex-con myself. Once when I was nineteen years old, I was out cruising with some friends and they burglarized a store. You can believe me or not when I tell you I didn't know that was the plan of my two friends when we started out and I knew nothing about it, but it ended up that they caught and convicted all of us. I spent a year in jail, and when I got out, I was a victim of ex-con discrimination, so I know what it's like. I couldn't get a job, but it might have been one of the best things that ever happened to me, because I went to junior college, then the university and I learned how to take care of myself. I've had a lot of luck and I have strip malls, apartment buildings and other wise investments. I do okay, and one of my missions is to help ex-cons get back on their feet. These two guys aren't the only ones I helped."

"I understand. That's an impressive story, Mr. Guzmano. You should be proud of what you've accomplished. How about Mr. Ryder?"

"He's a legitimate business man and a good tenant. Now I need a favor of you, detective."

"Sure, what is it?"

"I don't want it known that some of the guys working for me are ex-cons. These guys are getting a good start at a new life and I want it to stay that way."

"I understand. I'm mute. You have my word."

"Thank you, detective. I hope I was some help to you."

"You were, Mr. Guzmano. Good to have met you."

"Same here, detective"

Galinski returned to his office. He turned on some quiet music, sat, and thought. First, I still have a solid suspect in a murder case, George Gilmer. Second, I can't find any connection to drugs, but if it was a drug hit, how did they find out about Philip Matt in the witness protection program? If the Detroit drug gang did get him, where was the leak? They're out of business. Did they manage to arrange the hit from their jail cells? Or, are we just spinning our wheels while the real killer is sitting in the slammer? No, this is a drug hit until proven otherwise. There's too much coincidence to ignore here. This guy, Brown-Matt put 'em all away in the slammer. I can't see them saying, 'I forgive you my son. He laughed to himself.

Two more things I've got to do. What about the kid who found the knife, Ronald Jones? He would have been number one had Gilmer not come along. He looked like a street kid to me. I'll have to question him again. I'll put a little fear into him and see what he knows and if he can be some help. This case is still wide open.

Next, Galinski needed to bring Doris Donaldson up to date. He called and gave her a phone report.

"We're still in no hurry, detective. We're in a hold and delay pattern. The only one in a hurry is Gilmer, but isn't that always the case?" replied Donaldson.

She called Michael Stuart and transmitted the same report. Stuart informed Gilmer and his reaction was one of disappointed resignation. Gilmer's only hope had been this unexpected drug development, but that had now gone up in a puff of smoke. Now he had to hope that he'd be labeled insane.

CHAPTER 56

Galinski tracked down Ronald Jones, taking the direct street approach. When he confronted Ronald at work, it was unmistakable that his suspect was agitated.

"What is it, man?" asked Ronald.

"I got some questions. Are you still sticking to the story that you found the knife?"

"I'm sticking to it 'cause it's true."

"That's bullshit and you know it."

Ronald leaped off his stool and stared at his interrogator. "That ain't bullshit. It's the truth. How many times you wanna hear it?"

"Why don't you admit you know something about the murder?"

"Man, but you lost it. I don't know a damn thing," he shouted and stuck a finger in Galinski's face.

"Galinski brushed his finger aside and said, "Fess up, Ronald. I know all about your drug connections."

"Okay, shit!" he exclaimed. "You got me, yeah, you got me. So I'm the godfather and my real name is Vito Ronald Corleone Jones. I'm gonna make you an offer you can't refuse. He looked the detective right in the eyes. "Your brain is fried, man. What you smokin?"

Galinski tried to mask his smile. "What have you heard on the street about the murder?"

"Nothin'."

"Okay," he said, trying to look serious. "We got your fingerprints on the knife, and you know it. We didn't book you because we got strong evidence against another suspect. We also got some evidence that a drug gang might have been behind the murder, so the investigation isn't over. We need your help. If you hear anything at all, I'm asking you to get in touch with me right away. Believe it or not, I'm on your side. You got lots of contacts out there, black and white. You can help us. In fact, I'll let you in on a secret if you can keep it quiet."

"What's that, man?"

"The guy that was killed, Philip Matt, blew the lid on a drug ring in Detroit. They were dealing drugs big time. Matt wasn't his real name, but when we found out about it we began to wonder. Was this a drug hit, or what? That's why we're looking again. You know all about the drug scene here, so I'm asking that you look around. Maybe you can help us."

"Okay," said Ronald, perked up because of this drug news. "If I hear somethin', I'll call you."

Galinski thought, this kid knows nothing about this case. Still, he suspected that it was possible he might have established some street rapport, and he got Ronald working undercover in a neighborhood and with a subject he knew something about. Stranger things have happened.

CHAPTER 57

Up to this point Galinski withheld all information from George and Gail. They had just begun to adjust to his situation, and Gail's parents had stepped in to fill the gap. Gail was trying to keep her mind occupied and found solace by volunteering at the church. She explained to the children that daddy was away because of illness, but she was sure he'd get better soon. They all prayed together at bedtime.

Unknown to Gail, Eve invited Burt to dinner at her parent's home. She and Burt drove to the far northwest suburbs with Burt in seventh heaven over the thought that Eve wanted to introduce him to her parents. He watched as she left the expressway, drove down a country road, and approached a large iron gate, which she opened with a remote control.

Burt stared in amazement at the tree-rimmed road, looking for the house. "Well you're through the gate," he said. Where's the house?"

"Further down the road."

"You got to be kidding," he said. "How much land do you have here?"

"I have none. My parents have eighty acres," she said with emphasis.

"Okay, lady, I got the message," he said as the house came into view. "Whoa, if we lived in that house, you could hide and I'd never find you. I'd have to report you to the police as a missing person."

Eve laughed. "You can be funny some times. I like a man with a good sense of humor."

"I'm glad, I need all the positive attributes I can muster to get you interested in me."

"It's time I told you."

"What?" said Burt with lifted eyebrows.

"I have ulterior motives in inviting you here, Burt."

Burt whistled and his eyebrows lifted further. "You mean your parents aren't home?"

Another laugh. "Oh, Burt, I still say you should have been a stand-up comic."

"What's the ulterior motive?

"I'm going to tell my father all about George Gilmer. George did some construction work for him; a beautiful fireplace mantelpiece and an outdoor deck. I'll show them to you."

"That should be interesting. I'm amazed at what these craftsmen can accomplish."

"My father thinks the world of George and I hope there's something he can do for him, so I may need your help to convince him George isn't a murderer."

"I'll do anything for you, Eve, and for George, as long as it's legal, moral and ethical—and fun—especially fun."

"We're on the same wave length, but for now the fun can wait."

Eve parked the car on a large circular driveway. They stepped on a rectangular front porch with four white pillars. Eve rang the bell. A woman's voice through an intercom said, "I saw your car coming down the road."

"Yes, it's Eve, mother."

They entered and Eve introduced Burt to her parents. His impression was that here were two people very much in love and protective of their daughter. Eve took him to the main fireplace to see George's mantelpiece and to the rear of the house to see the deck overlooking a well-manicured back yard and a duck filled pond. They enjoyed an excellent dinner followed by dessert and coffee in the family room. With Burt's help, Eve told George Gilmer's story to a very attentive and concerned Fred Worthey and his wife. Before Burt and Eve left, Fred smiled and said he would look into it, and he believed he would be able to help.

As they were driving back to Chicago, Eve said, "I know my father. When he gets that look on his face, there's nothing he can't do."

CHAPTER 58

The next morning, Worthey called his corporation's law firm. He asked to speak with his good friend Jerold Cronin.

"Jerry, this is Fred Worthey."

"Sure, Fred, how are you?"

"You guys are making millions from my corporation, right?"

"Give or take a few hundred grand here and there. What's cooking, Fred?"

"I've got a rush job for your firm. Tell your leading criminal lawyer I need all the information he can get within three days on a pending murder case. Suspect's name is George Gilmer—G-i-l-m-e-r. Get the records, talk to the lawyers. Get into the meat of it. He's got three days, max. You call me when he's ready and I'll come down for a report."

"What's this got to do with you, Fred?"

"You're wasting time. Move your ass. You do want to keep my business, don't you?"

"Got the message. You'll hear from me soon," said the lawyer knowing full well that the message received from Worthey came with an ultimatum

"Are you up off your chair?" said Worthey.

"As you speak, I'm rising."

"I'm waiting for your call back, and none of this lawyer crap like not calling back when you say you will."

"Guarantee; you have my word."

"I'll be waiting by the phone."

Three days later Worthey was in Jerold's office, seated across the desk from Sean O'Brien, Chicago's leading criminal attorney. Worthey listened to the entire report before responding.

"I know George Gilmer very well. My gut tells me that he's safe for release on bond. Don't you agree?"

"Yes, an' I do."

"Then that's it. Here's a check for fifty thousand. Get him out right away."

"Consider it done, me man."

George was astounded at his sudden release from jail. Still, he had no idea how or who arranged it.

"Daddy!" screamed the girls as he walked in the door. Gail was beaming.

"You see, kids," she began, "I promised that daddy would be better soon and come home."

"Who did this?" asked George after a jubilant family supper and after putting the girls to bed. "Who came up with that kind of money?"

"I have no idea, but I suspect Mr. Worthey. He's the only man we know who could afford it, and I bet Eve had something to do with it. I'll find out about that for sure."

"Man, I can't believe it. But, if it was Worthey, then how am I ever going to be able to pay him back?"

"We'll think of something," Gail said.

George shook his head. "I can't believe…" He looked at his wife… "Let's talk about that tomorrow when we get up," George whispered. "But, now…"

CHAPTER 59

After meeting with Galinski, Ronald Jones returned home. He still lived with his parents and a younger brother and sister. Born in Chicago, he grew up on the streets with two older brothers as his mentors. It took their sacrifice for Ronald to understand the ramifications of the drug culture. His older brother was serving time in prison for dealing drugs while the second brother died of an overdose. As a result of this experience, Ronald never got involved with drugs. Refusing all temptation, the warning of his father became a constant reminder. "If I ever find out you're using drugs, I'll kill you myself." Ronald had every reason to believe him.

Ronald knew that the police had nothing on him for the Matt murder, but he realized that the case was still open after the grilling from Galinski. He liked Galinski because he spoke the language and understood "what goes down." Ronald told the truth. He had about as much to do with drugs as he had to do with rocket science, but if the police were looking for a drug connection, he might be able to help. Ever since the episodes involving his brothers, Ronald had a heightened awareness of drug activity in the neighborhood. He knew the pushers, and he knew the users. He knew who they were and how they operated. He had no knowledge about where they got their drugs, but he could name every pusher that worked the neighborhood for a mile around in any direction. These pushers would rotate street corners and never stay on a corner too long. But wherever they went, their customers followed.

The pushers would either arrive on foot or drive up in fancy cars and transact business through the driver's window. Business was always brisk. If one pusher disappeared, there would be another to take his place. Then it hit him. During the last couple of weeks, Ronald noticed something that puzzled him, but he didn't think much about it until Galinski questioned him. Maybe there was a fit here?

Two strangers had replaced some of the steady pushers, whom he had been familiar with, but the interesting thing was that these strangers were white. That did not happen very often in his neighborhood, so Ronald wondered if there might be some connection that could benefit Galinski. These strangers drove up in a small, gray, closed panel truck. They did some business with people who drove by and passed some boxes to a few of the regular pushers in the neighborhood. Ronald spent the next few nights involved in his own personal surveillance. Then he saw them again.

This time he jotted down the license plates of the truck and cars that drove up. He also recorded the location where the transactions took place. He had no idea what, if anything, all this had to do with a murder, but maybe these new characters on the scene would be of interest to Galinski. Ronald assumed the role of a secret agent.

On the following day, Ronald showed up at police headquarters for a meeting with Galinski which he had arranged that morning. "I got something for you," he said, "I don't know anything about the murder, but here's something about drugs that might fit in."

"What have you got?" Galinski asked.

"I wrote it all down. Here it is. Two new pushers, white guys, license plates on the pusher's truck and license plates of the customers, and there's the address where it happened," said Ronald.

"Hey, nice work, Ronald. This could lead to something big. But, remember. I don't know you, and you don't know me. From now on, don't come here. What I want you to do is call me any time you have some important information. If I need to get hold of you, I'll call you at home. What name should I use?"

"Just say, 'Phil from work,' and if I'm not there I'll call you back," Ronald promised.

"Okay. Understand everything?" asked Galinski.

"Yeah, I do."

Although Galinski felt that Ronald's bit of intelligence would not bear fruit in the George Gilmer case, it might lead to some other information with a ripple effect that could prove useful. It wouldn't be the first time that an investigation of one case led to some helpful information in solving another case.

CHAPTER 60

Galinski involved Narcotics in the investigation and told them Ronald's entire story. They set up a surveillance video at the sight mentioned by Ronald. They used a small truck with a sign painted on its side, identifying it as a plumbing company. They parked it across the street of the location and did not tell Ronald anything about it. Within days, the gray truck appeared. The two suspects performed just as Ronald had reported: dealing with customers and passing boxes on to several unidentified men.

As these transactions were going on, two plain clothed officers transmitted information by radio to two nearby unmarked police cars. Everything was videotaped. One unmarked police car followed the unidentified men, the ones who had received the packages, to a nearby apartment building. When the two men who had been under surveillance had completed their work, they drove off and were followed by the second unmarked police car. They drove to a shopping mall. The men parked the car in the lot and entered the office of the shopping center. All locations were noted and videoed. The police brought the video evidence back to headquarters and called Galinski asking him to look at the tapes with them so he could help determine if anything was relevant to his investigation.

Galinski and the narcotics team viewed the tapes. They watched with rapt attention. No one said anything. When it was all over, Galinski spoke. "Get back to the part where the two white guys drive up in the gray truck and get out and start dealing."

They watched again as Galinski moved closer to the screen.

"We got something very big here," shouted Galinski.

"What?" demanded the narcotics chief.

Galinski replied with uncontrolled excitement. "Those two white guys were the same two that I saw in the supermarket of Philip Matt's father-in-law. Remember, Matt's father-in-law handed them a white envelope. These were the same guys who drove Mr. Guzmano's car. The tape also shows that they drove to the strip mall where his father-in-law's super market is located. See, right in the corner of the shopping center. They parked at the strip mall and went into the shopping center office and whose office do you think that is?" asked Galinski.

"Drop the bomb, begged Narcotics.

"A bomb is right. That's Guzmano's office," said Galinski. "We got our first lead here that could prove Guzmano's connection to drugs after all. Maybe Matt's father-in-law is involved too. Boy, did Guzmano give me a snow job with this great guy crap about helping ex-cons. 'But, don't say anything to anyone, officer. I don't want people to know what I'm doing. It might hurt my boys. Man, I want to barf. We might have a connection here. Guzmano, Matt's in-laws, the two ex-cons, drugs, and the Matt murder. Things might be taking shape," said Galinski.

The following day, Galinski went to the supermarket to speak with Alice Matt's father. He re-introduced himself and showed his identification.

"What can I do for you, officer?"

"I have some questions to ask."

"Sure."

"We're reinvestigating since we learned that your son-in-law was Thomas Brown. We've got reason to believe drugs may be involved, so, I'll just come out with it. Are you in any way connected to drugs, or, do you know of anyone who has a drug connection that knew your son-in-law?"

"That's easy, I've never been involved with drugs, and I don't know anyone who is. I'm just a businessman, and that's it."

"Do you know these two men?" asked Galinski who held out a picture of the two ex-cons taken off the video.

"Sure, I know these guys. They work for the landlord," he said.

So far so good, thought Galinski. "Do you ever come in contact with them?"

"Yeah, they come into the store and buy here, and they collect the rent for the landlord."

"Do you pay them the rent?" asked Galinski, probing for an explanation for the white envelope.

"Yes, I give them a check," he said.

"Who's your landlord?"

"Mr. Guzmano," he replied.

Still fits thought Galinski. "What do you know about him?"

"I've known him for years. He's a great guy. I'm lucky to have him for a landlord because he helped me when I first started this business. Years ago, he even gave me a pass on the rent when I was having trouble. Without Mr. Guzmano, I wouldn't have been able to make it. So, I owe him a lot. Did you ever hear of a landlord telling you that you didn't have to pay rent until you got going? Well, it paid off for the both of us. I'm doing well, and he gets his rent right when he should."

This is getting better all the time, thought Galinski. The jigsaw puzzle is falling into place. "Did Mr. Guzmano know Philip Matt?"

"Sure. He met him at the store. As a matter of fact, I invited him to my daughter and Phil's wedding. It was a small affair with only relatives and a few friends. I considered Mr. Guzmano a good friend after what he did for me."

"So, Guzmano knew your son-in-law well enough to speak to him?"

"Sure. He liked him, and he gave him a thousand dollars for a wedding present. How's that for a nice guy?"

"That's a great guy, alright. Thanks for answering my questions."

"Anytime, detective, sorry I couldn't help you."

You helped me more then you'll ever know, thought Galinski.

CHAPTER 61

While all these developments were taking place, Galinski was sitting in his office concentrating on another matter when the telephone rang.

"Hello."

"Is this Detective Galinski?"

"Yeah, who's calling please?"

"This is officer Mason, Detroit police department."

Galinski perked up. "Yes, sir, what can I do for you?"

"You sent us a photograph, and prints of Larry Benson?"

"Yeah, I did. That's right," said Galinski thinking of the giant Larry Benson, Matt's drinking buddy at Traficante's bar and grill.

"We have your man."

"What? You're holding him?" asked Galinski, unable to mask his surprise.

"Better than that; he's in jail."

"Jail?"

"We booked him for murder," reported Mason.

An astonished Galinski, sat upright, put the phone on his lap and tried to digest what he had just heard. "Uhh...murder? What else is going to happen in this case? I've got to talk to Benson about another matter. He was the last man to see a murder victim alive here. We've cleared him so far, but we need to ask him some more questions. Who did he kill there?" asked Galinski.

"A lawyer with drug connections. But there's more."

"What?" asked Galinski shaking his head, his antennae up and ready.

"It's about those prints and the blood and photograph you sent. We matched it, but not to Benson. We matched it to Steve Baltero, a long-time resident of Detroit."

"Steve Baltero? Hold it. Are you saying that Steve Baltero, whoever the hell that is, and Larry Benson are one and the same?"

"You got it."

"I'm speechless," said Galinski, shaking his head. "My head is spinning. I've got to talk to him. I'll get out there as soon as I can book a flight."

"Right, detective. We'll see you."

Galinski was stunned. He stared at the wall and shook his head. "What the hell is going on?"

CHAPTER 62

Meanwhile, Galinski busied himself obtaining available information on Thomas Brown, alias Philip Matt. and his destruction of the Detroit drug ring. He could not help but develop a grudging respect for what Brown had accomplished. Nevertheless, he had no idea what motivated the guy to risk his life in purging Detroit of a large drug distribution network.

He was able to arrange a meeting with the parents of Thomas Brown. The next morning Galinski flew to Detroit and checked into a motel near the Brown home. Their house was located in a blue-collar section of town. Mr. and Mrs. Brown greeted him at the door, and then escorted him into their living room.

"Thanks for coming," said Mr. Brown. "We appreciate whatever you can tell us about our son. If there's anything we can do, please count on our help."

"Thank you," replied Galinski. "First, let me express my sympathy for your loss. As you know, I'm investigating Thomas's murder. It was only through fingerprint analysis that we were able to identify him. Since you know the story, I won't repeat it. However, I hope there's some consolation in knowing that your son committed an incredible act of bravery."

"Yes, we're very proud of him," nodded Mr. Brown. "After what he did to the drug ring, I'm surprised they didn't get him long ago."

"Do you know about the suspect we have, George Gilmer?" asked Galinski.

"Yes. The FBI gave us the entire story," Mr. Brown said.

"We're investigating the possibility that these drug dealers killed your son. Still, we have no proof that the suspect we're holding is in any way connected to them."

"Then you'd better check again, detective," said Mr. Brown.

Galinski said, "We're doing that, sir. I want to learn everything possible." He paused to take a deep breath. "There is something else you need to know."

"What?" asked Mrs. Brown. She looked down and twisted a handkerchief between her fingers.

Galinski said, "Your son was married. I spoke to his widow, but she didn't know anything about you and your husband. She thought Philip's parents were dead."

Mrs. Brown gasped.

"Please understand, Mrs. Brown," said Galinski. "This had nothing to do with you or your husband. People in the witness protection program have to surrender their past lives. They have no choice. When I told your son's wife about you, she was hoping to meet you."

There was another long pause. The Browns stared at each other. "Yes," said Mrs. Brown, "it's the right thing to do. How long were they married, detective?"

"Six months."

"Let me tell you my son's story," said Mr. Brown.

Galinski listened for over twenty minutes. He learned that Thomas Brown went to work for a friend of his who turned out to be a relative of a prominent drug dealer. He ingratiated himself with the organization and worked his way up the ranks, but the police apprehended him during a drug delivery. Brown subsequently learned that the drug gang made him the fall guy and they warned Brown against incriminating them less he and his folks all pay with their lives. He took the fall, served two years in jail, and, after release, he worked with the Detroit police to expose the drug network. They all ended up in jail. Thomas Brown passed into the witness protection program only to surface disguised in Chicago as Philip Matt.

Galinski would have to come back, no doubt, to interrogate Steve Baltero alias Larry Benson indicted for the murder of a Detroit attorney. This case was taking on some unusual dimensions, a circular route that was making Galinski dizzy.

CHAPTER 63

George Gilmer now had a full agenda. First, he needed to reach Fred Worthey to thank him for paying bail. Worthey was the only possible benefactor despite his low profile. George wasted no time in phoning. "I don't know what to say, Mr. Worthey." I will repay you someday."

"It's Fred, George. We'll talk about that some other time. Will you be going back to work at the construction firm?"

"No. The foreman wants to wait until my case is settled."

"It will be their loss if they don't."

"I want to repay you for all your help and support, Mr. Worthey. Anytime you need some carpentry, I'd like to do it free of charge."

"Please. You owe me nothing. I intervened only because I believe in you, George. Before I did anything, I checked out the facts of your case. That was an amazing illness you had. Thank God the doctors cured you. Concentrate on getting this case over with and then we'll talk."

Worthey's unwavering support and generosity gave George a new lease on life. He resolved to take action and spoke with Gail.

"I can't just sit around. I need to talk to the detective who arrested me. Since they learned that the murder victim was into drugs, all sorts of things are possible."

Gail looked puzzled. "What can you do? You don't know anything about police work."

"If I don't do something, I'll lose my mind again, with or without the tumor."

"Not funny," said Gail. "Anyway my father used to tell me that when you've had a bad experience you need to figure out if there was anything to learn from it. Did you learn anything?"

George looked reflective. "I guess I did."

"What?"

"I learned I'm a lucky guy."

"Why?"

"Because I had such a good friend in Mr. Worthey and such a great friend in you."

"Always. Anything else?"

"I learned I'm pretty stupid."

"How come?"

"Because I thought I knew more than the doctors and didn't need to take the tests. I assure you that will never happen again. Look where I'm at now because of that stupidity."

"I blamed it on the tumor," said Gail, it caused you not to know what you were doing."

"Maybe, but I don't think so. I can still remember thinking the tests weren't necessary. It teaches me that when you deal with a pro you should take their advice."

"That's good," said Gail. They hugged.

"I'll call the detective now," said George.

Gail shrugged her shoulders. "I know I won't be able to stop you, so I just have to hope that you know what you're doing."

CHAPTER 64

Two days later George showed up at Galinski's office. "Thanks for letting me come and talk to you, detective."

Galinski looked up from his seat, regarding his visitor with curiosity. "No problem. What is it that you want to talk about?"

"I'm in a terrible spot, and I know it. I can't just sit and do nothing. I'd like to get involved in solving this case."

George's statement took Galinski by surprise. "I can tell that you're serious, but you're still a suspect. And the only one we've got."

"I know, but this drug business…"

Galinski cut him off. "That's a job for police. It's not your line of work, you know. Not to mention how dangerous it is."

George persisted. "My wife told me about the knife you were searching for at my house."

"Yes, that's right, and she couldn't find it. So what?"

George charged ahead. "Can I see the knife?"

"You want to identify it? That won't help your case any."

"Yes, I want to see it—if you'll let me."

Galinski hesitated, but seeing the intense seriousness of George's f ace, he said, "Okay, Come with me." He led George to another room, opened a file drawer, and removed a plastic bag. Inside was the red knife. "Leave it in the plastic, George."

George looked at the knife on all sides. "It's mine," he said with finality.

"Are you sure?"

"I'm positive." He held the plastic bag close to Galinski's face. "See where the red paint is chipped off the bottom. That happened a long time ago."

Galinski's mouth fell open. "You just admitted to owning the murder weapon."

"It's my knife, but that's all I'm sure of. I don't remember carrying it with me that night and I'm not admitting to the crime. I want to talk to the man who found it," said George.

We've already interrogated him. We picked him up along with some gang members in a routine sweep. He denied any connection to the gang, and the gang members confirmed he wasn't a member. When we searched him, we discovered your knife. He claims that he found it. We've checked everything. He's in the clear."

"I want to talk to him," he said. "What's his name?"

"I can't let you meddle in police work."

"I'm not doing police work. I just need his name and address. What I do when I leave here is out of your control, right?"

Galinski stared at George. He was a new man, cured of the amazing malady that had so changed his life. He was firm and insistent. Galinski knew that George meant business. What the hell, he thought. The guy's right. I have no control of where he goes or what he does. "Wait here," he said, going into the file room. He returned with Ronald's full name, address and telephone number.

"I appreciate this. Can you tell me something about the guy?"

"Sure. His name is Ronald Jones. He's a twenty-one year old black man who lives near Roosevelt Road and does security work at a hospital not far from his home. Here's his address."

"Which hospital?"

"Broderick Memorial."

George reached for Galinski's hand and shook it. "Thank you, sir. I hope we'll talk again soon.

Galinski accepted this weird turn of events, but expected nothing to come of it.

CHAPTER 65

Later that afternoon George showed up at Broderick Memorial. He learned Ronald was at the security station adjacent to the emergency room entrance. George found him seated at his post on a tall stool in front of an elevated desk. Tall, good-looking, well built, he wore a starched blue uniform bearing his name and photo: Ronald Jones, Security.

"Mr. Jones?"

"Right, sir. What can I do for you?"

"My name is George Gilmer."

He sat up in his seat, his eyes fixed on George's face. "You know me. Am I supposed to know you?"

"You might. I know they cleared you in a murder case. You found the knife."

Ronald looked startled. "Who are you, a cop?"

"No."

"What business is it of yours then?"

"They're accusing me of the murder."

Ronald jumped up, clutched his holster with one hand, and glared at George. "What you want, man?"

George held his ground. "I'm in the same boat as you are, Ronald. We've both been accused of the murder and we both didn't do it."

"So?" said Ronald, staring a hole through George's forehead. "I didn't do it, and the cops know I didn't do it. So what do they know about you, huh?"

"They know me inside out, but they got new information now. The murdered guy was into drugs. He ratted on his bosses."

"So what's that got to do with me?"

"Probably nothing, but I'm trying to clear my name. Since you've been through it, you know what I'm talking about. I'm looking for any lead I can find. I need help."

"I don't know how I could help you. I never dealt or took any drugs, but we sure got plenty of drugs around here."

George's eyes flashed. "How do you know there's plenty of drugs around here?"

Ronald laughed. "You kidding, man? Go out on the streets and watch 'em deal."

"Where do they deal?"

"Different places."

"Name me one and make it a busy place."

The men were starting to trust each other.

Ronald answered, "Go to the corner of Arbor and Oak about seven or eight o'clock at night."

"How do you know?"

"I oughta know, man. I live near there. I see what goes on."

"I figured that. I can't see you holding down a job like this if you were into drugs."

"Well you got yourself some sense at least."

George had the information he needed. "Thanks for the help. I appreciate it. Maybe we'll be in touch again."

He left Ronald to plan his evening at Arbor and Oak, but did not intend to tell Gail.

Armed with a small still camera and a video camera, George found some men and boys congregating on the street corner. His heart was pounding, yet he managed to snap a few still pictures and some video action. His surveillance continued for three days. On the third day, two white men drove up and started to deal. George captured it on a hidden video recorder. He realized the improbability that any of his evidence would help his case. Yet he wondered if the police knew about the drug trafficking that went on at this particular location.

CHAPTER 66

George returned to Broderick Memorial Hospital to show Ronald the photographs he had taken of the drug dealings.

"Remember me?"

"Sure, man."

"I took your lead. Do you remember telling me about Arbor and Oak?"

"Course I do."

"Well, you were right; plenty of action going on. I took pictures. I really flipped out when I saw these two white guys dealing. Look here."

Ronald took the pictures and smiled. "I'll be damned. The cops talked to me, too. They told me to keep my eyes open. I saw the same guys. I got the license plate number off some gray truck. Hey, I didn't tell the cops you talked to me."

George was excited. "I think we've got something. I'm not sure if it'll help me, but what the hell? What's with these two white guys out there dealing drugs? Let's get this to the police," said George.

They met with Galinski the next day. Galinski was surprised to see the both of them together, but he kept his surprise to himself.

George told Galinski, "We got something for you detective. We caught some guys dealing drugs. They're white, working a black neighborhood. It's all down here: pictures and video, two new pushers, license plate numbers on the dealer's truck, the plates of the customers, and where it happened,"

Galinski studied the pictures and without letting on that he already knew much of this, he said, "Let me borrow those videos for a few minutes. I'll have copies made that we'll keep under wrap. This could be big. Okay. Understand?" asked Galinski.

"Got it" They chimed in together.

"Great. You guys did some good work here. Keep it up, but be careful. Don't forget that you're on your own." That was good work by George, Galinski thought. He smiled at the pun.

CHAPTER 67

Galinski arrived in Detroit to see Officer Mason who was holding Steve Baltero alias Larry Benson, the murderer of an as yet unknown attorney. The murder had taken place at the lawyer's office.

Galinski learned that Steve refused to talk and met every question by silence. With the help of Steve's parents, Mason pieced together his life story. The Balteros cooperated although their son in police custody hit them hard, since both were quite frail. Steve's mother suffered from metastatic breast cancer, and his father, who was sixteen years her senior, had advanced emphysema after a lifetime of cigarette smoking.

Mason told Galinski the following: Steve, now thirty-four-years-old, had been born and raised in Detroit. He was an only child. In grammar school, he was quiet with average grades and few friends. His father enrolled his son in martial art classes when he entered high school. Steve loved the training, and the timing was excellent. He was experiencing a rapid growth spurt and soon became a mass of walking muscle.

By the age of fifteen and a high school sophomore, Steve was six foot five inches tall and weighed two hundred forty-five pounds. He achieved brown belt status and was on his way toward becoming a black belt. Steve's classmates feared competing against his powerful bulk. In school, when Steve triumphed against his class in the sixty-yard dash, the football coach could no longer contain himself. He approached Steve about trying out for the team, but Steve was not interested. He had never played football and was aiming for his black belt. Yet when the coach heard 'black belt,' he urged him to reconsider. He reassured Steve of his strong potential, promising a career of fame and fortune that would not interfere with his goal of black belt status.

In fact, he would encourage him to continue the martial arts as it would be good for his football career.

With his father's prodding, Steve tried out for the team and made it. His speed, strength and quickness astounded the coach. He made first string as a middle linebacker. He proved himself so valuable that the coach also played him on offense.

Soon Steve fell in love with the game and put all his energy into improving his skills. He made all-state his sophomore year and led his team to the city's semifinals, a position they had never before attained. His coaches were considering him for All-American status, a college scholarship, and a National Football League career. The experience transformed Steve. As a high school hero, he came out of his shell and was more approachable. He continued martial arts training between his sophomore and junior years, and college coaches began to take note.

Then, one day everything changed. Steve, a friend, and his friend's father were driving to class when a drunk driver broadsided their car. Paramedics rushed Steve into emergency surgery for a lacerated liver. Although he survived, he underwent subsequent surgeries to repair a fractured knee and right hip. A fractured pelvis that kept him bedridden further prolonged his rehabilitation. Throughout most of his junior year, he was recuperating in the hospital and a rehabilitation center.

The accident, which occurred before the opening of the football season, eliminated Steve from that year's competition. This major disappointment, made him retreat into his shell. Not until the doctor reassured him of his ability to resume playing did Steve begin to mend.

When Steve appeared to have recuperated, and after medical clearance, the coach put him back in the lineup his senior year. He began to regain his skills, throwing himself back into the game as if he had never sustained an injury. His amazing skill and potential enabled him to amass a record that college coaches could not overlook. Many came to watch him play.

In the midst of all that joy, lightning struck again. Steve had just intercepted a pass, attempting to power his way through his opponents and score a touchdown, when the other team brought him down. He felt his knee twisting beneath him, and he suffered an anterior cruciate rupture. Both the season and his career ended that day.

Filled with anger and bitterness that he could not control, Steve became depressed. College coaches turned their attention elsewhere. He felt that everyone was conspiring against him. His new life was marked by doctors, surgery, and unfulfilled dreams. Coming face-to-face with such adversity, he could accept the inevitable and take a new direction, or he could revert to bitterness and forgo any further education.

Steve chose the second path. He dropped out of high school and became a trucker.

Intermittent pain was a constant reminder of what could have been and fueled his anger. Yet, according to his father, in time Steve's lifestyle far exceeded that of the average truck driver. He had a beautiful townhouse, an expensive car, and fine clothes. When his parents asked how he could afford such things, his answer was simple. "I work hard." He had reverted to his behavior before football. He was quiet and secretive. That's about the story on your man, detective," said Mason.

"I'd like to talk to him," said Galinski.

"Well, detective, like I said, he won't tell us anything. Since he's not a suspect in your case, I see no harm in you talking to him. Maybe you can get some info out of him. Let's go see him."

Galinski approached Steve and saw a sullen looking man staring angrily in Galinski's direction.

"You remember me, don't you?" inquired Galinski.

"Yeah, I do."

"What do you want me to call you, Larry or Steve?"

"You know my real name now, so call me Steve. What am I supposed to talk about? I had nothing to do with the Matt murder. We settled that."

"Right. We couldn't hold you without evidence. But after you left, we discovered something new. I'll bet you can tell me what we learned."

"I don't know what you're talking about."

"I don't believe you, Steve."

Steve's face reddened. "That's your problem, but I still don't know what you're driving at."

"All right, Steve. I'll tell you. Philip Matt was not Philip Matt."

"What? You trying to screw with me, detective?" said Steve.

"You heard me right. Philip's real name was Thomas Brown. He was a member of a Detroit drug gang."

Hearing the news, Steve froze.

"That's right. Thomas Brown. Drugs."

Steve rapidly recovered his composure and smiled. "Oh, man. You never know who you hang out with these days."

"Now maybe you know why I'm here. Both of you: impersonators with fake names. Sounds kinda funny, don't it? I'm a pretty good detective, and I can't let that pass without a few questions?"

"Okay. Go ahead," he grinned. "But you're asking the wrong guy. How many times I got to tell you I don't know a damn thing?"

"This is tough work. You should feel sorry for me. I got a suspect who says he didn't do it, and you don't know a damn thing. Help me out here."

"You got me all choked up."

"How about drugs? What do you know about that?"

"Not a damn thing."

"I think you're hiding something, man," said Galinski with a smile.

Steve laughed. "This has gotten stupid. You're bugging me, and you got the goods on some other guy?"

"That's right, but you know what?"

"What?"

"He says he's innocent."

Steve laughed again. "They all say that."

Galinski quickly added, "And you've said nothing about this murder case in Detroit. Why are you keeping your mouth shut?"

Steve looked away.

"Who you protecting?" demanded Galinski.

Still no response.

"What were you doing in Chicago under the name of Larry Benson?"

"Working."

"Why Larry Benson? Why not Steve Baltero?"

"I took a new name" Benson said nonchalantly checking his finger nails.

"You're making it tough on yourself, Steve. I think you're withholding evidence. Keep that up, and you know where you're heading."

"Don't worry about it. I'm not worried, so why should you be?"

"I worry plenty when I don't solve a case."

"Get off my ass. You solved the damn murder. It's the guy you got. Get me outta here," he hollered.

Mason had kept silent until this moment. "Calm down, Steve, and tell him what you know. You're only hurting yourself. All we want you to do is cooperate with the Chicago police. What you got to hide?"

"Screw off. This is bullshit. Get me out of here now!"

"I'd better go," said Galinski. "We're getting nowhere. Thanks for setting up the meeting, Mason, and as for you Steve, if you change your mind about talking, let officer Mason know."

"Don't hold your breath," barked Steve.

Mason eyed Steve. "You know that you're making a mistake, Steve. Detective Galinski could be barking up the wrong tree with this drug thing, but if there's some truth to it, then why sacrifice yourself for them? What the hell do you owe them?"

"You're wasting your time," Steve muttered.

CHAPTER 68

Armed with the new information, the Narcotics Division of the Chicago Police Department held a high-level strategy meeting. They got permission to step up the investigation because of their surveillance data. Both Guzmano's ex-con employees were involved in regular scheduled drug transfers. The sighting was not an isolated event. Besides acting as drivers, the two suspects also collected rent from apartments and shopping center tenants of Guzmano's far-flung real estate empire.

Staffers swung into action, hiding electronic bugs and stringing wiretaps. One young technician with a promising future slipped into Guzmano's office during the evening hours to set up a police band frequency. Officers assigned to tail the suspects and capture their transactions on tape set up telephone wiretaps at drug safe houses.

What had begun as an investigation into the murder of Philip Matt was taking on a life of its own and becoming a major drug investigation, the likes of which Chicago had seldom seen. The investigation confirmed the existence of a sophisticated drug network connected with Guzmano, who had appeared to be a wealthy and respected citizen, a prominent real estate developer, and a generous philanthropist. The principle location for drug trafficking was centered in Guzmano's office, the drop site for drug shipments that were stored in cardboard boxes and delivered by unmarked trucks. The two men under surveillance were the drivers. These boxes were stored in a small room hidden behind a false closet wall. The closet door opened to reveal only suits, shirts, coats, ties, and shoes. A hidden control above the door entrance, when pressed three times activated the rear closet wall. The wall then swung open to expose a small storage room used to hide drug shipments. Only

Guzmano and his two loyal confidants knew of this setup. Their job was to pick up and distribute the boxes throughout the city.

Little doubt remained about Guzmano as the kingpin of this operation. A bureaucratic organizational chart began to emerge. The Narcotics Division geared up for a major bust.

Galinski flew back to Detroit. He wanted to talk to Steve again. This time he took George with him. After all, as he said to George, "You helped us uncover all this."

CHAPTER 69

This time Galinski learned a great deal more when he and George landed in Detroit.

Attorney Jacob Wagner, killed by Steve Baltero alias Larry Benson, proved to be involved in interstate drug transfers. Galinski commented to Mason, "At least you've learned what you're dealing with. The FBI should be a big help."

"We're working with them," said Mason,

Galinski asked "Any other businesses the attorney was involved in?"

"Four others, and my men are looking into them now."

"Any that stretch to Chicago?"

"So far, none. If we uncover anything, we'll let you know, detective."

"This means that since Steve killed this drug dealer lawyer, he must be tied in somehow."

"You got that right," agreed Mason.

Before arriving in Detroit, Galinski had learned the name of Steve's public defender, Max Brundage. Galinski met and briefed him on the latest developments. Both agreed that in light of their new findings it was urgent to interrogate Steve Baltero again. Galinski and Brundage showed up at the jail with George in tow.

Steve was waiting when Galinski, George, Mason, and Brundage arrived. It was clear from his expression that Steve was displeased about the renewed questioning.

"What the hell is this all about?" asked Steve. "I told you everything last time."

Galinski confronted him. "Last time we asked if you had drug connections. You denied it and played dumb."

"I still deny it."

"Bullshit. We know for certain that the lawyer you're accused of killing was into drugs and was getting them into Chicago."

"I'll be damned. Who'd a thought it?"

"You're surprised?" asked Galinski.

"You got that right, man."

"How dumb do you think we are? You were the last one to see Matt in Chicago alive. Now you've killed a lawyer involved with drugs, and you say you know nothing about it?"

A smiling Steve nodded his head.

"Let's cut the bull. I think you can clear a lot of things up and save your own neck. Why not come clean? Who you willing to die for?"

"Man, you're wasting your time. I know nothing about the Matt murder. I got nothing to say about the lawyer and I don't know shit about drugs."

"Okay, Steve. You're on your own." Galinski decided to leave any future questioning to the Detroit authorities. His next plan, and final hope, was to confront Steve's parents.

But George, who had been silent to this point, blurted out, "Make peace with yourself." This sudden statement surprised Galinski.

Steve stared at George. "Who the hell are you?"

"George Gilmer."

"You a priest or something?"

"No," said Galinski, "George has been accused of Matt's murder."

Steve stared in disbelief, his mouth agape. "You must be kidding or else the world's gone nuts. Do you let murderers walk free in Chicago?"

"George's free on bond. He's trying to prove his innocence."

"Is he the guy you told me about with his fingerprints and blood all over the murder weapon?"

"Yes."

For several seconds Steve gaped at George, then he yelled, "Get me back to my cell. You all got shit for brains."

"You're facing the death penalty," George reminded him. Don't die with a lie on your lips. I'm talking about the murder here in Detroit. There's no evidence against you for Matt's murder, but there's drug traffic between Chicago and Detroit. Maybe you got the power to stop it. Think about all the people you could save."

"I don't know any drug bullshit. I got nothing more to say, so why not you get off your soap box and all of you get the hell out of here." Steve turned his back and waited for the guards. The moment he left, Galinski said, "Well, I can't say that I'm surprised."

"Me neither. I didn't try to respond because I knew it wouldn't help. I get the same BS you just got," said Brundage.

"Would you mind calling Steve's parents and let them know I want to speak with them?" asked Galinski.

"Sure thing. Glad to do it," said Brundage"

"George, nice try," said Galinski.

"Thanks. Detective."

CHAPTER 70

Detective Galinski and George Gilmer arrived at the Balteros later that day. Mr. Baltero looked frail when he greeted them at the door. He walked with short, halting steps and he spoke in staccato sentences because of shortness of breath.

"Hello, detective," said Mr. Baltero.

"Pleased to meet you, Mr. Baltero. This is George Gilmer. Is your wife here?"

"No. She's at the hospital getting chemotherapy. I'll pick her up later."

"I'm sorry. I hope she does well. Thanks for seeing us."

"I don't mind, detective. How can I help you?" he asked, guiding them into the living room.

They all sat down and Galinski said," I've been investigating a murder in Chicago. Someone killed your son's friend, Mr. Matt. The murder victim had turned State's evidence against a Detroit drug gang. We've been trying to track this down, and our trail led to your son here in Detroit."

Mr. Baltero looked grim. "What can I do?"

"I get the feeling your son might be protecting somebody, or something. We've questioned him about the crime here and the one in Chicago, but he won't even tell us anything about the murder that they accuse him of. He denies any drug connection, and yet there are too many coincidences. Have you spoken to your boy?"

"I get nothing out of him either," said Mr. Baltero. "He won't speak to me. He never did. All his life he's been a loner. When he did good in football, he opened up. But then he was injured, and..." he put his hands over his face and wept.

"That's okay," said Galinski. "Take your time."

"I'm sorry," said Mr. Baltero, wiping his face before continuing. "His injuries set him back. He quit school after that and went his own way."

"I know how painful this must be for you, Mr. Baltero, but I hope you understand. I'm here only because I think you're our last hope. Steve refuses to talk to us, but maybe he would confide in you and Mrs. Baltero."

"I'll do what I can," he promised. "My boy has no idea how sick his mother is. Doc says it might only be weeks. I have a bad heart and lungs. Smoked too many damn cigarettes. I can hardly breathe. God only knows how long I've got. The wife and I, we're coming to the end of the line, and our son…" Baltero choked up. He was wheezing and his words came in spurts. "You know, detective. You may be on to something with this drug business. Steve was living pretty high on the hog as a trucker. Never could understand it."

"You've been very helpful, Mr. Baltero. Stay in touch with your son's attorney, and also with the police. We've got drug connections from Detroit to Chicago, and now there's a dead attorney. Let's hope your son can give us some clues."

"I'll try, Detective. Maybe I can save him from himself." After showing the two men out, Mr. Baltero got into his car and drove to the hospital. His wife was finished with chemotherapy by the time he arrived. On their way home, he recounted the story of Detective Galinski's visit. She broke down and sobbed.

"We'll go there tomorrow and talk to him." If Steve's involved like the detective thinks, maybe we can help him. I pray to God that it's His will to save our boy's life, and that He keeps me alive long enough to see it happen." Mrs. Baltero cried again as she reached for her husband's hand.

When Mr. and Mrs. Baltero arrived at the jail the next morning, Steve was waiting behind a wall of glass and wire. He looked shocked when he saw how thin his mother was. She seemed to have aged ten years. Steve stood up to get a closer look as his parents walked over, arm-in-arm, to greet him at the glass partition. They sat opposite one another.

"What's the matter, Ma?" said Steve speaking into the telephone. "You don't look so good."

"I'm okay, son. I had a touch of the stomach flu for a while, so I haven't been eating anything."

"Neither one of you looks too good. How are you doing, Pa?"

"Not bad. But remember, Steve. I'm getting older, too. And don't forget that I married a child bride," said Mr. Baltero smiling. Then, he sat straight up and cleared his throat. "How are you doing, son?"

"I'm fine, Pa."

"The detective from Chicago was at the house, and…"

Steve interrupted before his father could finish his sentence. "Damn that guy!" he shouted. "He got no right talking to you. I told him I knew nothing about the murder in Chicago."

"I know," his father replied. "On that one he said you were in the clear, but he's tracking this drug thing down. The guy seems to think you might know something." Mr. Baltero observed his son's sullen face and added, "He's just doing his job, Steve."

"He's wasting his time."

"He's only trying to help you. If you know something about the drug business and don't talk, you could get the death penalty." Mrs. Baltero started to cry.

"Don't talk like that in front of Ma," said Steve to his father.

"She already knows everything, Steve. She's the one who insisted we come here. I believe the detective and I think he's on to something. I never saw a trucker live the way you did. Maybe I should have figured it out then."

"I'm telling you there's nothing to it." Steve insisted. "Ask the cops. They looked into it and knew the trucking company I worked for was legit."

"We don't want you to die," his mother said, dabbing her eyes.

"I won't, Ma," said Steve. "Don't worry."

"Think about what I've told you," cautioned his father. "Don't take the fall for anyone, son."

"Enough of this crap! I don't know a damn thing!"

His parents knew it was time to leave.

"Okay Steve, your mother and I will leave now," Mr. Baltero said. "We both love you."

Steve saw his father's anguished look and softened. "I love you, too, Pa and you too, Ma."

The Balteros never saw the tears that rolled down their son's face.

CHAPTER 71

The Detroit police continued their vigorous pursuit of the trail that led from Chicago. They investigated the dead lawyer's cases. He only had ten active high-volume personal injury cases, none of which seemed to have drug connections. Other cases involved severe industrial injuries and major automobile accidents.

The dead attorney had also been involved in five major corporations, as either director or company owner. The only one of importance was a manufacturing concern that made electronic chips. The chip company boxes were the same ones used to transport the drugs.

The Detroit Police Department had many details concerning the lives, business, and professional activities of the murdered attorney. But then the trail stopped cold. The drugs made their way to Chicago. No one could implicate Steve Baltero in this scenario. He continued to remain silent, insisting he knew nothing about drugs. He also remained silent about why he killed the lawyer. This continued to be a source of great frustration to the police, attorney Brundage, and Seve's parents.

A psychiatrist examined Steve. His conclusion: fit to stand trial.

CHAPTER 72

The Chicago police were closing in. They were gathering evidence at an ever increasing pace, defining the linkages of the principals involved while mapping out the flow of drugs. Most important was the phone tap of Guzmano's office, which revealed the arrangements for a significant meeting: "Allegretti's Restaurant, small meeting room, 6:00 o'clock Thursday."

Undercover police officers set up a second meeting at Allegretti's for a so called Amber Corporation, and scheduled it the night before Guzmano's meeting. Electronic experts arrived for dinner dressed in business suits and carrying brief cases. After coffee and dessert, they requested the door remain closed for a special business meeting. Within an hour, they wired the room to disclose its secrets, and the so-called businesspersons left a substantial tip for their waiter's excellent service.

Six men showed up the next night. First to arrive was Guzmano; the other five arrived ten minutes later. A hidden camera recorded the proceedings for positive identification later. Two of the six were from Detroit, Guzmano represented Chicago, and the other three were unidentified. These were the kingpins of the drug trade. The actual meeting convened after dinner service had begun.

"We're here to inform you of the sudden disruption of our Detroit distribution network due to the unexpected death of the principle distributor," reported an older gentleman who resembled the retired chairman of a major corporation. "We assure you the situation is temporary, and we're working to reestablish the network. It may take time, so we're asking for your understanding. We'll notify you when we're ready, but just how that notification will occur will be a surprise. Nevertheless, I can assure you you'll learn about it."

Although all the drug kingpins knew each other, those at the vice presidential or middle management level didn't know their counterparts in other cities. This matter was for the Detroit division to resolve. Chicago would take an interest, but only if the solution was ineffective and disrupted the functioning of their operation. The Detroit division was following ethical organization standards by calling this meeting and advising its members.

"We ask your patience while we rearrange management," continued the speaker. "We assure you that we will take care of this matter just as we did in Detroit. This problem, however, will go much faster."

They switched to small talk, finished drinking, and adjourned.

Back at police headquarters, Galinski stopped the video near the start. He spoke to the narcotics division personnel in attendance. "You're not going to believe this. See this guy," said Galinski.

They all crowded around the screen, staring with great concentration where Galinski was pointing.

"This is a big break." said Galinski. "That's Leo Carlin, the owner of the house where Matt got killed. He's the one who called the paramedics."

As the viewers stared in disbelief at the film, Galinski said, "Damn, Carlin is part of the drug trade. They made the hit in front of his house so he could confirm it, I bet. We'll keep this to ourselves for the time being while you narcotic guys work on the last pieces of the drug puzzle."

"Good advice," said the narcotics chief.

Then Galinski said, "There's more. Listen to this on the last part of the film." 'We ask your patience while we rearrange management. We assure you, that we will take care of this matter just like we took care of the problem in Detroit.'

"Did you get that?" inquired Galinski. "Are you thinking what I'm thinking? If this isn't proof that the Matt hit was a drug hit, I don't know what is. And it was arranged from Detroit. We still can't prove anything, but it's damn suspicious in my book. If we assume that's what he was referring to, then where does George Gilmer fit in? Nothing we have exonerates George yet. I'll get hold of the Detroit Police. They've got lots of information on the narcotics traffic right down to the local source out there.

"I'll give the FBI the scoop on the Allegretti meeting. Since this crosses state lines and represents an interstate drug effort, they need to get involved here too, and we'll take all the help we can get," said Galinski. "We're close to blowing the lid on Chicago's operation, but I think it's smart to hold back. If we do anything to shut down the operation here, the druggies will close up in Detroit, lay low, and the police there will be stymied."

"Right," replied the chief of narcotics. "We'll keep getting evidence and work with Detroit since they had to develop a new distribution network to Chicago. I'm sure Guzmano will be ready for his drugs no matter how they come in. So keep your eyes and ears open and give me a report about anything new the moment you hear about it."

When the narcotics chief left police headquarters, Galinski replayed the message from Detroit: 'We will take care of this matter just as we did in Detroit.'

The way I see it, thought Galinski, The new drug dealers plus the jailed druggies in Detroit took responsibility for avenging Brown's, or Matt's, double-crossing of the Detroit dealers. What else could it be, for God's sake? If Gilmer were a drug hit man, then case closed. But since I don't believe that, we're left with a random killing by an insane man who, by some amazing coincidence, killed Matt before the Detroit boys could do it. If that's true, then Detroit is taking credit for a killing they didn't do. No way do I believe that either. The Detroit boys did it. That's it.

Although Chicago had accumulated enough evidence to indict, they continued to collect more. They were hoping to help the Detroit police come up with the source of drugs that led into Chicago. Meanwhile, Detroit made good on their promise to reinstate a distribution network; shipments began showing up again at Guzmano's office. The source remained a mystery. The fact that they resupplied Chicago and nobody knew the origin was puzzling. It was even possible that the origin was not Detroit, but there was no evidence yet to suggest that.

CHAPTER 73

Attorney Stuart could not hold off much longer without a breakthrough from Galinski. He had exhausted all delay tactics for George's case, and pressure from the court mandated them to move forward. Besides, George was rational and very impatient. Stuart's only hope now was Donaldson.

Stuart asked her, "Have you heard from Galinski?"

"No. I'll try to reach him now and get back to you," she promised.

When Donaldson called, Galinski had nothing positive to report about any progress on George's case. He glossed over details of the narcotics probe since it was undercover work.

George was tightlipped about his surveillance, disclosing nothing to anyone but Gail.

Galinski promised to call Donaldson the moment he had a break.

Preparations for the George Gilmer hearing were under way.

"I'll call you the minute I hear about the trial date," Donaldson told Stuart. Meanwhile, Stuart intended to level with George to prepare him for what was to come. The meeting took place the following afternoon.

Stuart said, "It's time we get moving on your case, George."

"I know," he replied, "yeah and I'm dreading it. This waiting is tough. Did you learn anything new about the drug business?" he asked, masquerading as ignorant.

"No. The detective has been working hard, but nothing so far that could help you," said Stuart.

"I was praying for a break. Now what?" asked George.

"Our next step is to have an insanity hearing before the judge. First, we need to establish that you were legally insane when the murder was committed and not responsible for your actions."

"Will the psychiatrists have to be there, or just their reports?"

"They'll both be there, and with their reports. You know they've already confirmed your insanity at the time, and no way can a judge rule against unanimous expert opinion."

"Does that mean I'm off the hook after the hearing?"

"No. First they decide if you're competent to stand trial."

"When is that decided?"

"It could be done at the same time, or at a later date."

"Then the best I can hope for is being labeled 'guilty but insane.' It's damn depressing. There's got to be a reason for all this, Mr. Stuart. Someday I hope it'll all come out."

"Better than the death penalty, George."

"I know, but Gail is afraid that nobody will ever hire me again. Why, even my old job won't take me back until everything's finished."

"Hey, George, you're not responsible for getting that crazy tumor. I admire how you've come to accept your fate. A tumor like that might affect anyone's brain. People understand, you know. We all get sick, but we also hope for a cure. You're one of the lucky ones. That's what happened to you, and what counts is how you are now."

"I know. I'm just scared."

"Sure, and that's normal. If you weren't scared, then we'd all be worried you were still sick. You've got to look strong. If your discouragement shows and you look ill, that could spell trouble for us when we try your case. You have one big battle to get over, so focus. Get over the hurdle and forget about the future. Let it sort itself out. Don't try to leapfrog more than one hurdle at a time or you'll fall flat on your face. We'll prove that if you did this thing, it wasn't your fault. Your job will be to prove that you're cured and normal. I know you can do it," said Stuart.

George nodded. "You're right. I need to concentrate on one thing at a time, and I'll try hard."

"I know you will. I promise to let you know when we're ready to begin. It shouldn't be too much longer," Stuart said, as he stood up to leave. "I'll be in touch."

Stuart advised James Kantor before consulting with Donaldson. They felt prepared, and so did the psychiatrists. All that remained was to get a date for the hearing and that information came forth within two days. The court set the date.

Donaldson notified Galinski about the date. Galinski said to her, "I can't elaborate, but we have good reason to continue this investigation even though nothing turned up on the Gilmer case lately. A lot is happening, and I'd consider it a personal favor if you would delay the hearing a bit longer. Once you hear it you'll understand."

"The judge has already set the date," reported Donaldson.

"Could you delay the hearing on whether George is competent to stand trial?" asked Galinski.

"That could work. The judge might go along with it as long as plaintiff and defense agree. I doubt Stuart would have a problem with this. After all, we've been working together."

"I'm counting on you. It's important," stressed Galinski.

"I'll tell Stuart."

"Great. Not only does George thank you, but, as you may find out later, so does the whole city."

Donaldson looked surprised, but knew better than to question Galinski. "I'll be patient, detective."

The hearing commenced on time with Judge Kaufman presiding.

"Your Honor," said Donaldson, "we are prosecuting George Gilmer for the murder of Philip Matt. The fact that it has been determined that Philip Matt of the witness protection program was Thomas Brown of Detroit, Michigan, complicates the case. Brown turned State's evidence against drug dealers and was responsible for ending their Detroit reign. Now they're in prison. Thomas Brown assumed the alias of Philip Matt. I'm sure that even defense counsel will agree that the accused, George Gilmer, is guilty of murder by virtue of overwhelming evidence: A positive DNA match, the defendant's blood and fingerprints on the murder weapon, and the defendant's blood on the victim. Having said that, I agree with the defense attorney that George Gilmer was insane at the time of the murder. A tumor rendered him incapable of coherent thought and action. This is a rare disease, and George Gilmer had a most virulent form of the illness. You will hear details later. I have present, Your Honor, as does the defense, a distinguished psychiatrist who will attest to these facts."

"Thank you, counsel. May I hear from the defense, please?"

"Your Honor, I'm in full agreement with everything stated by the prosecution," said Stuart. "Mr. Gilmer was indeed insane, and the defense psychiatrist will attest to this fact. I also have affidavits from three physicians, Dr. Pollard, Dr. Crowell, and Dr. Godwin, the doctors who treated George Gilmer the evening of the murder. These doctors are all on staff at Covenant Hospital. They've certified that George Gilmer was insane at the time of the murder and not responsible for his actions. I submit these affidavits to you."

"Let me see, please," said the judge, reaching over to get the documents from Stuart. He checked them page by page before asking for the witnesses' testimonies.

First called was Dr. Geary who presented a brief description of hyperparathyroidism, his experience with the subject, and a review of the literature. Of special concern were the statistics about the type of psychosis that correlates with varying degrees of calcium elevation. He attested to George's insanity on the day of the murder when he attacked Carly Godwin and then was hospitalized. Next, Dr. Carey presented her evidence and arrived at the same conclusion as Geary.

The attorneys approached the bench.

"Congratulations on the cooperative effort that both of you have made for the sake of the defendant," said Judge Kaufman. "It is indeed a pleasure to see co-action for the sake of justice. There is no doubt the defendant was insane at the time the crime was committed."

Both Donaldson and Stuart felt genuine relief as they returned to their seats. Judge Kaufman announced that he would delay the competency hearing and announce the time later.

"We did it," laughed Donaldson. "Maybe someday we'll even find out what this cloak and dagger stuff is all about." She notified Galinski that Gilmer was insane at the time of the murder and that he delayed the competency hearing.

"That's great, but I'm still not able to deliver anything that would exonerate him," said Galinski.

While all this was going on, Chicago police were considering the possibility of waiting for Detroit. Although they had amassed enough evidence to strike and thereby end Guzmano's operation, this was a bi-state effort. Striking too soon could disrupt the investigation in Detroit.

The FBI was eager for a multi-state sweep, but maintained a low profile while continuing the surveillance. They thought it unlikely that Guzmano, once arrested, could be convinced to implicate other drug networks in other states. Thomas Brown had been unique.

CHAPTER 74

"All leads seem to point to Steve Baltero," said George, "but there it ends. Why not try getting to him through his parents? Everyone else has failed and he won't say anything to anybody."

"Even if he opens up there may be nothing there to help you. We've got nothing on him as far as your case is concerned," replied Galinski.

"I know. But until there's no hope left I can't rest, and I don't have much time. I want to talk to Steve's parents."

"Well, George. I guess I can't stop you. Since you started us down this road, let me call Brundage and see about his arranging for you to visit the parents. You have every right to participate in your own defense. I'll go with you."

Three days later George and Galinski were visiting with the Balteros whose concern about Steve gave them a powerful incentive to remain alive.

George sat before them nervously looking for the proper words. "From where I sit, your son not talking tells me that he's hiding something, said Steve."

"We know," said Mr. Baltero. "The drug business explains a lot. The way I see it, they've got a gun to his head."

"No one could get through to him. Not his lawyer, not the Detroit cops, not even the detective from Chicago. Steve seems willing to go to his death without a blink of the eye. You're his only hope, and mine, too," said George

"What can we do?" asked Mrs. Baltero, looking very frightened.

"Steve's only hope is to come clean about the murders. The murdered guy was dealing drugs, so maybe Steve knows something. If he tells how the drug business works, he could save his life," said Galinski.

"Yes. But still, what can we do?" pleaded Mrs. Baltero. "He never listened to us. Never."

"Can I ask a few questions, but if I get too personal, just shut me up," said George.

"Go ahead," replied Mr. Baltero.

"I heard that both of you are pretty sick. Is it true, Mrs. Baltero, that you've got cancer?'

"Yes. I'm pretty sure I'm going to die soon."

"Does Steve know?" asked George.

"No. How could I worry him with all that he's facing now?"

"And you, Mr. Baltero. You're sick, too?"

"My lungs. Yeah. I been on a respirator twice, but no more. I told the wife that if it happens again, not to resuscitate me, and I signed a living will."

"Your son needs to know this," said George.

This sudden unexpected statement cause Mrs. Baltero to shake her head vigorously. "No. I can't do that. He got enough to worry about."

Galinski jumped in recognizing that George was on to something. He said to the parents, "Nothing will happen to Steve for a long time. Even if he gets the death penalty, with all the appeals and stuff it could take years. But, Mrs. Baltero, you don't have years and maybe Mr. Baltero doesn't either. George here is making sense. I think Steve should know, and maybe you could tell him. Why not tell him that neither of you wants to die knowing he's going to be executed. If he's got a chance to live by fessing up, he owes you that before you die."

They both stared at George and Galinski and then at each other.

George added, "Think of what he could do, Mr. and Mrs. Baltero. He could bust the whole drug trade."

Mrs. Baltero started to cry. "He's right," she said, taking her husband's hand. "He's right. We have to do it." They stared at each other, a slow understanding crossing their features.

"I'll go see Steve's lawyer," said Mr. Baltero.

CHAPTER 75

Mr. Baltero arrived at Max Brundage's office.

Max said, "I'm up against terrible odds with Steve, Mr. Baltero. Your son knows about the evidence. Nobody saw the shots being fired at the lawyer, but there is no question that Steve was admitted into the office where the attorney was. The witnesses testified that Steve and the lawyer argued for about five minutes behind closed doors. Then they heard two gunshots. Steve came out of the office not saying a word and got into his car. The witnesses called the police, and they picked up your son. He didn't resist, and he had the murder weapon. They couldn't trace the weapon, but the bullets found in the victim matched the gun. Do you want me to go in with you to see Steve?"

"No. I'll go alone. My wife wanted to come, but she was too weak.

"Good luck, Mr. Baltero."

Mr. Baltero went to the prison where he intended to confront his son.

"Where's Ma?" asked Steve.

"She couldn't come," replied his father. "She's pretty sick."

"What's the matter?

"It's bad news, Steve...she's got cancer and it spread all over. She hasn't got much time."

"Damn." Steve buried his head in his hands. "Ma said she had the flu, but I had a hunch it was more. She got so skinny."

Mr. Baltero observed his son's naked emotion, unlike the face he had been wearing for so long.

Steve looked up with tears in his eyes and softly said, "How much time has she got, Pa?"

"The chemotherapy isn't doing any good, son. Your mother asked to stop the treatments."

"How much time?"

"Maybe weeks, but..."

"Can't I see her?" interrupted Steve. "Can't she come here?"

"I could bring her, but...your mother's in a wheelchair now, son."

"I need to see her," said Steve.

"Sure, Steve. I'll bring her right back."

Despite her weakness, Mrs. Baltero was eager to see her son. Her son's death penalty loomed over her like a dense fog, and she vowed to do everything within her power to prevent it. She fortified herself with pain medication, and then left with her husband to return to the prison.

The glass partition prevented any physical contact, but the expression on his wife and his son's faces brought tears to Mr. Baltero's eyes. After a moment of mother and son touching through glass, he managed to speak.

"Steve, your mother knows everything," he said. "We know you killed that guy, but...we can't figure why...you won't talk. Are you protecting someone? It's drugs, yes? You owe them so much you're willing to...to give them your life? Please, don't just sit and accept a death penalty. For the sake of your mother...she doesn't have long. Don't let your mother die thinking you will die...without a whisper on your lips."

Steve's eyes burned a hole through his mother's head.

"You know, son, we're very ordinary...your ma and me. When we die, no one will know any different. All we did was raise a son and try to be good citizens. I'm pretty sick, you know. I don't have long either. You got a bad break, Steve. Maybe you would have been a Hall of Fame football player, but it wasn't to be. If you're gonna die and you got something on the drug gang and take it to your grave, your passing will go unnoticed like...your mother and me. But, if you got something to say, son....something that could make the world a better place after you're gone, then say it. Please, son," he pleaded. "We want to die happy...and proud. Let us rest in peace."

Steve had been listening with his eyes closed. Then, after his father finished, his eyes blinked open. First, he looked at his father and then turned to gaze at his mother. His face reflected relief as he said, "Yeah, I killed that guy and the police know it. I have a lot to say and I'll say it. Tell Mr. Brundage to come here, and to bring a recorder, and tell him to bring a priest too." With that he smiled, radiating such calm as they had never seen before.

Back in Chicago, the case against the drug gang was tightening. No question about Guzmano being the Midwest's principle distributor. They identified at least three safe houses with drugs largely due to Ronald Jones and George. Galinski recommended Ronald get two years of college and apply to the police force. He already was street smart and had security experience. "You'll make a hell of a cop," he told Ronald.

CHAPTER 76

The meeting with Steve took place early the following morning. A pair of armed guards, Attorney Brundage, a technician, Detective Mason, Galinski, George and a Catholic priest were present.

"We're all here, Steve," said Brundage, "this is Father Morfeld, the priest you asked for. You've already met George Gilmer and Detective Mason. Also, the technician that you asked for to record everything is here."

Steve had an aura of confidence and composure that Brundage had not seen before. Brundage knew that they would hear the full story at last.

Steve spoke into the mike. "I would like to make a confession," he said. "I wanted a priest to hear it too. Is that okay, Father?"

"This will be the first time I have heard the confession of someone with others present. Under the circumstances, I'm sure that God won't mind."

Steve drew a deep breath and started. He turned to the technician and asked," Are you ready, sir?"

"Ready to go," answered the technician.

Steve started. "I confess to the killing of the lawyer. I shot him. I knew him for a long time, I worked with him, and I knew what he was up to. But I want to start at the beginning because plenty of people are involved. Also, I want my mother and father to hear my confession when I'm finished because it's really for them that I'm doing it." He paused.

"When I left high school, I started working and got a job with a trucking company. I made deliveries in Detroit. It was a nice company to work for. As far as I knew, the business was legit and everything was on the up and up. One night I was sitting in my truck in the lot behind the company warehouse when I spotted a car drive in with no lights and park. Two guys just sat there. I figured they were waiting for someone and didn't think they saw me since it was dark. Then I saw another man coming out the back door. It looked like he was walking toward his own car when all of a sudden, two guys jump out of their car and run towards the guy heading to his car. I could see by the moonlight that one man had a knife. It was pretty clear they were going to kill him. I jumped out, tackled the two guys, wrestled the knife away and knocked them out. My black belt came in handy. The guy I saved got some rope from the trunk of his car and we tied up their hands. They weren't going no place. Then he got on his phone and made a call. I got no idea what he said, but five minutes later another car drove up and four men got out, put the two guys in their car, and took off. As soon as we were alone, the guy I saved thanked me for saving his life. He asked all kind of questions and he offered me a job. He didn't have time to go into any details because I had to get going, but I told him I'd like to hear more about it later. He told me he was a friend of my boss in the trucking business, and that he'd tell him what I did, and that since I saved his life, he'd return the favor. So we made arrangements to meet two days later." Steve took a sip of water.

"Who was this guy?" asked Brundage.

Nodding, Steve continued. "When I met the guy later, I found out his name was Ben Clark. He was a customer and good friend of Harry, my boss. Harry picked up and delivered for Ben's operation. Ben offered me a big increase in salary. I'd be his driver and deliverer and bodyguard, but still truck for Harry. I stayed on Harry's payroll, at the same salary, but was to get two times that amount in cash. The cash would come from the person I'd deliver to who was a lawyer. That was big bucks and I couldn't turn it down. Bigger salary, less work, so I grabbed the deal and my boss said Ok.

"Things were going great. Ben meant what he said about returning a favor, and at Christmas I'd get a big fat bonus. It turned out that Ben was a big shot drug dealer. I learned about the operation and met the big shots. The packages I picked up for Ben had drugs, and I delivered them at night to the office of the lawyer I killed. He was the collector and distributor. At first we got along, but everything changed after Ben died in a plane crash. Probably you read about it in the papers. Pretty soon I stopped getting paid on time because the lawyer was holding out and making promises he couldn't keep.

"I had other friends there, but I couldn't make a stink about it because they were friends of the lawyer too. I didn't have the power to change things. Meanwhile, the lawyer put tabs on me and I didn't like it. The organization kept me busy with other matters and gave me plenty to do. I was out of town a lot, and when I got back I tried to collect my back salary from the lawyer and he told me to get lost. He said he owed me nothing, and if I knew what was good for me I'd forget all about it and mind my own business. He also told me that he made other arrangements for shipments and was satisfied with the way things were going. He threatened me, and said I had a bad attitude. He was right. I finished him off with two bullets." When Steve ended his monologue, he bowed his head and refrained from making eye contact with anyone.

"Is that the end of the story?" asked Brundage.

"No," replied Steve. "They caught up with me and threw me in jail. Soon as I got there a guard handed me a note that said if I blew the lid on the drug operation, they'd bump me off right away, jail or no jail. They said they don't like to shoot old people, so they would commission some friends to get rid of my folks. I kept my mouth shut to protect them, but then I find out that my mother's dying of cancer and my father's pretty sick too. My folks begged me not to protect anyone, and that if I had to die for the murder, I could go out doing some good for the world. They thought it might even help me beat the death penalty and then they'd die happy. I made a lot of mistakes, but now I'm making up for them. Last night I wrote everything down that I know about drugs. Here, take it," he said handing the papers to Brundage. "Now it's up to you. Please call my folks and tell them what I did and play them the tape."

First to respond was Mason. "I have two questions, Steve. One: Who was the guard who gave you the note, and two: Did you do any Chicago deliveries?"

"Oh, yeah," replied Steve. "I got the guard's name written down. As for the drug deliveries in Chicago, I would drive to a small farm about forty miles northwest of Chicago. There was a small house on the farm. An older guy would be there and I would pass the drugs to him. This would always happen late at night.

"I'll be damned," said Mason. This was their breakthrough. "Do you know who this older guy was you delivered to?"

"Don't have a clue. I'd knock on the door and he'd come outside and I'd transfer the drugs into a shed on the side of the house. Once though, the light was on in the house when he walked out and I got a look into it and I saw a doctor bag on a table in the hallway."

"Are you sure? A doctor bag?"

"Yeah."

"Do you know the name of this doctor, or person, or whoever it was who you'd deliver to at this small farm?" asked Galinski.

"No, and I was told not to say a word to him, just drop the stuff and leave."

"Could you tell us the directions how to get there?" asked Galinski.

"Yeah, that's no problem. I'll write it down for you."

"That's great. Anything else we should know."

"No, that's it," said Steve. He was more subdued when he returned to his cell.

George smiled to himself. He now understood why he had developed the tumor.

Galinski knew what he had to do when he arrived back in Chicago.

CHAPTER 77

Galinski returned to Chicago police headquarters late in the afternoon. The department honored him and the chief of the Narcotic's Division. They planned strategy to identify the "doctor" and the farm in the northwest suburbs who received the drug shipment from Steve. "We'll meet here tomorrow morning. We got a big day ahead of us," said Galinski.

They also congratulated Ronald Jones for his clandestine role. He had big plans for the future. His new friends on the police force were going to recommend him after he finished his two years of college.

Max Brundage had what he needed. When Steve turned state's evidence, they indicted the refurbished Detroit drug cartel, eliminating drug flow into Detroit and Chicago. Brundage had the ammunition he needed. Confident that he could spare Steve the death penalty, he took appropriate steps.

Mr. and Mrs. Baltero wept when they saw their son's confession on film. His mother lived long enough to read the newspaper account of the story and learn of Steve's accomplishments. When she died, Steve received permission to attend her funeral and his father described his mother's final moments.

"Your ma had a good chuckle before she died, Steve," said his father. "On her deathbed she said, "They can't get me now because I beat them to it. Our son's a hero." Those were her final words, son. She said them with a smile." Mr. Baltero put his arms around Steve, and continued. "I'm proud of what you did. You're gonna live," he said with tears. Your mother knew too, and she died happy. I know it." He choked as the tears flowed.

Within one week of his wife's funeral, Mr. Baltero died also. So, thought Steve, he beat the drug dealers to it too. He laughed and cried at the same time. After the second funeral, Steve felt an inner peace that he had never known before.

Though they acclaimed Steve for lifting the lid on organized crime, he knew his greatest achievement was enabling his parents to die with peace and contentment.

That night Steve fell asleep. He dreamt about football. It was the final two minutes of the Super Bowl, and his team was ahead two points. The other team was on the four-yard line, with four yards and four downs to go for victory. Steve was the middle linebacker. First down: the center snapped the ball and the opposing fullback took the ball off left tackle. He managed to go just half a yard before Steve stopped him. Second down: three and a half yards to go. A pass to the tight end on the goal line. Steve took a mighty leap and batted the ball away from the tight end's outstretched hands. Third down: a run around right end. Steve discarded two blockers and tackled the runner for a one-yard loss. Fourth down: a field goal attempt. Steve, managing a four-foot vertical jump, deflected the ball with his fingertips. No goal! Victory! Super Bowl ring! No sooner did Steve awaken than he summoned the guard for sheets of writing paper and a pen.

CHAPTER 78

Galinski and his crew learned that a person named John Wagner owned the small farm in the northwest suburbs of Chicago. He was indeed a physician, duly licensed and practicing medicine in the Chicago area with an associate named Burt Crowell. They planned to arrest Wagner, but since they didn't know anything about his associate, they decided they would speak with him at the same time they arrested Wagner. Checking with the hospital, they learned that Dr. Crowell was signed in there.

Galinski looked up Crowell's office phone number and made a call. "Good morning, I'm Doctor Nelson. Is Dr. Crowell there, please?"

"No sir, doctor, he would be at Covenant hospital all morning. Can Doctor Wagner help you with anything? He's here in the office."

"No thank you. I'll reach Dr. Crowell at the hospital." He hung up and spoke to his associates. "Okay, Wagner's in the office. Get him and read him his rights and bring him in. Call me as soon as you book him. I'll go to Covenant and talk to Crowell and see what I can learn."

As soon as Galinski learned that his men had arrested Wagner, he went to Covenant and had Dr. Crowell paged.

"Hello, this is doctor Crowell."

"Doctor Crowell, this is Detective Richard Galinski of the Chicago Police Department. I have something very important I need to talk to you about."

"What's it about, sir?"

"I can't discuss this over the phone. I'm in the hospital lobby at the main entrance. Can you come down, or can I meet you someplace?"

"Uhh...I can come down. Give me two minutes."

When he arrived, Galinski showed Burt his identification and said, "Doctor, is there a place around here where we can speak in private?"

"Oh yeah, sure. The outpatient department is right over there. I'm sure they've got an empty room we can use."

When they arrived, Burt asked, "What can I do for you, detective? Is this about one of my patients?"

"No, doctor. I'll get right to the point. Your associate, Doctor Wagner, has been arrested for illegal drug dealing." With that bombshell, Galinski observed Burt's reaction. What he saw was a young man who said nothing and just stared with unchanged expression as if he had been hypnotized. Burt's mouth dropped open as if he was attempting speech, but nothing issued forth. This was a non-verbal expression of legitimate shock that crossed Dr. Crowell's features thought Galinski. This guy's innocent. "Do you know anything about this, doctor?"

He slumped in his chair. Galinski interpreted his expression as… you can't be joking about something like this. You made a trip here to tell me that, so it must be true. What the hell will happen now? "No. I don't know anything about this, detective," he said shaking his head.

"I believe you, doctor, and we have nothing on you, but we're going to have to ask you a lot of questions, so let me know when you have some time to come down to headquarters and be interviewed. Here's my card. Call me as soon as you can."

"Yes, I will. But can you give me a little clue now how this all came about?"

"It's a long story, doctor. Let's save it for our meeting."

"Yes sir, I'll save it. I better get back to work now."

"See you later, doctor."

Burt walked up to the medical floor in a trance-like state. He spotted Eve charting at the nursing station. In a daze he went to her andIn a monotone he said, "I've got some important news, Eve. Same restaurant tonight? Same time. I need to talk to you."

"Jeez, Burt. You look like shit. I'll be there."

CHAPTER 79

Back in Chicago, Galinski held his final meeting with Donaldson. "We've got nothing new from Gilmer, but the importance of what your investigation uncovered will never be forgotten," said Donaldson. "I've got the feeling that they'll be teaching this one in criminal justice classes and law schools across the country."

"Thanks, that's nice, but don't forget, I had lots of help. Has the date been set for George's trial yet?"

"Yes. I couldn't stall the judge anymore. Two weeks from today."

In Detroit, Steve spent the better part of the day writing, taking extra care to make sure that they would understand his poor penmanship. He finished that afternoon and told the guard about the importance of the letter that his lawyer needed to get at once. Brundage, notified immediately, was there within forty minutes.

"You wrote all this?" asked Brundage surprised, after scanning the document. The paper was several pages long, dated, and signed.

"Every word," responded Steve. "Read it all. I know you'll know what to do with it."

Brundage sat down, adjusted his glasses, and proceeded to read. When he had finished, he looked up at Steve and smiled. The two men shook hands. Not another word passed between them.

Later that day, a staff secretary interrupted Galinski in the middle of a meeting. "There's an urgent call for you," she reported.

"Who is it?"

"A Mr. Brundage from Detroit."

"Brundage? Sure, I'll take it," he said, as he picked up the receiver. "Hello, Brundage? What's up?"

"Good talking to you detective. I have something you'll be interested in. What's your fax number?"

Galinski gave it to him. "What are you sending?"

"I'll let you read it," replied Brundage.

"It's coming now?" asked Galinski

"This minute. I'm hanging up."

"Sarah, bring in the fax from Detroit the second it comes through," said Galinski. He adjourned the meeting and rushed to his desk. As soon as he sat down and poured himself some coffee, Sarah brought him the fax. He put on his reading glasses and read:

> Dear Mr. Brundage
>
> I have something to tell you but mostly this letter is for the detective in Chicago. Also for the guy who was with the detective. I cleaned my soul when I confessed to the murders of the lawyer drug dealer here in Detroit and I know my folks died happy. That detective in Chicago is a pretty smart guy because even though he had the goods on the guy who was in prison for the murder of Matt, he had a feeling there was more to it. They never had nothing on me but I know all about that murder in Chicago. Just read on for the whole story.
>
> Philip Matt who was Thomas Brown in Detroit ratted on the Detroit druggies. He did a good job because they're all in jail now. But before the Detroit guys went to jail, they sent Thomas Brown's picture to their drug friends around the country and a few left in Detroit. Well they found Brown alright. They spotted him in Chicago under a fake name strictly by a fluke.
>
> When he got married in Chicago one of the guys at the wedding was a big shot drug dealer by the name of Guzmano. When he saw Matt, he got suspicious. He took a couple of pictures of Matt at the wedding and sent them to the prison where the Detroit boys were. They were pretty sure it was Brown but they had some experts compare the pictures of Brown and Matt. When they put

Matt's nose and hairdo and mustache on Brown, they knew they had their man and the hit was on. It was just a stroke of luck for the druggies and bad luck for Brown. Ever since I saved Ben Clark's life I had a good reputation with the drug gangs so one of the big Detroit guys told me to move to Chicago and find an apartment near Matt get to know him and take him out when the time was right but make it look like a mugging. I would get a hundred grand up front and another hundred after doing the job. I had six months to take care of it.

I got a new identity a new social security card and Larry Benson moved to Chicago near Philip Matt. The Chicago drug guys didn't know I was there except for Guzmano and one guy Leo Carlin who had Detroit connections too. First I spent time casing Matt and got to know his habits. I knew he went to this local bar and grill called Traficantes so I started going there too and got to know him. I also got a day job driving a truck for a bakery. I spent a lot of time there getting to be friends with Matt and waited for the right time. I would get him outside and the weather conditions had to be just right. It would be easy because he was a little guy.

One Friday night the conditions were perfect. It was cloudy and dark. We had the usual Friday night fish fry and some beers and then we went our separate ways home. That night I wore a pair of shoes that were two sizes too small in case of footprints. I bought them at a flea market. I took along a folded hunting knife and cap and gloves that I also bought at the flea market. The cap was to leave no hair and the gloves were to leave no prints. I also took along a black plastic folded raincoat to wear over my clothes so I wouldn't leave no fibers.

Me and Matt left Traficantes and walked to the corner. He went one way and I went the other because our apartments were in different places. I knew what way Matt would walk to go home. He would pass by

Leo Carlin's house so I got instructions to make the hit there if conditions were right so Carlin would know I did it. I put on my gloves, hat and raincoat as soon as I left Matt. Then I ran to meet him around another corner the opposite way he was coming toward Carlin's house, which would be about one block before he got home. It was a dark night because the moon was behind the clouds.

Just as I turned a corner, I ran smack into a really weird guy. I wanted to keep on going but this guy grunted and made some strange noises and lunged at me with a knife. He acted nuts. He didn't know what he was doing so I grabbed his knife and knocked him out and kept right on going to meet Philip. I think I cut his hand when I took the knife away. The whole thing didn't take more than ten seconds.

The knife I took from that crazy guy was a large pocketknife with a three inch blade so I decided to use it on Matt instead of the one I was carrying. I hid and waited for Matt. When Matt turned the corner, I saw him coming so I acted like I was hurt and got on my knees. He came up to me and I tackled him and stabbed him three times. It happened just that fast. I took off and dropped the knife. I figured there might be some false leads on it. I knew I got him so I left town and went back to Detroit.

We followed what was going on in Chicago. We knew about the guy they had under wraps so I wasn't afraid to come back. I knew that Traficante could testify that I was there in his place and eating with Matt so I figured I would be wanted for questioning. Using that crazy guy's knife and dropping it there was a damn good idea.

I'm sure the guy you're holding for Matt's murder is the one who was here visiting me. Gilmer is the guy I bumped into and took his knife away, cut his hand

and knocked out. But whoever you got is innocent because I'm confessing to Philip Matt's murder just like I confessed to the murder of the lawyer here in Detroit.

Steve Baltero

Galinski just stared at the letter and shook his head. His hunch was right after all. This was what made police work so rewarding. He lived on such sense of accomplishment. Donaldson needs to hear all this right away, he thought.

CHAPTER 80

Donaldson read the letter twice. "If this is true, then we have no reason to hold George and this case is over."

"Don't you think he's telling the truth?" asked Galinski.

"Probably, yes. His letter explains everything very well. Gilmer's fingerprints, the matching blood, it all fits. Now I've got a new suspect, Steve Baltero, but I've got only his word to go on. A confession is just another piece of evidence. Steve just confessed to the murders in Detroit. Could he have made this whole thing up? Is he trying to be the good guy and get the 'crazy guy' off? He'll probably get life no matter what he says now. Sure, I think he's telling the truth, but that doesn't mean a judge or jury will agree. We could finish this case for good if we had some evidence connecting Steve to the crime scene. I've got great evidence against Gilmer, and he'd probably get off for reasons of insanity, but make my life easier, detective, get me some evidence on Steve Baltero."

"You're right, but you've given me an impossible task at this late date. We never looked for evidence with Steve in mind. We'll have to talk to him. Look, his blood was not on the victim, and his prints weren't on the murder weapon. He tells why in his confession and the explanation sounds good to me, but our only hope is to get the gloves and clothing he wore that night. Problem is it's been such a long time, and after reading his confession and seeing how thorough he was, I doubt those clothes even exist anymore." He sighed. "Okay. I'll go back to Detroit right away and see what I can do."

Galinski reached Brundage by phone, explaining what he needed to do and requesting that he accompany him to see Steve in Detroit. Then he called George.

"Are your wife and kids there with you?"

"Sure. What's happening?"

"Put your wife on too."

We're both on, detective. What is it?"

"Steve confessed to killing Philip Matt."

"Oh, my God!" said Gail. George's shoulders slumped and he embraced his wife as tears flowed from them both.

Galinski filled them in on all the details. "Tomorrow I'm leaving for Detroit to try and get some evidence from Steve. Come with me, George. You deserve to be there. I'm hoping to close this case."

George gasped. "Yes. Oh, yes!"

They took a taxi from the airport to the prison where Brundage and Steve were waiting to greet them.

"You did a great thing, Steve," said Galinski, resting a hand on George's shoulder. "You may get an innocent man off. But we need some direct evidence from you to prove your confession. If we can get that, the attorney could then move to dismiss all charges against George."

"All you got is my word." Steve looked glum.

"How about your gloves and the clothes you wore?"

"You can forget them. I put everything in a bundle and threw it away."

"You threw the clothes away? Where?" asked Galinski.

"I wrapped them up in my plastic raincoat and packed them in my bag. Then I went back to Detroit. The next day I was driving along Interstate Highway 94 and threw them down a steep ravine. The brush is so thick that even if a car went over the side there, no one would find it."

"Do you know exactly where?" demanded Galinski.

"Yes, exactly. About 100 yards past exit 122, there's a long bridge over a deep ravine, and on the north side, at the far end of the bridge, that's where I stopped and tossed the package. You can't miss the spot."

George shook Steve's hand. "Thank you, my friend. Thanks from all of us and my whole family."

"No problem," said Steve. "You sure look good compared to that night I bumped into you in Chicago."

Galinski, George and two Detroit detectives arranged to take Steve and a cadre of police capable of rappelling down the ravine to retrieve the discarded clothes.

Early the next morning, the assembled group arrived on the scene and Steve pointed out the precise spot where he had remembered tossing the parcel. "It landed right about by that clump of trees in the middle of all those bushes. It's probably right there because there's too much brush for it to roll anyplace."

George positioned himself behind the guardrail, where he would get a good view of the action. The police used powerful binoculars, but failed to detect the bundle. Four men proceeded to rappel down the bank. They stopped before the clump of trees then explored every inch above, around and below them. A half hour into the search they discovered the package wrapped and in good condition, protected from the elements by the plastic raincoat. Steve's directions had been perfect. Galinski beamed, and he and George returned to Chicago where they gave the evidence to the crime lab for analysis. A sample of dried blood from the right glove was an identical match with both Philip and George's blood type.

Donaldson was satisfied with the evidence. They were also doing DNA analysis, and those results would take additional time, so they had to postpone the trial date until they received results.

At last, the findings came back: a perfect match. Everything fit in place. Steve had been telling the truth. The gloves that he wore had Philip and George's blood on it.

CHAPTER 81

When Detective Galinski, Paul Stuart, and Ruth Donaldson brought their new evidence before Judge Kaufman, he dismissed the case against George. He was a free man.

Steve Baltero awaited his disposition, but with new resolve and contentment. He was happier than he had been in years, and he would handle whatever happened now that he no longer faced the death penalty.

Doctors Pollard, Crowell and Godwin wrote a case report on hyperparathyroidism published in a leading medical journal.

Ruth Donaldson, Paul Stuart, and James Kantor published a similar article in a legal journal.

All this superb police work dealt the drug trade a crushing blow. Leo Carlin, who turned out to be a drug financier and money launderer, went to jail along with his compatriots in the drug business.

The murdered Detroit attorney, Jacob Wagner turned out to be the brother of Doctor John Wagner, partner of Burt Crowell. The nice little family business the Wagner brothers had going came to an abrupt end because of a parathyroid adenoma.

John Wagner MD received twenty years in a federal penitentiary.

Hugh Adams dropped the malpractice suit against all the doctors and the hospitals. However, when he told Matt's widow his decision, she begged him to sue the drug dealers for her husband's murder. The suddenness of her demand conjured up the vision of ending up in cement boots, so he declined, stating that he no longer felt the case had any merit and that she was free to seek legal counsel elsewhere.

All the doctors implicated in the malpractice suit were relieved to have the case against them dropped. Pollard remembered his threat to

Adams about an abuse of process suit, but decided against it in favor of continued Emergency Department responsibilities and a clear mind.

George went back to work as a carpenter for the large Chicago area construction firm. He was much the wiser and humbled by his experience and his work was better than ever. It would take him a long time to comprehend the magnitude of what his BRAINSTORM had created—and then accomplished. In his spare time, he began a new project with Fred Worthey and refused any payment.

Burt Crowell, interrogated and cleared of any complicity in his associates' criminal enterprise, continued with his now solo practice. The evening he told Eve about the news of Dr. John Wagner, he asked her to marry him. She suggested he ask her again if the dust from the emotional trauma he just experienced had resolved and his new solo practice was satisfying and successful and his mind was clear and content and, most important, his sense of humor remained intact even after the trauma he had experienced. He agreed. He waited. When he was ready, he and Eve went to their favorite restaurant where they had one drink, splurged on the most expensive meal in the place, and during desert—he popped the question. She answered yes.

Eve called Gail and gave her the good news about her impending marriage. 'Would you do me the honor of being my matron of honor at my wedding, and your husband one of the groom's men?" Eve asked.

"Oh my God. You and Burt! We'll be there with bells on. I'm so happy for you, Eve. Everything looks so beautiful now."

THE END